THE AVIGNON AFFAIR

VATICAN SECRET ARCHIVE THRILLERS
BOOK FOUR

GARY MCAVOY

RONALD L. MOORE

LITERATI
EDITIONS.

Hardcover ISBN: 978-1-954123-20-5
Paperback ISBN: 978-1-954123-21-2
eBook ISBN: 978-1-954123-22-9
Library of Congress Control Number: 2022910390

Published by:
Literati Editions
PO Box 5987
Bremerton WA 98312-5987
Email: info@LiteratiEditions.com
Visit the authors' websites:
www.GaryMcAvoy.com
www.RonaldLMoore.com
R1123

BOOKS BY GARY MCAVOY

FICTION

The Confessions of Pope Joan

The Galileo Gambit

The Jerusalem Scrolls

The Avignon Affair

The Petrus Prophecy

The Opus Dictum

The Vivaldi Cipher

The Magdalene Veil

The Magdalene Reliquary

The Magdalene Deception

NONFICTION

And Every Word Is True

PROLOGUE

Believed to be suffering from terminal lupus, in April 1314 Pope Clement V lay on his deathbed in Avignon, the recently established seat of the Holy Roman Church.

Raymond Bertrand de Got—the French Archbishop of Bordeaux who had taken the regnal name Clement V when he was crowned pope in June 1305—had largely assumed St. Peter's Chair through King Philip IV's influence, having bound himself to the French monarch before his elevation as Christ's vicar on earth. And with Philip's encouragement, Clement—disinclined to face the violent chaos in Rome after his election—insisted that the papacy be moved to Avignon, which was then part of the Holy Roman Empire. Thus was established the first pope in Avignon rather than Rome in what was later known as the Babylonian captivity of the papacy.

His body swollen and agonized, knowing death loomed close, he summoned his brother, Cardinal Florian de Got, for one final but important assignment. At his bedside lay two rolled parchment scrolls bound by hemp.

"Florian," the pope rasped, "I am not long for this world. God forgive me, but I must confess to you that I have amassed a

1

great fortune during my papacy, and I am leaving it to you alone. The treasure is safely hidden, and I will disclose to you how to find its location when you return from handling one final burden I must ask you to assume.

"Those scrolls, the ones on the table. They are most valuable, and terribly dangerous in the wrong hands. I want you to take them to Notre-Dame immediately. Give them to the archbishop there. He will know what to do. The scrolls are not safe here in Avignon, especially if Philip should name my successor, someone not of my own choosing. Should the king see the confessions in one of the documents, he will hardly be able to contain his wrath."

The young French monarch ruled his kingdom with a silver tongue and an iron fist. Known as Philip the Fair for his handsome features, he was anything but when it came to governing his empire, something Clement knew only too well.

Philip had been only seventeen years old when the crown passed to him on the death of his father. Plagued by fiscal deficits owing to the many wars he either inherited or incited—most notably with Aragon, England, and Flanders—Philip was deeply in debt to both the Jewish merchants of Lombardy and the Knights Templar, the latter of whom established international banking much as it operates in modern times.

In a shrewd maneuver of fiscal handiwork, Philip expelled all the Jews from France and confiscated their property, including several Jewish silver mints, thereby not only gaining substantial wealth in the process, but also escaping repayment of his debt to them.

Not content with that, he had convinced Pope Clement V to free him of his great debt to the Templar monastic order by claiming the movement was a state unto itself and abolishing it entirely.

The contents of the scrolls Clement now handed to his brother could incite wrath from Philip against both Clement and his family.

"Make haste, dear brother, for when I die, I cannot guarantee your safety. You will travel incognito, dressed in bishop's clothing to avoid Philip's troops who are watching for papal envoys. And I shall provide you with an official bishop's escort, so you will be well received as such. Now go, and may God's grace be with you."

Cardinal Florian de Got left Avignon shortly afterward—not as a prince of the Church nor the brother of the pope, but as a mere bishop. Unfortunately, he died during the difficult eight-hundred-kilometer journey to Paris, with the hidden scrolls sewn securely into the sleeve of his right arm.

Uncertain what to do, his entourage—who themselves were unaware of their master's true identity—dutifully proceeded on to Paris carrying the body of the presumed bishop for the rectors at Notre-Dame to deal with.

As THE GREAT cathedral of Notre-Dame was in the final stages of its construction—now some one hundred and ten years after it began—Jerome Baudette, the esteemed Bishop of Bordeaux who succeeded Raymond Bertrand de Got, had paid handsomely to be interred in the foundation of the grand cathedral at such time as he passed away. This privilege was granted to a rare few and was largely contingent on their recipients' influence in the Church, not to mention the tithings they pledged to secure their crypts.

As it happened, Baudette was attending a conference of European bishops in Lisbon, Portugal, when he took ill and shortly afterward died. It was decided that his body would be taken by ship from Lisbon up to the French port of Le Havre, and from there down the Seine River to Paris and his final resting place at Notre-Dame, according to his wishes.

But those wishes were never to be realized. The English ship carrying Baudette's body, the *Shoreham*, sank during a ferocious storm in the Celtic Sea off the coast of France. There were no survivors, and Baudette's casket plunged to the ocean floor.

By sheer happenstance, Florian de Got's body had arrived at Notre-Dame in Paris at the same time that Bishop Baudette's corpse had been expected. And since no one yet knew of the shipwreck, and this man was dressed in bishop's attire, the rectors assumed he was the venerable Bishop of Bordeaux, and they interred him in Baudette's prearranged crypt deep in the catacombs beneath the cathedral, dressed just as he had been when he arrived, with the secret scrolls still hidden inside his sleeve.

POPE CLEMENT V died many days later and eight months after that, King Philip died in a hunting accident at the age of forty-six. His three sons each took their turns as king, but none of them lasted long and died relatively young themselves. Ultimately, the throne passed to his nephew, Philip, Count of Valois, head of the Capetian House of Valois.

Avignon served as the seat of the Holy Roman Church for the next sixty-seven years and home to seven popes, all of them French.

∾

PRESENT DAY

Notre-Dame Cathedral – Paris, France

A CHARRED LATTICE of ten-meter oaken trusses, roughly hewn from their original construction between the years 1163 to 1260, had toppled onto the floor of the great cathedral during the accidental fire of April 2019, which was likely linked to restoration work taking place in the spire at the time.

Some three years later, the oak beams still lay where they had fallen, while a team of archeologists and forensic specialists combed through the debris, seeking what could still be salvaged from the ruins as the interior underwent extensive cleaning.

In a surprise discovery, a fourteenth-century lead sarcophagus had been found in an excavated crypt just beneath the cathedral floor. And ground-penetrating radar used to determine the stability of the underlying floor revealed an even older pit, one likely dating as far back as 1230, when the cathedral was undergoing its original construction.

But once excavators cleared out the centuries-old detritus in that lower pit, they made another stunning discovery: beneath thick layers of dirt and the ample offscourings of time lay an ancient crypt obviously buried beneath subsequent construction that occurred over many hundreds of years. Clearly it held someone of prominence, for the crypt was elaborately fashioned. But strangely, there was no apparent indication of the identity of the person whose remains lay within.

When the crypt was later opened and the tightly sealed coffin disinterred, forensics specialists determined the person to have been a distinguished religious figure, noting that the ornate garments covering the body were in surprisingly good condition given the sealed crypt's apparent age.

But examiners discovered peeking through the thinning fabric a flat, tightly rolled set of parchment scrolls apparently sewn into the garment's sleeve with embroidered threads of gold, and with the hemp cord surrounding it having bonded to the paper itself. It would take extreme caution to separate the hemp from the scrolls for later analysis.

The Archbishop of Paris, Cardinal Anton Gauthier, was consulted as to the disposition of the scrolls. Considering their fragility and likely esteemed provenance, the cardinal decided this matter would best be handled by the archival specialists at the Vatican. He summoned Father Michael Dominic, prefect of the Vatican Secret Archives, to oversee the extraction and analysis.

But as it happened, Father Dominic had already received another official invitation to be in Paris at the same time.

CHAPTER
ONE

At eighty-nine, the First Lady of France, Jacqueline Valois, was dead. Her hearse, a vintage black 1960s Citroën, began the slow funeral cortège from Élysée Palace to the Hôtel national des Invalides, some twenty minutes distant.

A Mass for two hundred family members, close friends, and select dignitaries was planned at Dôme des Invalides, the former royal military chapel in the revered complex of buildings honoring the military history of France. Jacqueline Valois had been a fierce advocate for disabled war veterans, prompting her husband—a highly honored war hero himself—to push parliament to enact legislation supporting expanded benefits and retirement facilities for veterans of the French Republic.

Surrounded by a phalanx of security personnel lining both sides of the barricaded streets—vacant save for the massive, mourning crowds bordering the procession route—Jacqueline's husband of fifty-seven years, French President Pierre Valois, walked behind the hearse with his two sons, Philip and Lauren. Tears streamed down Pierre's and Lauren's faces each time they looked up at the tricolor-flag-covered coffin, while Philip remained stoic, glancing at his watch as he walked slowly down the Champs-Élysées.

That both sons had been appointed roles in their father's administration had been a sensitive subject for the French people, with modest catcalls of nepotism in the press and among opposition political parties as both sons were perceived as riding on their respected father's coattails. Now in his fourth and likely final term—for he was a sprightly ninety-two himself now— Pierre Valois deftly handled dissent on the matter from within his own party and, owing to his reputation as one of France's favorite sons, few others spoke up against his decisions.

Helping matters was the fact that both sons performed their respective duties capably, if not admirably—at least in the view of their party's supporters. As Minister of the Interior, Philip oversaw all law enforcement and public safety agencies in the country: an exceedingly powerful position equivalent to the United Kingdom's Home Secretary or the United States' Secretary of Homeland Security and Attorney General combined. He also was formally consulted on the appointment of Catholic diocesan bishops throughout the French Republic, a role giving him significant influence in relations with the Vatican.

As Minister of Culture, Philip's younger brother Lauren attended to the country's cultural heritage, including historical landmarks, national parks, museums and galleries. While his wasn't as inherently powerful a position as his older brother's, Lauren was perfectly suited to the job, hobnobbing with the rich and powerful whose philanthropic impulses could be of tremendous value to his own political maneuvering. The arts being a historically significant standard of French culture, Lauren had his finger on the pulse of the country and knew which ways the winds were blowing—and he wasn't opposed to pointing his sails to take advantage of those winds.

The two brothers were usually at odds with one another as they fought for their father's attention. Many of Lauren's pursuits had escaped his father's attention, and Pierre considered his younger son a bit foppish and flamboyant, a darling of the art crowd. Lauren was closer to his mother in that regard, for her patronage of the arts was just one of the many reasons she was considered a national treasure by the French people.

While Pierre Valois loved both his sons, it was clear to Lauren that his father favored Philip in nearly all ways. For Lauren, his mother's death was the loss of a grounding influence. For Philip, it was merely an unexpected inconvenience.

For Pierre, though, Jacqueline's passing was a sorrowful milestone in his long life, and he knew his own time was coming sooner rather than later. He had been in and out of hospitals of late, battling a series of conditions he had kept discreetly hidden from the public.

Only he and his personal physicians knew that he was dying.

At the official reception held in the Élysée Palace, Pierre and his sons greeted friends and dignitaries who had come to pay their last respects. Apart from pandering cabinet ministers and others who sought political favor with their appearance, notable among the guests were Baron Armand de Saint-Clair—one of Pierre's closest friends who had served with him during World War II—and Hana Sinclair, the baron's granddaughter and Pierre's goddaughter, who was escorted by the decorated French *Béret vert* Marco Picard in full dress uniform.

Behind them in the receiving line was the pope's personal representative from the Vatican, Father Michael Dominic, who had known the Valois family through Enrico Petrini's—now Pope Ignatius's—close friendship with Pierre. Though he would have preferred to have been there himself, the pope knew his presence would disrupt the solemn occasion for his dear friend, but on hearing of Jacqueline's death, had consoled Pierre for some time by phone.

The solemn funeral cortège and the dignified reception were marred only by a sizable number of protestors kept distant by the Police Nationale, forces under the direction of the Ministry of the Interior. Owing to burdensome fiscal policies and the surge of refugees from the Middle East and Eastern Europe, bands of frustrated young Frenchmen—out of work, hungry and angry, roaming the streets of Paris looking for trouble, especially during an official state function—had been forced to protest several blocks away from the government palace.

Aware of the volatile political climate before sending Father Dominic to Paris, Pope Ignatius had insisted that the priest be accompanied by one of his most loyal Swiss Guards, Sergeant Karl Dengler. As the two already were close friends, Michael Dominic didn't mind the company, though he balked at needing protection at all, since he had visited Paris often for both Church business and to visit his longtime friend Hana Sinclair.

Dressed in a dark plainclothes suit, Karl Dengler mingled with other security details lining the Grande Salle des Fêtes, the official banquet hall in the west wing of Élysée Palace. Looking out the window, in the distance he could see the protestors now becoming more agitated, gathering around the tall Egyptian obelisk at the Place de la Concorde just off the Champs-Élysées. It was clear the crowd was growing larger as more people—mostly young, masked men—joined the fracas. The Swiss Guard was only mildly concerned, given the strong police blockades lining the barriers, but he instinctively shrugged and settled his shoulder to ensure his holstered SIG Sauer was readily available.

Looking back to the packed grand salon, Karl saw Marco Picard making his way toward him through the well-dressed crowd. Marco had been employed by Hana's grandfather some time ago to guard his granddaughter after an attempt on her life. As Karl and others knew, their relationship had grown from bodyguard and charge to something more over time.

"Bonjour, *mon ami*," Marco said as he shook the young gardist's hand. The two had been bodyguards for Hana and Michael in the past, enjoying many hours and much action together as they stood by their charges. "It's good to see you again, Karl. I assume you're here as Father Michael's escort?"

"I am, yes. The pope asked for me personally, and he's kind of a hard man to turn down. Besides, though I love Vatican City, it's good to leave it from time to time. Life there can be a little confining, if you know what I mean." Both men turned to the tall, arched windows to observe the protests down the long boulevard.

Sensing Karl's disquiet as he watched the disturbance, Marco offered, "I wouldn't worry too much about those *décadents*. The National Police have them under control. France is well known for its anarchists, especially black bloc ideologues who oppose authority and capitalism. But then, revolution is in our blood." He laughed as if it were an inside joke. Karl just kept staring out the window, unamused.

Turning back to the guests, he noticed an intriguing couple talking with Father Dominic: a tall, aristocratic gentleman wearing a blue satin sash across his chest with a cluster of military decorations pinned over his heart, and on his arm a striking woman of regal bearing sporting a sleek, black Dior skirt suit with a large, broad-brimmed black hat and a conspicuous Jardin Mystérieux cultured pearl-and-diamond necklace that drew attention to her ample endowments.

"Who are those people talking to Michael?" Karl asked. "They look like royalty."

Marco's head turned to the trio across the room. "*Oui*, they are *la noblesse*, nobles of royal blood. That is His Grace Jean-Louis Micheaux, the Duke of Avignon, with his wife, Duchess Sabine. The duke is believed to have his eye on the presidency when Valois retires, which is quietly expected soon in certain circles. But he will be up against a strong opponent, for the Defense Minister, André Bélanger, is also known to covet the job. If you ask me, Bélanger would be a catastrophe. He is a hardline conservative calling for a return to traditional values, and a repugnant xenophobic nationalist to boot. Nor does he care for people of your stripe, my friend."

"Homophobic, eh?" Karl muttered discreetly. "I hope he loses by a landslide."

"On the other hand, Duke Jean-Louis Micheaux is an ardent supporter of liberal issues and is more inclined to give the people what they want: more generous government support, shorter working hours and higher salaries, sexual freedoms, and a welcoming hand to those seeking refuge—to the extreme by some standards. There is a distinct clash of cultures between these two men, and you see both sides playing out across France now. It should be an interesting election when that time comes.

"But," Marco continued, "the man to keep an eye on is Philip Valois, the president's elder son. He, too, is a hardliner and has close relations with Bélanger. Look at him"—he nodded to the Minister of the Interior huddled with the Minister of the Armed Forces in a far corner—"he is little more than a scheming power monger, and a scoundrel at that. I'm sure the two are taking bets now on how long Philip's father has left to live. I do not trust the man."

Just then, Michael and Hana emerged from the crowd and headed for the window where Marco and Karl were standing.

"Hey," Hana said, smiling as she reached for Marco's hand, "what are you two scheming over here? Looks like a serious discussion."

Marco leaned down to kiss her forehead. "We were just discussing the political dynamics of the room. You did not miss anything, *ma chérie*, just idle chatter."

"I had a fascinating conversation with the Duke and Duchess of Avignon," Michael said. "Really nice people, though she's quite the firecracker. It's clear who wears the pants in the Micheaux family. I imagine Duchess Sabine is a force to be reckoned with, and I'm not sure I'd want to tangle with her. But I really liked Jean-Louis. Do you know them, Marco?"

Marco was pensive for a moment, crafting a proper response.

"Who doesn't? They are well known all over France. But I can't say I know them all that well personally. And I do not like his politics. He seems to want to buy his popularity with free this, government-funded that. Some days I feel like I'm supporting myself and a bunch of strangers, and right now, France has more strangers than it can afford. But he would open the doors even wider.

"And yes, I agree with you on the duchess. Keep an eye on that one. She is known as one of France's leading social influencers. She has a tremendous following on the internet. Always dresses in black. She considers herself the queen of French fashion and culture and, as you may have seen, her image appears frequently on billboards and magazine covers. She even calls herself a queen: *La Reine Noire*. The Black Queen."

CHAPTER

TWO

The wide streets of Paris from Élysée Palace south to Montparnasse Cemetery had been cleared of traffic as the funeral procession made its way to Jacqueline Valois's final resting place.

The motorcade had taken a circuitous route to bypass the protestors gathered at Place de la Concorde, but it was clear that, with their rapidly growing numbers, the agitators had begun to spread out even down into the 14th Arrondissement where the ancient cemetery rested. Apparently, wide media coverage of both events had incited more provocateurs to join the fray, and many of them mingled among the legitimate mourners lining the route.

The cemetery grounds at Montparnasse had been encircled with barricades by the National Police with the assistance of the city's local gendarmerie, and the Ministry of the Interior had deployed a Quick Reaction Force to stand by in case extreme measures were needed to protect the dignitaries. Security was tight.

The motorcade of limousines and black sedans was led by police motorcycle escorts through the narrow cobblestone lanes to the Valois family's burial crypt, where the First Lady's casket had already been placed for final interment. The tricolor flag of France lay draped across the coffin, and a six-man cadre of honor guards stood at attention on either side of it.

As a smaller group of a hundred or so family members and select guests were taking their seats for the memorial service, Marco and Karl stood back with the other protective security details, all of whom were cautiously surveying the outer perimeter of the cemetery. Despite the barricades and police presence, some three hundred protestors surrounded the grounds, and they were rapidly being joined by others.

Marco walked up to one of the other security people standing next to Philip Valois's limousine. "Bonjour, Bruno. Have you got any intel on these demonstrators? Clearly, their numbers are growing. Should we be concerned?"

Bruno, the beefy, nearly two-meter tall bodyguard and chauffeur for the Interior Minister, glanced down at Marco with disdain. He paused a moment, his hand pressed against his coiled earpiece as he listened to chatter from other colleagues. Then he responded.

"I was informed by ministry officials that there is some online chatter about those *connards* initiating a disturbance, but it is nothing we cannot handle ourselves. Just keep your eyes on your own man, Picard."

What's with him? thought Marco as he coldly turned away. *Bâtard grossier…*

He looked for Armand, Hana, and Michael among the mourners, took note of their positions beneath the large, white, open tent canopy erected for the service, then turned back to Karl.

"I'd like you to stay with the car, *mon ami*, and keep the engine running as a precaution. No telling yet how this is going to play out. Hopefully, it's a quick ceremony." Despite wearing aviator shades, he held up his hand to shield his eyes from the glaring overhead sun, again surveying the demonstrators surrounding the cemetery. He noted that many wore distinctive yellow neon vests—the kind French drivers are legally obliged to carry in their vehicles for roadside emergencies—but which also are popular among French activists, who earned the label "Yellow Jackets" as a known collective of hostile provocateurs. Marco could easily hear their shouting and cursing from where he stood, which was too close for his comfort. Even peaceful crowds can be dangerous, but when politically frenzied—as these people obviously were—the threat level increased substantially.

As Cardinal Anton Gauthier, the Archbishop of Paris, was reading verses from scripture to the assembled guests, the service seemed to be going smoothly when Marco noticed Sabine Micheaux look at her watch, then reach for her husband's hand as they both stood up and walked quietly but with purpose to their waiting Peugeot 607 Paladine limousine. As if by prearrangement, the chauffeur had already pulled the vehicle out of line and was idling in the access lane, waiting for the duke and duchess. He got out of the limo and opened both doors for them, then drove south, away from where most of the demonstrators had gathered, and out onto Rue Froidevaux, where the limo merged into Parisian traffic.

Then, suddenly, a loud "BOOM" in the distance shook the mourners. Everyone was startled by the commotion, which was followed by more thunderous sounds and clouds of tear gas descending where most of the demonstrators had assembled.

Now on full alert, Marco homed in on the quickly escalating action not far from the funeral service. The number of protestors had grown significantly, outnumbering the police forces, who were using batons and shields against a swarm of people wearing double pairs of black denim jeans, combat boots, layered hoodies, elbow and knee pads, and thick leather gloves. Many were equipped with black bicycle helmets, mirrored sunglasses, and respirators. Clearly, the rabble had been expecting the use of rubber bullets, pepper spray, and tear gas.

And in a flash, they were overrunning police lines and

jumping over the barricades, heading for the group of dignitaries with presumably nefarious purpose.

Instinctively, Marco and most of the other security specialists drew their weapons and raced across the cemetery, weaving through the headstones, to fetch their protectees from under the large, white canopy some distance away. Karl had moved their rented Range Rover out into the lane, ready to take off when Marco returned with the others and gave the order.

A swarm of Yellow Jackets and black bloc protestors had already raced to where the dignitaries were assembled, while most of the esteemed guests were still seated in frozen disbelief, shocked that this could actually be happening at all. One of the protestors produced a large dagger and expertly cut through one of the lines holding up the tent, which partially collapsed over the people still seated there. Pandemonium reigned; people started screaming.

Michael Dominic reflexively drew Hana close to him, protecting as much of her body as he could as he gathered her grandfather Armand as well while trying to find a route of escape from beneath the nylon canopy, which had now collapsed over everyone after the other tethering lines had been cut.

"I've got you," Michael assured her confidently. "We'll be out of this soon." She leaned into him without question, accepting his guidance and protection.

Meanwhile, Marco had just reached the collapsed tent and the covered crowd of mourners. Lifting one of the sides near to where he knew his charges to be sitting, he saw Michael was protecting Hana, then found and put his arm around Armand, shielding him with his own body.

"Michael!" he shouted. "Follow me!"

The priest pulled Hana with him as he kept lifting the canopy behind Marco and Armand to reach the side of it and escape from the smothering white nylon. They could hear gunshots outside the tent, which Marco assumed—or at least hoped—

were warning shots from the detail of security personnel guarding the French president and his family.

Having finally escaped from beneath the canopy, all four ran through the graveyard, dodging the multitude of gravestone monuments, until they reached the Range Rover. As they piled in, Marco shouted to Karl, *"Go! Now!"* and the SUV raced away from the scene, over which clouds of tear gas were now billowing.

"Are you okay?" Michael asked Hana as she settled herself in the back seat, his arm still holding her tightly.

"Yes, but a bit shaken. I can't believe what just happened! What was that all about? Grand-père?"

At ninety-two years of age, Armand seemed remarkably calm considering the circumstances. "Yes, my dear, I'm fine. Just dispirited that this great and proud country has fallen to such mayhem."

Marco, adrenaline still coursing through him, leapt to respond angrily. "I've dealt with a lot of demonstrations over the years, but nothing so outrageously bold as that. I am shocked they were allowed to get as close to the president as they did. Someone's head will roll for such a reprehensible fiasco, and it's likely to be the president's own son, Philip Valois's. He's in charge of the National Police, who apparently were not prepared for that kind of excessive protest. Those people meant business. And it was obviously well organized, not random at all."

There was a moment's pause until Karl spoke up.

"Did anyone else see the duke and duchess get up and leave while the ceremony was still in progress? And it was just minutes before all hell broke loose. Don't you find that odd?"

"I didn't notice, but then, they were sitting behind us," Hana said. "Maybe they had a prior engagement."

"Yes, I saw that too," Marco said, a pensive note to his voice. "Seems an unusual breach of protocol, not to mention courtesy, especially for the funeral of the First Lady of France with the president in attendance. But as they were sitting behind him, he likely missed it as well. *Alors, la noblesse…*they have their own standards of conduct."

Michael's adrenaline had him on edge. "After all that excitement, I need to get a run in before dinner. Karl, you up for joining me?"

"You bet I am. I could burn off some energy too."

"So," Michael wondered to the group, "where are we staying tonight?"

"I've put you up at the Park Hyatt Paris Vendôme, far away from the demonstrations," Armand replied. "With my compliments, of course, I insist. But shall we have supper together later, say, eight o'clock? I suggest the Pur' - Jean-François Rouquette, which is conveniently located in the hotel. A superb restaurant, I might add, and dinner will also be on my account there."

"Great! I've actually stayed there before, for a conference a couple of years ago," Michael said. "Baron, you're too good to us."

"Nonsense, my boy. You took fine care of my granddaughter back there. It is the least I can do."

Marco shifted uncomfortably in the front passenger seat but remained silent as he watched the road ahead.

CHAPTER

THREE

A fter checking in at the Park Hyatt, Michael and Karl went to their rooms to change into running gear. Before heading to the elevator, the priest had asked the hotel concierge for a map and route that might circumvent the demonstrators. Well aware of the city's protests, she happily provided him with a safe, five-kilometer jogging circuit.

As they emerged from the hotel entrance into the long, twilight shadows of sundown, both men were grateful they had brought windbreakers, for the autumn air was brisk but invigorating. They started off heading down Rue Danielle Casanova which, after branching out onto Avenue de l'Opéra, took them down toward the Seine, where they ran along the peaceful bank of the flowing river.

Michael had much on his mind. Having recently confessed to his life's mentor—who also happened to be Pope Ignatius—that he was in love with Hana, he had been consumed with thoughts of the different futures potentially awaiting some kind of decision on his part.

Of course, that decision was not entirely up to him. There would be no point in leaving the priesthood for a woman who did not share his feelings. He knew he needed to talk to her about this, but from a certain standpoint, he was afraid to. Either answer she might give had serious implications for his future, and he was not sure he wanted to face either of them. If she professed her love for him, was he ready to leave the priesthood? If she did not share his same feelings, where did that leave him? There was a certain peace in not knowing. He could just continue for a while with things the way they were, and not have to face a serious decision that could reshape the rest of his life. He just wasn't self-assured enough to make a decision of that magnitude.

On the other hand, he could not let it go on forever. Not making a decision was a decision in itself, just one that was the coward's way out. No, he would have to face it at some point, and soon. That was only fair to Hana. But before he spoke to her, he needed to know his own heart, and right now he just wasn't sure. There was an authentic bliss to being a priest, and he enjoyed a coveted position within the Church. His work in the Vatican Apostolic Archives provided untold treasures of knowledge and had propelled him into several adventures already. What other untold secrets in the Archives could be waiting for him?

But there were periods when the cloistered and silent halls and rooms of the Archives whispered only loneliness, and his mind drifted to those few precious times when he and Hana had shared moments of intimate closeness. They had only kissed once, but the memory of that incident still burned in his mind. Her touch was electric. He longed to hold her. To protect her. To be with her. He couldn't deny those feelings, but did they mean he had to act on them? Or, like so many priests before him, must he learn to control and suppress those feelings, not just for himself, but for the sake of those people he served, and for the Church?

Dare he speak of this to Karl? To share the burden and gain some kind of insight from a close friend? As they ran in silence—the cadence of their breathing and their rhythmic footsteps the only sounds—he decided to chance it. After all, Karl had come out to him on their first run together two years earlier, and they had developed a strong bond since.

"I'm in love with your cousin," he blurted out as his gaze was turned to one of the ships passing up the river.

"Yeah, me too," the young Swiss Guard said, laughing and shaking his head. "She's an amazing woman."

"No. I... I meant it in a different way, Karl. I really *do* love her." As he repeated the words, Michael suddenly seized up, feeling dizzy and nauseous. His pace slowed until he began walking in tight circles, breathing heavily, his hands resting on his hips. His eyes teared up as he looked at his friend. "And... I don't know what to do about it..."

Karl had stopped as well, now looking at the priest in a different light.

"You're serious, aren't you?"

Michael looked away, largely to keep his emotions in check, then took a couple of deep breaths. Turning back to Karl, he laid out the truth of his longtime desire, including the spontaneous forbidden kiss that occurred in the dim light of the underground Archives several months earlier, and the obvious dilemma he now faced.

"Am I crazy to even be talking like this? I figured you're the only one I can turn to. What do I do?"

"Do you know if she feels the same way?"

"That's just it—I don't know! And if I did, and she shared my feelings, well, what then? Leaving the priesthood doesn't seem like an option, and yet I can't have it both ways."

"If only the Church were more enlightened on this issue, not to mention situations like mine, where I have to keep my own relationship with Lukas secret. It isn't fair, and the rules are archaic. But, they're still the rules, Michael. We either choose to keep to them or not."

"If I only knew how she really felt about me, it might make a decision easier. Has she ever mentioned anything to you?"

Karl rolled his eyes and put his hand on Michael's shoulder. "My friend, she's smarter than that. I know she cares about you, like we all do, but she'd never come out and actually say how she feels in that way—especially since you're a priest! She barely even mentions how she feels about Marco."

"And there's that too. I'd hate to come between Marco and Hana if there was something special there—which I don't really sense in a more meaningful way, I might add. It's just a feeling, though I'm not sure I can trust my own judgment on that. God help me..."

"Why don't you just ask her? That's the simplest way to know for sure, don't you think?"

The priest froze. "Sure. Just ask her. Why didn't I think of that?" he deadpanned.

"Well, let's burn off this energy with a few more kilometers. All the more reason to run!" Karl laughed at the double meaning as he picked up the pace, with Michael catching up.

"This isn't over, you know."

"Yeah. I know. But you'll figure something out."

FOUR

J ust across from the Musée du Louvre in the historic Palais-Royal lies the French Ministère de la Culture on Rue de Valois. The very core of French identity rests firmly on its culture—architecturally, artistically, musically, theatrically— and has since the Renaissance, when Louis XIV, the Sun King, established himself as a leading patron of the arts, though mainly in ways that enshrined his own image in sculpture, portraiture, and dance. In fact, Louis had been classically trained in ballet, his favorite of all pastimes, and personally starred in some eighty roles in forty major ballet performances, most while reigning as king.

Such determined self-aggrandizement aided him in escaping the malign influences of his cabinet ministers and a coterie of mistresses, though his subjects justly poked fun at the monarch, expecting more responsible government and less self-idolization. But the supremacy of culture Louis instilled in his countrymen blossomed, and through the centuries, all things French became international symbols of aspirational refinement.

No one knew that better than Minister of Culture Lauren Valois, whose own passion for the arts was well known and admired by all but his father and brother—though as president,

Pierre Valois astutely knew that putting his son in charge of cultural affairs was among his wiser decisions. The people loved Lauren.

When word came to him of the discovery of a body and its concealed scrolls in the lower pit of Notre-Dame, Lauren knew immediately whom to call for advice and disposition: the Vatican's own Father Michael Dominic, prefect of the Secret Archives and a prominent authority on ancient manuscripts.

Also, these particular manuscripts, Valois was informed, required specialized technology to extract them from the ancient garments to which they had adhered. Further considerations included the subtleties of how to access their contents, for the fragility of the documents was evident even to the excavation crew, who had no formal training in such matters.

And Lauren knew the Vatican was among the few institutions in the world possessing such technology, so it was only logical that Dominic be summoned to assist in the process.

RETURNING to the hotel after their run, Michael and Karl went to the front desk to retrieve their room keycards.

Recognizing the priest, the desk clerk said, "Ah, *bonjour*, Père Dominic. You have a message." She handed Michael a small envelope. As he and Karl made their way to the elevator, he opened it and read the gold-embossed card within.

"Interesting. It's from the Cultural Ministry. Lauren Valois himself, in fact. He wants to speak with me about a matter involving Notre-Dame. Wonder what that's about."

When he got to his room, he called the Cultural Minister's office. After a few moments, the minister's secretary put him through.

"Father Dominic?" asked Lauren Valois after picking up the phone.

"Yes, Minister, I'm here."

"Michael, please, call me Lauren. Are you by any chance available tomorrow to come by Notre-Dame on a matter of some importance?"

"May I first ask what this is about?"

"Yes, but I must insist that you keep this confidential for now. While excavators were in the process of completing a preventive dig under the cathedral floor—in order to install a thirty-meter-high scaffolding to reconstruct the great iron spire—they discovered a lower pit, a crypt of sorts, deep beneath the marble floor. They not only found a lead sarcophagus, which you've likely seen in the news, but something else we have yet to disclose publicly: another unmarked, tightly sealed casket. Specialists from the National Institute of Preventive Archaeological Research, or INRAP, have opened it but have yet to identify whose remains it contains.

"Curiously, the person was dressed as a bishop; that much we know. But sewn into the inside of his garment sleeve was a set of ancient scrolls, which, for whatever reasons, seem to have been purposely hidden. They appear to be in remarkably good condition, except for having adhered to the fabric of his pontifical vestments over time.

"Michael, the manuscripts are tightly rolled up in typical scroll fashion, though flattened against the garment, and opening them could surely destroy them, given their age and fragility. I am aware that you have specialized equipment in the Vatican that can analyze such documents without unrolling them. Is that correct?"

"Yes, Minister, we do use microtomography to detect the presence of iron in specialized inks—those typically used between the twelfth and nineteenth centuries anyway—all without having to unroll the original scrolls. It's been quite effective in our work in the Archives and, yes, it does sound as if that process might help in analyzing your discovery, which would seem to be a pretty exciting find."

"So, you will meet with the INRAP team tomorrow, yes? You

will have full access to everything in the pit, of course, and be able to make the necessary arrangements with the rector for transferring the scrolls to Rome if needed. As you can imagine, few people are allowed inside Notre-Dame now, especially in the lower pits, so this should make for an interesting experience. And naturally, you can call on me at any time. We want to know what's in those documents, Michael, and how it contributes to our history."

"Of course, tomorrow works fine for me, Minister. Will you be there?"

"No, I'm afraid I have other commitments. But when you arrive, ask for Père Pascal Roche, the rector of Notre-Dame. He will introduce you to the appropriate personnel."

BARON ARMAND de Saint-Clair had reserved a table for five at Pur' - Jean-François Rouquette, the Michelin-starred restaurant at the Park Hyatt Vendôme. When the party arrived sharply at eight o'clock, the maître d' seated them at his finest table. The baron was not only a longtime patron of the establishment, but the master of the house knew, naturally, that he was in Paris for the funeral of France's First Lady, making him an especially important guest.

"And what would Monsieur le Baron prefer in the way of wine or champagne?" he asked Saint-Clair.

"*Oui*, Sébastien, we'll start with two bottles of the Krug Grande Cuvée, the 168th Edition, please. And rather than order from the menu, kindly ask Chef to prepare for us five special entrees of his choice."

"*Très bien*, Monsieur. Chef Rouquette will be honored to surprise you with his favorites. I will have the champagne brought over at once."

As the maître d' went to fetch the sparkling wine, Armand looked around the table. "Such a sad day. Jacqueline was one of my oldest friends, and of course her passing reminds us all of how short a time we have on this earth. At least it does me."

"Oh, Grand-père... you'll probably outlive us all," said Hana. "You're as strong and feisty as you were when I was much younger, or at least that's how I remember you. But let's not dwell on the maudlin. How was your run today, Karl? Michael?"

The priest suddenly reddened, unprepared to discuss *anything* about today's run. Sensing his discomfort, Karl quickly stepped in.

"It was great! We ran along the Seine and up to the Louvre, over to the Eiffel Tower, then back here to the hotel. Not a long run, but it was good to get out into the fresh air after the funeral. What did you guys do this afternoon?" He looked at Marco and Hana expectantly, giving Michael time to collect himself.

"Hana had some writing to get done in the apartment," Marco said, "so I watched a football game on TV while she worked. France shut out Portugal three to zero, so that was something to celebrate."

"And what about you, Michael?" Hana persisted. "Anything new to speak of?"

Having regained his ground, Michael replied, "Actually, I just received an invitation from Lauren Valois to meet with some people tomorrow at Notre-Dame. I didn't think there was much going on there except restoration from the fire damage, but as it happens, he's requested my services on a special project. I'm afraid I can't go into detail about it yet, but hopefully I'll be able to tell you more soon."

"Well, that doesn't sound intriguing at all," Hana said tauntingly, her eyes fastened on Michael's. "You can't even give us a clue?"

"Not even a small one," he replied, smiling back at her. "But maybe you might like to meet me there? We can have lunch afterward."

"Lovely! It's a da— plan, then," Hana said, catching herself. Blushing, she quickly turned the conversation.

"Oh, I forgot to mention it, but my editor has hinted she might expand my investigations purview to our Rome bureau. There's much happening there now that affects France's largely Catholic population, and our main competitor, *Le Figaro*, is already making inroads there. So I may be spending more time in the Eternal City."

Marco looked up abruptly. "You have not mentioned this to me! But... France is our home. Are you sure that is something you really want?" He glanced across the table at Michael, a faintly sour look on his face.

Hana leaned toward him, whispering her reply. "I only said she was thinking about it. And I'm telling you now. You know I have to go where the stories take me. Don't make a big thing of it, Marco, please."

He leaned back in his chair, miffed at the prospect of leaving France. Michael just kept his head down.

After the team exchanged small talk and sipped on champagne, a troupe of waiters arrived at their table, each carrying a cloche-covered plate. Each took his place to the left of a diner and then, in a show of culinary theater, they simultaneously laid down the plates and removed the silver domes, revealing stunningly colorful dishes. Sébastien began describing the chef's specialties.

"For Mademoiselle Sinclair, Chef has prepared morel mushrooms picked this very morning from the Fontainebleau Forest, stuffed with walnut sabayon, leeks, and fava beans in vinaigrette. For Monsieur le Baron, knowing your fondness for prime beef, Chef has grilled Japwagyu over a barbecue with grapevine shoots, salsa verde, and brocolettis—and may I say, the Wagyu is superb, flown in from Kobe, Japan, just last night. Monsieur Picard, you have the crab and cuttlefish, with fennel and a coral emulsion with coconut milk. For Père Dominic, our most fitting catch of the day: monkfish with grains of paradise, kohlrabi, and wild garlic. And finally, for Monsieur Dengler, pan-fried abalones dressed with black beans, red pepper chutney, and pomegranate molasses.

"Is there anything else I might get for you, Mademoiselle et Messieurs? More champagne, perhaps?"

"No, Sébastien, no more champagne," the baron replied, looking at the wine list, "but would you bring us a bottle of the Chateau Latour '98? And for those having fish, let's give them the Remoissenet Chassagne-Montrachet Maltroye Premier Cru 2019."

"Of course, Baron, excellent choices. *Bon appétit!*"

As everyone oohed and aahed over their dishes, Karl asked, "How did he know our names?!"

Armand smiled. "The maître d' of any fine restaurant makes it his business to know the names of favored guests, and my assistant, Frederic, provided him with a list when making the reservation." Young Karl looked at the baron in wonder, impressed by how such details mattered.

"Marco," Armand began, his face more serious now as he turned to the Frenchman, "I want to make sure you and Hana remain inseparable in the days ahead. These protests seem to be getting worse, and I don't want any chances taken with her safety." Then, looking at Hana, he added, "Forgive an old man his overbearing concern, my dear. But I truly do fear for everyone's safety just now. These anarchists are dangerous and unpredictable; look at what we witnessed this morning as evidence. Stay away from the volatile areas, and remain close to Marco here."

"Yes, Pépé, I promise." She took Marco's hand, then glanced at Michael, who seemed forlorn. She said nothing, reluctantly turning her gaze away.

AFTER DINNER, as everyone was getting up from the table, Marco pulled Michael aside.

"*Mon ami,* would you join me in the men's room for a moment?"

Michael glanced at his friend. "Does my nose need powdering?"

Without responding, Marco gently guided Michael by the elbow to the men's room. Once inside, he looked at the priest sincerely.

"Look, Michael, I'll get right to the point. I love Hana. I think we might have something very special. But I get the feeling from her that she's holding out hope that you might decide to leave the priesthood and marry her. It's like fighting a ghost. I like you. *Zut!* I've saved your life a couple times! So I think you owe me this. I'm asking you to tell Hana that you are taking a step back. Give me a fair shot at this. I think if she wasn't secretly pining over you, that we'd really have a shot at making a happy life together. Can you do this for me?"

"You know, Marco, I've been thinking about that quite a bit recently. I've been praying for some kind of a sign as to what to do. Maybe this is it. I do owe you my life, yes, and I want Hana —and you—to be happy. But I don't like lying to her."

"Tell her you are anticipating some additional duties at the Vatican, helping out your father or something, some secret project. You seem to keep attracting those anyway. She won't suspect anything. Just tell her you need to take a step back. Please."

Michael looked pensively at his friend, conscious of their mutual predicament. "Okay, Marco. I owe you that. But you make her happy, don't hurt her."

"No need to worry about that, my friend. And thanks."

CHAPTER

FIVE

Considered one of the finest examples of French Gothic architecture ever built, Notre-Dame's twin stone towers loomed seventy meters high above Father Dominic as he approached the central portal of the stern façade. Having taxied to the Île de la Cité, an island in the Seine on which the cathedral had been built in the thirteenth century, the priest was cleared for entry by the rector, Father Pascal Roche, who escorted him into the building.

"Oh," Michael said to Roche as they headed toward the entrance, "I have a friend who will be stopping by later, Hana Sinclair. Would you kindly permit her access when she arrives?"

"*Mais oui*, Père Dominic. That will not be a problem. One of the foremen will escort her in." He spoke to one of the men standing nearby, then rejoined his guest.

On passing through the great doors, Michael found dozens of men and women working with obvious expertise—stonemasons, sculpture and fine art restorers, carpenters, ironworkers, and others—scattered about the interior, cleaning the massive, six-thousand-square-meter space. Cranes, ladders, and scaffolding were visible everywhere as people meticulously scrubbed walls, floors, ceilings, and vaults, and gently cleaned the large, stained-glass rose windows. Restoration had begun up in the higher sections of the cathedral and progressed downward to preserve areas which had already been cleaned. Thin layers of dust and ash, a good deal of it composed of lead particles, coated the entire interior after the massive fire, and Michael saw many people using fine brushes with soft bristles to pore over tiny, dust-laden cracks in the statuary and sculptured columns and walls, and vacuum up the soot and fine powder in specialized backpacks as they attentively moved on to the next area.

As he and Father Roche climbed down ladders into the lower vaults and the pit containing the sarcophagus, the rector explained some of the problems they were facing.

"You see, Michael, the archeologists have a clear mission as regards any new discoveries in antiquity that are made during this process, and those appear to be many, and of significant importance. Under the auspices of the Ministry of Culture, their job is to unearth, identify, and protect anything of cultural value to France, and they take their roles quite seriously.

"On the other hand, we are bound by French law in matters concerning the dignity and respect for human remains, areas which fall under the domain of the police and Interior Ministry. The two are constantly at odds over these new finds, both the sarcophagus and now this unknown bishop. And of course, as you probably know, both ministries are overseen by the rival Valois brothers, which doesn't make my job any easier. After a good deal of political maneuvering, it was finally determined that the casket could be opened, and later re-interred when the crypt is restored."

"Yes, as to that, Pascal... I would very much like to see the scrolls Minister Valois mentioned to me, the ones INRAP needed help with."

"Of course," Father Roche said, pointing. "The coffin is over there. Careful now, there are many stones and loose slabs all around us."

Having been given hard hats with LED headlamps, the men

made their way down to the site of the casket as their beams of light pierced the dim underground chamber in wildly shifting directions, highlighting fine dust particles lingering in the dank air.

"Shouldn't we be wearing respirators or something?" Michael asked.

"No, it's perfectly safe here. We breathe the same particulates most everywhere else, we just don't see them so clearly as we do in such dark, confined spaces as this, lit by our headlamps."

Michael looked back up through the opening in the floor and could still see the scaffolding and people working on the upper vaults of the cathedral. The noise of drills, hammers, vacuums, and moving equipment was deafening, even down below where they now found themselves.

Leading the way after climbing over centuries-old detritus, Father Roche finally stopped in front of a closed wooden coffin set back in a corner. Its elaborate design clearly identified its occupant as a person of prominence. Michael observed that it was in a remarkably fine state given its age and was adorned with carved depictions of biblical scenes in bas-relief. Standing there looking down, both priests made the sign of the cross as each said his own silent prayer punctuated by the construction sounds above.

"Michael, if you'll give me a hand opening the crown... you take that end. I'll manage this one. It just comes straight off, there are no hinges." Together, they carefully lifted the lid off the casket and gently set it on its edge against a wall.

Resting inside was a skeleton dressed in fine liturgical garments in surprisingly good condition. The skull was covered by a wreath of, and rested on a pillow of boxwood leaves, which were used to preserve bodies of the religious and social elite of the time.

The colors of the garments were still vibrant, and the ornamentation did seem to indicate to Michael's studied understanding that this could be a bishop from the fourteenth century.

Especially notable was the bejeweled bishop's miter above the skull. The chasuble and alb were made of white wool and silk—fabrics only available then to the wealthier classes—and a jewel-studded cincture went around the waist. Across the chest was a purple stole with a golden hem.

Michael bent down to peer more closely at something that caught his attention; something few others might have recognized at first glance: the man was wearing the ecclesiastical ring of a cardinal.

"It seems we have something of a contradiction here, Pascal. Come, look at this. That is the ring of a cardinal, not a bishop," he said confidently. "A cardinal's ring during that period was usually set with a sapphire, while the inner side of the bezel bore the arms of the pope conferring it. Would you mind if I removed it for a moment?"

"Not at all! Though I must admit, I'm quite surprised by this."

Reaching inside the coffin, Michael easily slid the ring off the bony left hand of the skeleton lying there. Reaching inside his backpack, he withdrew a magnifying glass, then aimed his head-lamp at the now brilliantly glowing, deep blue sapphire. Turning the ring on its side, he read aloud the inscription inside the bezel.

"'*Clement V PP,*'" he said, astonished. "This was from Pope Clement V! The 'PP' stands for '*Pontifex pontificum,*' the suffix for a pope's regnal name, meaning 'pontiff of the pontiffs.' This is amazing! There's just no way a bishop would dare wear a cardinal's ring given to him personally by the reigning pope. So, you're likely not dealing with a bishop here, Pascal. This man was much more important.

"But that's a mystery for another time. As for the scrolls, where did you say you found them?"

"Just here, sewn inside his right sleeve." The rector carefully folded back the stiff hem of the fabric, revealing the rolled edges of apparently two aged and flattened parchment manuscripts.

"As you can see, over time, it appears the parchments have

adhered to the fabric. We're afraid to try to extract them, but as you are the expert in such things, I'll leave that to you."

His headlamp aimed directly at the objects, Michael inspected them more closely, further rolling up the sleeve ever so gently to prevent any tearing of the scrolls. The garment itself was somewhat inflexible, making the process slow and tedious.

As he was about to touch the parchments to check their own pliability, he heard his name being shouted from above. It was a woman's voice.

Removing his hand from the sleeve, he walked back to where he could see above the floor, and found it was Hana calling him, standing next to one of the foremen who had accompanied her in. He noticed that she was standing at the edge of the pit by a makeshift railing. He could barely hear her over the noise. He still had much to do here, and she had arrived earlier than he expected.

He had planned on talking to her face to face, but he was dreading that moment. Since she was early, he would just have to talk to her from here.

"Hana, I can't be with you now," he shouted, looking at her anxiously.

She turned her ear toward him and shouted, *"You can't what?"* Just then, her phone rang and he saw her put it to her ear. It was Marco.

As she answered, she heard Michael shout, *"I said, I can't be with you!"* this time with exasperation.

Instantly, the look on her face changed to one of confusion or dismay or maybe remorse; Michael couldn't interpret it from some eight meters away. And whether it was from his words or the phone call, he couldn't tell either. *"You can't be with me?"* she shouted.

Michael quickly replied, *"I need to take a step back."*

"What *is* it, Marco?" she snapped, holding the phone tightly to her ear.

"Where are you?!" he asked heatedly. "You know you

shouldn't be alone now. I'm coming to get you." Upset at what Michael had just told her, Hana simply said, "Fine, pick me up at Notre-Dame." Then she abruptly ended the call.

Turning back to Michael, she shouted down into the pit, *"I'm going to be with Marco. I... I'll see you later."* She turned away, emotion clouding her face.

Michael was stunned. *Maybe Marco had talked to her too?* he thought. *Well... I guess that's that, then.*

Despondently, he walked back to the coffin and Father Roche. *I hope this was the right thing to do.*

CHAPTER
SIX

Returning to the tomb of the unknown bishop-cardinal and focusing his mind on the task at hand, Michael happened to notice something on the crown of the coffin leaning against the wall where Father Roche stood. Shining his headlamp on it, he discovered a small inscription in French, hidden in the shadows. Leaning over, he read it aloud: *"Ici repose Son Excellence Monseigneur Jérôme Baudette."*

"'Here rests His Excellency Bishop Jérome Baudette.'" Michael looked quizzically at Pascal. "I still think this is a case of mistaken identity. I'll have to do some research once I'm back in Rome, though I'm inclined to go with cardinal. But why the disguise of a bishop, I wonder? Well, in the meantime, what to do with these scrolls?" He leaned back down over the body to reexamine the sleeve, then looked up at his companion.

"Pascal, I'm afraid we're going to have to perform a little surgery here. It would be pointless to move the entire body to Rome just to remove the scrolls. But I will have to separate the sleeve from the rest of the garment. That's something that can more easily be restored at a later time, should you find it more respectful, though I don't think it's all that necessary for his garments to be intact at the time of reburial. We only need the scrolls. Do I have your permission to extract the sleeve, then?"

"*Oui*, by all means, proceed. It is more important that we have the documents to better understand who this man was and why he was buried here."

Michael opened his backpack and grabbed a pair of white cloth gloves and a Swiss Army knife that Karl had once given him. Retracting the small pen blade, he very gently sliced through the stitching of the upper seams of the garment at the shoulder. Being hundreds of years old, the threads gave little resistance to the blade, falling away with each cut.

"Parchment is composed of prepared animal skins, and is impressively durable over time," Michael muttered absently to Father Roche as he kept working. "Exemplars have been discovered dating as far back as 2500 BCE, so it's not surprising these are in such good condition. You certainly have my interest in deciphering them. Our tomographic analysis should reveal their contents fairly easily, I would think."

"Forgive me for saying, Michael," Roche murmured, wringing his hands nervously, "but you must ensure their return to Paris as soon as possible. They will be placed in the Louvre until Notre-Dame is restored."

Michael looked up at the priest with a slightly indignant smile. "Rest easy, Père Roche. The Vatican already has far more manuscripts than we know what to do with. It's not like we're on a scavenger hunt for more. You'll get them back promptly once we're finished with the analysis that your government has requested."

Turning back to his task, Michael clipped the final strands and, with a little gentle persuasion, separated the sleeve from the shoulder.

Sliding it down the skeletal arm, he examined the scrolls more closely under the headlamp light as best he could. Having been folded flat and sewn-in for centuries, it was immediately apparent that, once removed, attempting to unroll them could very well cause the manuscripts to chip or even crack. There was no doubt they would need to be analyzed using the specialized X-ray equipment in Rome—but the gold threads woven into the garment sleeve would present interference with the imaging, so ultimately all traces of the garment would need to be separated from the scrolls themselves.

"I don't know how long the process will take, but I won't chance trying to unfold them. Our technology can read through the layers of parchment and identify what is written on each of them, despite the multiple layers caused by the folds."

"We will leave all that to you and your team, Michael, with my personal gratitude for your assistance. I very much look forward to your analysis. Are we finished here?"

Michael looked around to see if he could find anything else intriguing, then replied, "I think we're good to go for now, Pascal." Removing a large, acid-free calico conservation bag from his backpack, he gently placed the sleeve and scroll inside it, then returned it to his pack. "I'll find a proper box for this once I get back to the hotel. But now, let's get back upstairs, shall we?"

Climbing back up the ladder, Michael and Father Roche returned to the main floor of the cathedral. The noise was even louder now: saws cutting timber, vacuums sweeping up wood and iron dust, men shouting in French from all directions.

As they paused at the exit, Michael thanked his host for the opportunity to assist with such a remarkable find and summarized what would happen in the coming days.

One of the construction workers who stood nearby moved closer as if to pick up a bit of debris. Then, out of the corner of his eye, he watched as the two men shook hands before the priest walked away toward a line of waiting taxis.

Stepping outside, the worker pulled a cell phone out of his pocket and made a call.

~

ENTERING THE ARCHING, blue-tiled, translucent façade of the new *Le Monde* headquarters in Montparnasse, Hana proceeded up the elevator to her office on the fourth floor, keen to hear of recent developments in the protests around the French capital, which had begun yesterday during the cemetery fiasco, but she thought had died out through the night and morning. Eager to see Michael today, she had gone a bit early to Notre Dame, only to be heartbroken by Michael's statement that he needed to step back. Then Marco had been insistent when he called that he should have accompanied her, setting her on edge even more.

When she arrived in the newsroom, gaggles of reporters and editorial staff were clustered around flat-screen TVs hanging throughout the expansive room, all of them shocked at the spectacles they were witnessing live across their beloved city.

"What's happening, Martine?" she asked her editor.

Martine Deschanel turned to her with a grim expression.

"Hana, it is beyond terrible out there. Yesterday's protests began again this morning. So far, there have been more than two hundred arrests, and one Yellow Jacket was shot and killed, though no one knows why or by whom. Several dozen protesters were admitted to hospitals for treatment of exposure to tear gas and pepper spray, and others with broken arms or shoulders from police baton strikes. Many suffered severe bruising by bean bag guns shot indiscriminately by police officers roaming the streets in armored vehicles. Reports of fires being set, mainly in trash bins, are coming in from everywhere.

"The duke has even called for official inquiries into both the apparent lack of adequate preparation for these marches, and the overzealous reactions of the police in dealing with protesters, most of whom are simply peaceful demonstrators. They treat them all as if they were those detestable anarchists, which is always a much smaller number of opportunists.

"He even hinted that he may call for a vote of no confidence in the Valois government. Obviously, the duke senses political gain amid the chaos.

"Where have *you* been, by the way?" Martine asked. "You're missing all the excitement."

"Oh, I had some family business to take care of," Hana replied, expanding on reality. "But getting through the crowds in the streets was excitement enough, thanks."

"I know this isn't your beat, Hana, but I want you to work on this for page one. You've got twenty-four hours to turn in a thousand words, and be sure to include that bit about the duke."

"You got it, Martine," Hana said, taking a seat in her cubicle.

Just then, Hana heard the muffled sound of a phone ringing and checked her bag. Pulling out her phone, she saw Michael Dominic's name appear on Caller ID.

"Hi, Michael," she said simply, still stinging from their earlier encounter.

"Hana, I just wanted to say… Well, I'm sorry we couldn't speak at the cathedral. But Karl and I are now on our way to the airport, heading back to Rome. Lauren Valois asked me to handle something important for him, and I need access to our lab in the Vatican. Do you see yourself coming to Rome any time soon?"

"No," she said flatly, "there's really no reason I can think of at the moment. I've been assigned a page one piece on the riots which will keep me busy for the next day or so. And there are likely to be follow-up pieces."

There was an awkward silence as neither spoke for a few moments. Then, "Well, okay, I guess we'll see each other when we see each other," Michael said. "Do take care in the meantime, Hana, and make sure Marco is with you while Paris is still in flux."

"Thanks, Michael, I will. You take care of yourself too."

She hung up the phone and stared at the blinking cursor on an empty page of her word processing display. She had hoped for a lunch conversation with Michael, one that would fill her life with answers for her future. Instead, her future was as blank as the screen before her now.

CHAPTER

SEVEN

T
he main concourse in Terminal 2F of Paris Charles de Gaulle Airport was a bustle of construction activity as workers erected a series of new kiosks between the Duty Free shop and the Alitalia gate. Though the concourse was sectioned off with safety barriers, workers still had to weave around a nonstop stream of arriving and departing passengers as they went about their work.

Michael and Karl had just passed through the security inspection area and were heading to the Alitalia gate for their flight to Rome. Having had to check his weapon with their luggage, Karl was feeling disarmed in more ways than one, especially since he was responsible for Michael's safety, not to mention their valuable cargo: the sleeve and scrolls of the unknown bishop or cardinal, now stored safely in an acid-free acrylic box they had bought at an artists' supply shop on the way to the airport.

While Karl surveilled the area, he noticed that Michael seemed lost in thought as he stared at nothing in particular while they walked. He wondered if he was thinking of Hana...probably was, in fact. Ever since his visit to Notre-Dame the day before, he had been quieter than normal, less enthusiastic. The

Swiss Guard didn't envy his friend's quandary. It had to be tough on him, he thought, but if he wanted to share his concerns, he would in his own time. Meanwhile, he would stay close to him.

Karl was just about to ask Michael if he wanted to stop at Starbucks for coffee when he noticed a construction worker approaching them—a fit chap with a safety vest, hard hat, leather gloves, tinted safety glasses, and dust mask—as he carried a long, two-by-four length of lumber over his shoulder. The young Swiss Guard was trying to make sense of why his alert radar was up, but he trusted his instincts.

In an abundance of caution, he positioned himself between Michael and the wholly unrecognizable worker as they continued on to the gate. *I can't even see the guy's eyes... and why the dust mask? No one else is wearing one...*

Then the man suddenly turned, and the two-by-four swung around swiftly, heading directly for Michael's head. In a split-second, Karl grabbed Michael by the shoulders and put a foot behind his knee, to pull him back and down, along with himself, as the lumber flew over their heads.

Suddenly, the worker dropped the board with a loud *clack* on the floor and made a grab for the box Michael was holding. As the priest struggled for balance, uncertain what was happening, he tried to keep the box from being jostled. Meanwhile, Karl was on his way back to his feet when the worker made another reach for the box.

Catching the man's left hand with his own right hand, Karl twisted the man's hand up and back, pulling him away from Michael. Karl then used both hands, forcing the assailant's hand farther back and driving him onto his back. The workman rolled from his back in a somersault and came up in a fighting crouch.

So much for him being just a construction worker, Karl thought. As he squared off, putting himself between Michael and their attacker, the shrill screech of a police whistle split the air. Two airport security officers were running in their direction from fifty meters away, yelling for them to stop and stay put. Glancing in their direction, the workman turned and ran, making a break for the exit. Racing through the open automatic doors, mowing down people as he pushed them out of the way, he leapt into the passenger side of a waiting small, white Toyota pickup truck idling at the curb. The car sped away as the passenger door was still closing.

"Well, that was unexpected," Michael said angrily as he brushed himself off. "Who the hell *was* that guy?!"

"I can tell you one thing: that was no accident. He was waiting for us, that much is clear, and the getaway car proves it. Did you notice how he was geared up, obviously camouflaged to avoid being identified? He wanted that box of yours pretty badly, Michael. But who else even knows you have it?"

Just as the priest was about to respond, the *gendarmes* returned from their luckless chase of the escaping workman to interview Michael and Karl.

"*Messieurs*, please come with us." Each officer grabbed an arm of the two men and marched them down a long hall and into the security office.

"But we might miss our flight!" Karl protested. "And we're the victims here, by the way. That guy tried stealing something from us! What kind of workers do you hire here, anyway?"

"It's okay, Karl, they're just doing their job," Michael said amicably, then turned to the *gendarmes*, "but we *were* just minding our own business when we were suddenly attacked. How can we help you further?"

One officer, keen to assert himself, assumed control. "May I see your identification, both of you?" he demanded curtly. Michael and Karl presented their passports and Vatican credentials, neither of which impressed the lead *gendarme*. He scanned the documents into his computer, then began asking them various questions about their encounter with the construction worker and entering details of the incident in a computer terminal on the interview desk.

GARY MCAVOY & RONALD L. MOORE

"And what is it you have in the box, monsieur, that this man was so eager to acquire?"

"Since it passed through security without issue, I fail to see why that should matter," Michael said politely but emphatically, gripping the box more firmly. "We are on Vatican business here at the request of your government—by Cultural Minister Lauren Valois himself, in fact. We can call his office now, if you'd like. I'm sure he would be happy to discuss the matter with your superiors."

Correctly perceiving the challenge as a threat, the lead *gendarme*'s face tightened. As he was about to take more forceful action, a senior officer entered the room, having heard the commotion from the open door to his office. The two *gendarmes* snapped to attention.

"What is going on here?" he inquired, noticing Michael was wearing clerical garb. "And why have you detained a priest?"

"*Mon capitaine*, we—"

Michael took the opportunity to take control, speaking in French. "As I was telling your good officers here, we are on Vatican business as a personal favor to Minister Lauren Valois. As we were walking to our gate, we were suddenly ambushed by one of your construction workers. Since he tried to steal our Vatican materials here, my colleague—one of the pope's most capable Swiss Guards—took appropriate evasive action, as was clearly needed. We have done nothing wrong, *Capitaine*, and hope not to miss our flight." He glanced at his watch. There were just minutes left to board.

The captain, probably a Catholic since his eyebrows arched in appreciation at the mention of the pope, resolved the matter quickly. Addressing his officers, he declared, "Release these men at once. And in the future, show respect for the Vatican and the authority of a Swiss Guard on duty. *Messieurs*, if you will permit me to escort you to your gate; please, come this way."

Hustling Michael and Karl out the door and down the hall,

he cleared a hasty path to the Alitalia gate just as the boarding agent was about to close the door to the jetway.

"My apologies, gentlemen, and have a safe flight." All three shook hands and Michael thanked him, then he and Karl ran down the jet bridge to take their seats as the flight attendant secured the aircraft door.

THOUGH CHAGRINED by having been scolded, the lead *gendarme* back in the security office dutifully sat down to complete his report of the incident, entering the names of the victims and noting the unfortunate fact that the culprit had gotten away.

Unbeknownst to him, a hidden subroutine in the computer's database code flagged the report as containing a name on a confidential Watch List: Father Michael Dominic. The program automatically produced two secret copies of the report and instantly sent them by encrypted email: one to an address in the Interior Ministry, and one to another governmental office. The subroutine then deleted the logs which documented that the file had been copied and the emails sent.

In his office at the Interior Ministry, Philip Valois's computer chimed, noting an email had been delivered to a special mailbox. Sitting at his desk, Valois opened the decrypted message and read the report. He sat forward in his chair, steepling his fingers in thought. *Interesting*, he mused.

Though he was responsible for having the secret subroutine added to all law enforcement databases throughout France, Valois was unaware that the IT technician who had implemented the code had—as instructed by a much higher authority—added a second email address to the bot that scanned all filed law enforcement reports for flagged names and keyword alerts. The IT tech had been given specific confidential instructions that such requests were to be secretly routed to another office, one that President Pierre Valois had established to monitor domestic surveillance efforts—aware that it paid to know who was watching whom, and for what reasons.

As THE WHITE Toyota pickup truck sped away from the airport, the passenger opened the glove box and took out a cheap prepaid burner phone. He dialed a number from memory.

A man's voice answered, *"Allô?"*

"The project at the airport was not completed."

"Complications?"

"There was interference. The project had security."

"Crew status?"

"Operational, no compromise."

"Okay, return to the warehouse. I'll inform the project manager."

"Copy that." Snapping the phone in half, the passenger tossed it out the window. "Back to the warehouse," he told his companion.

The driver nodded, pressing down harder on the accelerator pedal.

CHAPTER

EIGHT

S tanding under the hot Parisian midday sun, a long line of mostly young men—perhaps a hundred or so, nearly all of them immigrants—snaked down the block from the Pôle Emploi Pigalles unemployment office on Rue des Martyrs. Many clustered in small groups, chatting restlessly as they waited their turn when the office would reopen after its long noon mealtime. While French shops and offices traditionally enjoyed a leisurely two- to three-hour midday meal, these men could afford no such luxury. Most of them were destitute, scrabbling for work and food to support their families.

Just across the street from the queue, a white Toyota pickup truck with a full cargo bed pulled up to the curb, its emergency flashers blinking. Two men emerged from the cab dressed in jeans, boots, and flannel shirts beneath reflective orange city workers' safety vests. The hard hats, earmuffs, safety goggles, and dust filter masks they wore conveniently obscured their facial features.

After placing orange safety cones around the truck, they removed a number of wooden two-by-fours, battery-powered drills, screwdriver bits, and long screws, and quickly assembled a makeshift scaffolding on the sidewalk, set up against a cinderblock wall of the adjacent building. Once complete, the men hoisted a heavy, thirty-liter beer keg onto the scaffolding, then stacked two dozen boxes of nails, screws, and nuts around the keg in a half-moon facing across the street.

One of the men retrieved a black plastic box about the size of a cigarette carton from the truck's cab. Mounting the scaffolding, he pushed an eight-centimeter metal cylinder with a wire dangling from it into a hole on the top of the beer keg. He then connected that wire to one sticking out of the black box and placed the entire assembly atop the keg.

Finally, they set up a portable DVD player with a small built-in TV screen on the scaffold, inserted a disc, turned up the sound, and pressed the Play button.

Finished with their work, the two men retrieved the orange cones, got back into the truck, and drove away.

It took a minute or so for the disc to load and play through the title and credits, but moments later, a few men across the street clearly heard the loud sounds of a woman experiencing pleasure. As more heads began to turn toward the unmistakably recognizable sounds, the men realized a pornographic video was playing, its explicit images vividly displayed on the small screen of the black box.

A group of younger men eagerly approached the TV and, after a few moments observing the images with wide grins on their faces, they motioned for others to come over and enjoy the show. As men farther away saw a crowd forming around the scaffolding, they too joined in, wanting to know what the commotion was about.

TWO BLOCKS DOWN THE STREET, a man of French heritage stood on the balcony of a sixth-floor apartment looking out over Rue des Martyrs, presumably considering the rental of the apartment. The leasing agent had been describing the unit's features to him when her phone rang. Stepping back inside to take the call, she left the man alone on the balcony.

Reaching into his jacket pocket, he withdrew a small pair of binoculars and peered down the street to the crowd of men forming around the scaffolding. He waited a few minutes for more of them to join the crowd watching the video.

Then, putting the binoculars away, he took out a two-way handheld radio made for the American ham radio market: one that had been modified to broadcast on the American FRS, or Family Radio Service, on frequencies that lay just outside the 440-megahertz amateur radio band. He depressed the Talk button, then keyed in a six-digit sequence on the radio's numeric keypad.

Back at the scaffolding, the cheap FRS walkie-talkie broke squelch and transmitted the tone sequence through an earphone adapter to the sound card of an Arduino microcomputer, which then—having received the correct series of tones—tripped the solenoid that was charged by the eight AA batteries powering the radio, the microcomputer, and the solenoid. Once the solenoid tripped, the charge that built up in several capacitors was directed into the blasting cap that had been inserted into the beer keg full of ammonium nitrate and fuel oil.

With a colossal explosion, the ANFO bomb detonated, projecting fiery, lethal nails, screws, and nuts at high velocity into the now-massive crowd of men watching the TV on the scaffolding.

The carnage was immediate and devastating.

The man on the balcony two blocks away turned, reentered the apartment, and closed the patio doors behind him. The leasing agent, still on the phone, turned and asked him, "What was that loud boom?" He merely shrugged his shoulders and replied, "Yes, I heard it too, but didn't see anything. Thank you, but I don't think this apartment is for me. I'll see myself out."

Leaving the unit, he walked down the six flights of stairs and exited the rear of the building, away from the line of emergency vehicles now streaming up Rue des Martyrs toward the area of the explosion. He got into his car parked in the alley behind the building and drove away, avoiding the ubiquitous surveillance cameras on the main streets.

FRENCH AUTHORITIES DID their best to contain the pandemonium at the blast area, focusing first on treating the wounded, then on attending to the casualties before beginning their crime scene investigation. Windows had been shattered by the shock wave for a couple of blocks in both directions. Little strips of singed paper were seen floating in the air more than a hundred meters from the explosion, having been tucked into the boxes of construction materials by the hundreds, including small slips of white paper on which were printed *France pour les Français*—France for the French—and *Les immigrés rentrez chez vous*—Immigrants go home. People well outside the blast area found them all over the place, blowing in the gutters and snagged on plants or trees along the boulevard. The authorities had no way of preventing these little messages of hate from being propagated, especially on social media.

By nightfall, crowds of angry young men, mostly immigrants bolstered by others sympathetic to their plight and opposed to the heavy-handed treatment of French authorities, gathered restlessly around the crime scene. Fearful that other improvised explosive devices might be hidden nearby, police had orders to keep crowds of people from gathering. But as attempts to disperse the crowds became more forceful, people's responses became more resistant, until full-scale rioting began to break out. As the livestreams began to fill social media, more and more angry and disaffected youths were drawn to the chaos and conflict. Windows were shattered in the nearby shopping district and looting broke out, prompting an even larger police response. For the first time in decades, a curfew was imposed in the City of Light.

. . .

IN THE EMERGENCY OPERATIONS CENTER, Philip Valois stood and watched the images flooding in on a wall of TV monitors. The timing of these demonstrations could not have been better, he considered silently, his mouth forming a subtle, grim smile. They almost seem to be coordinated; but by whom? Of course, he did not condone violence or the acts of domestic terrorism that certain members of the far right appeared to be perpetrating in his city, but he was more than willing to take advantage of them. The only question was, how?

His father, Pierre, was more ill than he let on, and it would not be long before elections were called for a new president. Having long positioned himself to appear as the favored candidate, Philip put great effort into doing things that made him seem more presidential in the eyes of constituents. As a law-and-order proponent, he knew a large segment of French society shared his views. His father had been too lenient with criminal punishment laws, and too liberal in his immigration policies, such that France was being consumed by too many unemployed immigrants: people who were turning to crime when their state assistance ran out.

The riots were a natural extension of that disorder. And the fear they engendered in the more conservative segment of society could be used to his advantage. The people needed to believe that Philip Valois was the man who could protect them from these dangers—real or imagined—so he needed to make that clear. And the best way to achieve that would be to go on TV and social media, getting his face before the people, and telling them those very things.

He reached for the phone to call his media advisor to get that ball rolling.

CHAPTER
NINE

S itting in a window seat, Michael gazed at the billowy cumulous clouds passing by as they flew over Switzerland en route to Italy. Looking down over the snow-capped Alps, his mind drifted back to his last conversation with Hana in the pit at Notre-Dame and later on the phone. Maybe he had misinterpreted her level of interest. Maybe she really was going to be happier with Marco. But if so, wouldn't she have been happier to have it settled?

Sitting in the aisle seat, Karl had his own concerns, certain they were up against unknown yet apparently skilled opponents. How could anyone else have known Michael had the manuscripts from Notre-Dame? Who could have leaked that kind of information? Having no answers put him at a distinct disadvantage in performing his duties, something that gnawed at him. The more he thought about it, the more concerned he became that the bad actors they had encountered in Paris were more than random thugs or part-time hoods; they were likely professional operators. During the two-hour flight, he stood and walked down the cabin aisle twice, back and forth, glancing at all passengers for anyone with a suspicious air.

· · ·

Arriving at Leonardo da Vinci Airport in Rome, Karl led the way down the jet bridge and into the terminal. As they weaved their way through the crowd of passengers waiting to board flights, he held a hand up for Michael to pause a moment while he scanned the area. He was looking for two things: first, anything that appeared to be out of the ordinary, despite the natural chaos of an airport concourse.

Secondly, he was looking for two people in particular. The first he soon found sitting at a computer rental kiosk facing the gate: it was Lukas Bischoff, pretending to be working on a computer while actually surveilling the concourse, something he had been doing for the past hour. As he saw Karl make eye contact with him, he pulled out a handkerchief and wiped his forehead, their all-clear signal.

"Michael," Karl said, "if you see anyone we know here, just pretend you don't know him. But if you recognize anyone from Paris, let me know right away."

Though Michael thought this a bit melodramatic, he accommodated his protector, casually looking around the area as they walked. Then he did notice someone familiar: a custodian pushing a trolley of cleaning supplies through the concourse. He was wearing white work pants and a white shirt, a white baseball cap, and sunglasses, with a pair of white earbud wires dangling from his ears.

Is that Dieter? he wondered as he watched the tall young man steer the cart through the crowd.

Just then, an electric shuttle cart pulled up in front of both men.

"This is for us, Michael."

"Come on... really, Karl? It's not a long walk, and I could use a stretch of the legs."

"Just grab a seat, please, on orders of the pope—more or less."

The priest sighed, then reluctantly took a seat on the back bench next to Karl. As the shuttle made a U-turn, Lukas stood up from his computer and jumped in the front seat next to the driver so he could monitor anyone approaching.

Behind them, the custodian had positioned his trolley to one side of the main aisle and pulled a mop out of a bucket. Placing a "Wet Floor" sign on the well-traveled linoleum, he began swabbing an imaginary spot on the floor, keeping an eye out for anyone showing interest in or following the shuttle cart.

"Why all the cloak and dagger?" Michael asked. "And was that Dieter I saw back there mopping a floor?!"

"Yes, but just ignore him," Karl replied. "He's watching our backs. After all that happened in Malta a few months ago, the Holy Father is concerned that the Swiss Guard needs to step up its security protocols in and around the Vatican; as well as the Secret Archives—and especially on your behalf. I think we both know the reason for that…"

Karl did not need to elaborate. The once-secret fact that Michael was the pope's son had been inadvertently leaked at an event in Malta months earlier.

He went on, "You'll also be seeing an increased security presence around the office. And for now, at least, you won't be traveling alone."

Though he appreciated the pope's reasoning, Michael was uneasy with all of it. He was a man of independence, comfortable in his own skin, and did not take well to being managed like this. As if he didn't have enough weighing on him now.

"By the way," Lukas said over his shoulder, "while you were airborne, there was a second terrorist attack in France. Somebody planted an improvised explosive device at an immigration center, and many were killed when it detonated. Police found anti-immigrant leaflets and right-wing slogans in the debris. Left-wing activists are retaliating, and anarchists are again taking advantage of the chaos. The authorities are overwhelmed, and the Interior Ministry has deployed additional personnel to restore order. Things are pretty tense in Paris just now."

"That's terrible news!" the priest exclaimed, then bowed his head in silent prayer for the victims and for the safety of others in Paris—especially one person in particular.

The shuttle having reached the baggage area, Lukas stayed with Michael while Karl waited for their luggage to appear on the baggage conveyor, along with his checked weapon. Once both bags appeared and were fetched, Karl escorted everyone out to a waiting black Land Rover. Sergeant Dieter Koehl, still in his white custodial garb, sat at the wheel, smiling to everyone as they got in.

"Just so you know, I'd never make a good janitor," he smirked. "Not enough action for me. And what damage can you do to someone with a mop?"

PASSING THROUGH ST. Anne's Gate at the Vatican, Dieter parked the Land Rover in the Belvedere courtyard lot. Grabbing his bag and the acrylic box, Michael went directly to his office with Karl in tow. A Swiss Guard in full dress uniform with a halberd at his side had been positioned at the entrance to the Archives building.

Michael looked exasperated. "This is going to get old fast, Karl. *This is the Vatican!* One of the most secure and impregnable places on earth!" he fumed.

"Well, the pope doesn't seem to think so," Karl said disparagingly, as if he took personal responsibility for the entire Swiss Guard corps.

Opening his office safe, Michael slid the acrylic box containing the sleeve and scrolls onto a shelf, then closed the door, spinning the dial a few times. As he turned around, he saw his assistant, Ian Duffy, stick his head in the doorway.

"Welcome home, boss," the Irishman enthused. "Good to have you back."

"Hey, Ian, how's it going?"

"Good, good. I hear you had some action in Paris, though. Everything turn out all right?"

"As well as might be expected, given the madness happening there now. But I did bring back a project for us. In fact, I even have a task for you now. I need a list of every bishop and cardinal in France around the turn of the thirteenth and fourteenth centuries, especially anyone who was elevated by Pope Clement V. Think you can get that to me yesterday?"

"You bet!" Ian said eagerly. "I'll see what I can dig up in our database, though it might be good to ask the historians here too. I'll take that on as well, Michael."

"Good idea, thanks. Tomorrow, we'll get our restoration lab working on some scrolls I brought back from Notre-Dame. I'll tell you more about that in the morning. But now I'm bushed and need some sleep. Don't stay up too late, Ian."

CHAPTER

TEN

Early the next morning, as a peachy pink glow lit the eastern horizon, Father Dominic had already dressed for his run and slipped out through St. Anne's Gate. After all that had happened in France, he really needed the exercise to clear his head.

He took off along his familiar route through the working-class neighborhood of the Suburra, focusing just on his breathing and the feeling of his body in motion. His muscles were tight, an indication of his body physically absorbing the stresses his mind was fabricating. He tried centering himself on the meditative sound of his footsteps, consciously taking in the morning aromas of wakening coffeehouses and the pleasant scents of honeysuckle and Chilean jasmine in flower boxes lining the streets.

But he found it difficult to maintain even the semblance of serenity. As he ran past newsstands, the morning newspapers being delivered featured banner headlines in Italian blaring "Massacre in Paris." He couldn't help but think of Hana, still there amid the chaos of a normally tranquil city.

And she hadn't even called. Generally, if something like this had happened, she would have called him right away, just to let him know she was all right. *Was she okay? Could she have been near the blast? Was she injured, or worse, dead? Marco would have called, unless he was there too. But if that were the case, Armand would have notified me, unless he was too grief-stricken to call.*

Enough! His mind reeled at the myriad possibilities, unlikely as they were, but he found it difficult to suppress his imaginings.

Stopping at the Edicola newsstand kiosk on the Piazza del Risorgimento, Michael picked up a copy of yesterday's late edition of *Le Monde*. Glancing at the bylines of articles on the front page, he flipped it over, his sweaty fingers leaving wet imprints on the paper. There, under the fold, was an article by Hana Sinclair, succinctly describing the latest political situation in Paris that was giving rise to such egregious domestic violence.

"Good grief," he murmured to no one in particular. Well, he ventured, at least he knew she was okay, since she had obviously survived the blast to be writing about it. But still, she hadn't called.

"Hey! You're dripping all over that paper," the kiosk attendant grumbled in fractured English, presuming Michael was American by his epithet. "You gotta buy it now. I can't sell it to nobody else."

"I'm sorry," Michael replied in Italian. "I'm just out for a run and didn't bring any money with me. But I was in France yesterday. In Paris. I just missed being there for this attack."

"Well, good for you. But what about this newspaper?"

"How about this… I'm a priest at the Vatican. If you set this aside, as God is my witness, I will come back here at lunch and pay for it."

"You better, or as God is *my* witness, I will complain all the way to the pope." He made the sign of the cross as he said this. "It's good for a priest to keep his word, yes? Hey, I'm Luigi Bucatini, like the pasta. What's your name?"

"I'm Father Michael Dominic," he said, smiling and extending a hand.

Bucatini exchanged the handshake. "Well, Father Michael

Dominic, I'm a good Catholic man, so I'm putting my faith in you. Don't let me down."

Michael laughed. "*Grazie*, Luigi. I won't let you down. You'll see me again later today."

AFTER A QUICK SHOWER and change of clothes back in his Vatican apartment, Michael headed down to his office. He retrieved the box containing the scrolls from his safe, then went to Ian's office and peered inside from the doorway. Ian was already there, typing furiously.

"Morning, Ian. I'm headed over to the Restoration Lab. How you doing with that list?"

"It's coming along, Michael. It's taking a little longer since I'm trying to incorporate birth and death dates so we can get the right age at the time of death. That kind of data is hard to locate."

"How many people are we dealing with, do you think?"

"I've identified more than a hundred so far."

"A hundred?! How did you find that many people so fast? What databases are you using?"

"Um," Ian stammered, "I'm not sure I can tell you that…"

"What do you mean, you can't tell me? Ian, I'm supposed to know everything that goes on here, aren't I?"

"Well, yes, I suppose that's true…" The Irishman fidgeted in his chair, clearly uncomfortable. "But something came up while you were gone, and I'm not supposed to be the one to tell you about it."

"I'm confused… What's going on? And if not you, *who* is supposed to tell me whatever *it* is?"

"Sorry, Michael. That would have to come from the Holy Father himself. Remember a few months ago, when he hadn't known about the safe in his office?—you know, the Petri Crypta? —well, he started a campaign to learn what else was being withheld from him, or what he was supposed to have been briefed on, but hadn't been.

"And one of those things came up while you were gone. They got me involved, but I was told it was absolutely confidential, and I'm not to talk to anyone about it who isn't already informed—and I *know* you will be, but you were away in Paris then, so…" Ian smiled weakly.

"Hmm," the priest murmured. "All right, I'll call Nick Bannon and get an appointment to speak with the pope about whatever it is. Meanwhile, you just keep working on that list."

"I'm nearly done, actually. Stop by on your way back from the lab and you can pick it up then."

THE SECRET ARCHIVES' Authentication and Restoration Laboratory was a state-of-the-art facility for identifying, validating, and reconstituting ancient manuscripts and other artifacts that were under the purview of the Vatican. Originally managed by the Franciscan Missionary Sisters of Mary for more than two generations, lay specialists slowly took over from religious personnel to handle the lab's delicate conservation projects.

Apart from handling its own treasures, such specialists were often called upon by museums, conservators, and other outside agencies to provide distinctive services for evaluating and restoring precious historical documents and other priceless objects, employing rare, delicate skills that were in great demand.

The center of the room featured a two-meter-square workbench composed of white Formica—immune to chemicals and grounded to prevent buildup of static charges—beneath which were storage drawers and shelves containing various scientific tools and instruments.

Individual workstations were situated on three sides of the lab, each topped with various but similar inert materials and with a variety of instruments—optical and digital microscopes, pH testing and deacidification tools, handheld steamers and HEPA vacuums, fiber optic light sheets, and other conservation equipment. Illuminated magnifiers on articulating arms hovered above each table. On the far wall, the only other door was labeled:

DANGER
X-Rays, High Magnetic Fields, Lasers
Authorized Personnel Only

As Michael entered the lab, Ekaterina Lakatos, the newest technician, was peering at a document through an illuminated magnifier at one of the workstations. She turned and stood as Michael entered.

"*Lachi tiri divés*, Father Michael," she greeted him in Romani.

"*Sastipe!* Ekaterina. *Sar si sogodi?*" he replied in her native language, asking how everything was.

"Good, Father. Oh, Uncle Gunari sends his greetings," she said brightly.

Michael thought back to the last time he had seen her uncle, Gunari Lakatos, the *voivode* or chieftain of a Roma clan, during an earlier operation in France involving Gunari's sons, Milosh and Shandor, and the Russian oligarch Dmitry Zharkov. The priest's ability to speak the old Romani language had formed a bond with the travelers, and a mutual trust—something the chary Roma did not give easily—had developed between the two men.

Ekaterina had earlier been relieved of her position in the Documents Section of the Forensic Science Laboratories of Carabinieri Force—something about a forged document the authorities had suspected, though couldn't prove, she might have been involved with. But, as a Roma, she was reflexively deemed untrustworthy in the disparaging eyes of her Carabinieri superiors and let go from her job—a job she had fought to get.

But, as it happened, she did come from a long line of forgers.

At the request of her uncle, Father Dominic had intervened with the Italian Art Squad, and the authorities had allowed the priest to take Ekaterina in as a ward, with a promise to keep an eye on her. Given her family's unique skills, he had given her a job in the Authentication and Restoration Lab. Who better to spot a forgery than a forger? Michael believed she would stay straight while working for him, both because the Art Squad was sitting on a warrant for her, and because there was now a debt to her uncle, one she would not dishonor.

"You've been home?" Michael asked her.

"Yes, just for the weekend," she said, then glanced at him ruefully. "But only to visit, not to work..."

Michael smiled knowingly. "Yes, Ekaterina, I do believe you. Is Giancarlo here?"

Ekaterina walked over to the far door of the X-ray room and knocked. "Dr. Borsetti," she shouted, "Father Michael is here for you."

Turning back to the priest, she said, "Ian told us you were coming. We can't wait to get started on your scrolls from Notre-Dame. Shall we open the box and get them set up for Dr. Borsetti?"

"Sure," said Michael, placing the box on her workstation table. "They're quite old, so exercise caution in handling them."

She looked up at him willfully, slightly insulted by the admonition. "Yes, Father, I'll be extra careful." She slipped on a pair of white cotton gloves.

To prepare the workstation for Dr. Borsetti's inspection, she opened the acrylic box, gently extracted the sleeve, and placed it on the sanitized stainless steel tabletop. She reached up to pull down a digital stereo microscope suspended from the low ceiling on an articulating arm and positioned it over the sleeve.

"Ah, Father Dominic," Borsetti said, emerging from the X-ray room. "I hear you've brought us something very special from France. I'm quite excited to see this artifact." Approaching the table, he reached for his glasses hanging from a strap around his neck and propped them low on the bridge of his nose.

After a few moments of adjusting the coarse and fine-focus dials on the optical microscope, he frowned.

"The scrolls might be an easy job for X-ray tomography, but I'm afraid these gold threads in the garment will obscure the analysis if they are not removed. We will have to extract them one by one from where they adhere to the surface of the parchments. That will take time, of course—maybe a week, perhaps two—before we will be able to conduct a reliable analysis."

"Yes," Michael said, "I thought those might present a challenge as well, Giancarlo. All right, please proceed as quickly and prudently as possible.

"Meanwhile, I need to get going. See you both later. *Achh devlesa*, Ekaterina."

"*Dja devlesa*, Father Michael," she replied, bidding the priest goodbye.

CHAPTER

ELEVEN

Returning to Ian's office, Michael picked up the finished list of bishops and cardinals who might be good candidates for their mystery man in the coffin at Notre-Dame. Identifying the body alone might surely provide a more-informed perspective on whatever contents were to be found within the scrolls.

Back in his own office, Michael picked up the phone and called the pope's secretary, Nick Bannon.

"Hello, Michael, what can I do for you?"

"Hey, Nick. I need a few minutes with the Holy Father. Apparently, something came up while I was in France that has some of my staff working on mysterious side projects on his authority."

Realizing his voice sounded mildly insubordinate, he regretted it instantly. "I'm sorry, Nick. That seemed harsh. I'm just curious to know what required a realignment of my department's resources while I was gone."

"Ah, well, I'm sure His Holiness will explain everything. And I expect he's curious about the funeral and your discoveries at Notre-Dame. He was hoping you could join him for lunch in his office at about noon. He is occupied with other duties for the rest of the day, but he still has to eat."

"Great, perfect. I'll be up just before noon. See you then."

Walking down the hall back to Ian's office, he stepped inside. "Hey, want to go down to the canteen and grab a latte with me? I'm feeling the need for a little boost."

"You bet! Me young Irish blood thrives on caffeine."

HAVING MADE their way down to the canteen and fetched their drinks, Michael and Ian had just taken a seat at a table by the window when Sister Teri wandered over with her own mug of coffee and a frosted cinnamon roll.

"Mind if I join you boys?"

"Don't mind at all, Teri. Have a seat," Michael said. "We were just about to discuss the identity of a person whose crypt was discovered under the foundations of Notre-Dame Cathedral. Since you love a good mystery, this should grab your attention."

"Ooh, well, that sounds right up my alley. Do tell me more!"

Michael paused a moment. "All right, but as I'm bound by discretion on this, I'll ask you to do the same. Besides, we can use your help.

"A few days ago, I was in France for the funeral of Jacqueline Valois, the French president's wife. And while there I was contacted about a newly discovered coffin found in a pit beneath Notre-Dame's altar during reconstruction after that fire a few years ago. The coffin itself was unusual in that it had a small inscription identifying the body as that of Bishop Jerome Baudette. The body was indeed dressed as a bishop, but the corpse was wearing the ring of a cardinal. Adding to the mystery, he had with him two parchment scrolls tied with hemp and sewn flat into the cuff of his sleeve."

"Parchment scrolls, you say? Have you learned what they contain?"

"No, not just yet. We removed the sleeve, and I brought it back here for conservation treatment and analysis. I have Dr. Borsetti in the Restoration Lab working on it now.

"Meanwhile, Ian's generated a list of both cardinals and bishops of that period who might be good possibilities for identification, but there's still work ahead to narrow that down to fewer likely candidates."

"But if he was identified as a bishop, why are there cardinals on the list?"

"As I mentioned, he was wearing the ring of a cardinal, one indicating he was elevated by Pope Clement V, which would make it between 1305 and 1314."

"Well, that is curious. At least that narrows the group down somewhat. Have you considered looking at death records from the churches within the diocese each cardinal hailed from? I'm sure, even back then, they would have recorded the passings of their cardinals and bishops."

"That's not a bad idea, Teri. I'll see how many of those records are in our collections. We might have to call quite a few dioceses and ask them to search their records. I was thinking of attacking the problem from the other end, seeing if I can learn more about Bishop Baudette that might confirm it's really him in the crypt."

"Why don't I help out?" Teri offered excitedly. "I need a meaty project to throw myself into. The Vatican's network is stable, and I can only answer so many phones before boredom takes over. Put me in, coach!" She looked pleadingly at Michael.

Ian glanced at Michael, who nodded approvingly. "Great!" Ian said. "See what you can dig up, Teri. Your considerable research skills will help a lot."

"Too bad this isn't happening today; in modern times, I mean," Michael said thoughtfully. "We could just get a DNA sample."

Ian looked away and bit his lip unconsciously, a tic Michael didn't notice.

"So... I'm gonna grab one of those cinnamon rolls and head back down to the office and keep working," he said, getting up. "I'll let you two know what I find."

"I've got to be heading out myself anyway," Michael said. "Good to see you, Teri. Thanks in advance for your research."

CHAPTER

TWELVE

ana Sinclair sat in the upper gallery of the National Assembly, France's lower House of Parliament, an iPad on her lap, a stylus pen poised to take notes on the most unusual proceedings taking place below her.

The 575 legislators, or *députés*, were taking their seats while the president of the National Assembly, Gaspard Barbeau, repeatedly brought his gavel down forcefully on the podium to bring the house to order. That he had convened this emergency meeting was unusual enough, but rumors circulating that he was intending to cede his time to the Duke of Avignon were causing an uproar. Pockets of *députés* huddled together, talking animatedly, arms waving, fingers pointing. The president's gavel sounded again and again, gradually forcing everyone to take their seats and settle down. When a modicum of silence had been achieved, he began his address.

"The Assembly will come to order. Over the last few days, we have witnessed some extraordinary events in France, the likes of which have not been seen in generations. We are a passionate people, yes, but we must temper that passion for the sake of our democracy. After the riot at the funeral of Madame Valois—which was so brutally put down by the security forces of the

Interior Ministry, and was followed shortly thereafter by the senseless and tragic attack near the Pôle Emploi, and the street violence that followed that—we, the representatives of the people of France, must examine the situation and determine what can be done, what must be done, to right the ship of state that seems so suddenly to be foundering. To that end, I am ceding the remainder of my time to His Grace, Jean-Louis Micheaux, the Honorable Duke of Avignon, who wishes to address us at this time."

Typical of boisterous parliamentary proceedings, a medley of boos and cheers erupted at the mention of Micheaux's name.

The duke, who had been waiting just offstage and out of sight, came up to the podium at a quick walk, smartly bouncing up the two steps of the dais to reach the lectern. Clearly intended to portray a picture of health and vitality, as compared to the sick and elderly president of France, Pierre Valois, his appearance attracted a mixed reception. Many people in the room owed their positions to the duke—or more accurately, to his money and support—for as a member of one of the oldest and richest families in France, he had money to spread around. His was a family of old, generational wealth, used over time to acquire vast tracts of land and industrial interests that now provided rents and dividends which only increased his prosperity. Micheaux had used his largesse to enjoy a profligate lifestyle and the trappings of power and influence that attained to his ancestral peerage. His supporters were encouraged by the optimism of his entitled position: one of their own was truly living the French ideal.

But there was another contingent, those on the right side of the political spectrum, who did not find him so charming. The duke understood that his influence depended on people's self-interest and greed, and he was more than willing to spend his fortune on giving the people what they wanted in exchange for his societal rank and influence. Jean-Louis Micheaux championed expanding the scope of free healthcare, government pensions and retirement support, food aid, rent control and subsidized housing, internet service fee caps, and other programs that favored the masses on the lower end of the socio-economic spectrum who significantly outnumbered the wealthy when it came time to vote. Those on the right were rankled by his benevolence, for which they had other uses, such as building up the military and police forces, and exerting French influence in foreign countries and markets.

Looking out over the Assembly with a confident gaze and a firm chin, he began his speech.

"My countrymen, this is a grave time for France. There is unrest in our streets. There is dissatisfaction in our homes. There is disquiet in our hearts. These are problems that cannot be solved with a baton or a bullet. It is a time for clarity; therefore, I will be blunt, direct, and forthright. Our leadership is failing. Our current president is old and sick and rightly grieving. And while France owes Pierre Valois a tremendous debt of gratitude for a lifetime of service to our country—from World War II to now—it is time for his generation to hand over the reins to younger and more capable leaders. Therefore, I call on the president of France to resign gracefully, immediately and without delay, and let there be new elections and a new government, one that is equipped to meet the challenges we face today. And if he will not resign, I call on this body to prepare a vote of no confidence. An extreme step, to be sure, but indeed these are perilous times, which call for drastic measures."

The assembly was stunned. An extended silence born from shock met the end of the duke's remarks. Having delivered his message, he turned swiftly and strode from the dais.

Hana turned off the recorder on her iPad and watched the reactions below. A sizable portion of the room had gotten to its feet and was applauding vigorously, while the conservative faction largely sat in silence or angrily walked out of the hall. There had not been a vote of no confidence in France for quite some time. This was practically a call for revolution. And yet everything the duke had said was true. There *was* great turmoil in France, and the current government did seem to be reacting harshly—though Hana placed that blame more on Philip Valois than on his father.

Still, she had some reservations about Jean-Louis Micheaux. If he were positioning himself for a run for president, and he intended to change the direction of the country, perhaps she should find out more about him.

THIRTEEN

Excited by her new project—and by once again being part of Father Michael's and Ian's research adventures— Sister Teri kicked off her flowered Converse Chuck Taylors and sat barefoot at the desk in her small room in the Mater Ecclesiae Monastery, nestled in the Vatican Gardens near the Fontana dell'Aquilone.

Launching the Safari browser on her MacBook Pro—a gift from her parents when she took her perpetual vows and became a nun—Teri first searched on the obvious name *Bishop Jerome Baudette* to see what she could find. Having worked at Google in her prior life, she was adept at technology and in using research and analytics tools in particular.

Early searches yielded little on the elusive bishop, though she did find a page dedicated to the history of the Catholic Church in France, one that listed bishops by diocese and years of service. It revealed that Baudette had been elevated to bishop in 1307 and died in 1314 while still sitting as the Bishop of Bordeaux. Scrolling to another link, Teri noted Baudette's name on a listing of the attendees of the Plenary Council of Lisbon in 1314, at which he gave a report to the Portuguese bishops on the findings of the Council of Vienne. The author of the web page posed his suspicion that the bishop had been on assignment from Pope Clement V to search for assets of the Knights Templar in Portugal, which, by order of King Philip IV, were to be seized and repatriated to France. The French delegation to the Plenary Council also included members of the Holy Inquisition, who were there to assist the bishop in his duties in Portugal.

Interesting, Teri mused. *The Council of Lisbon was the same year as the bishop's death. I wonder if he actually died in Portugal?*

She returned to the site where she had found the list of bishops, noting that the end of Baudette's term did not reference the month. But his successor was shown as having been appointed in March 1314. That would suggest that Bishop Baudette died in the first couple of months of that year.

Teri then searched for the Plenary Council of Lisbon. One of the sites she found listed the Council as starting in January 1314 and lasting thirty-seven days, though a start day wasn't given.

She was now convinced that the Bishop of Bordeaux had died in early 1314, which was about the right time to have been buried in Notre-Dame, given the ring from Pope Clement V and the approximate age of the crypt, and what was known about the building of the cathedral.

But if the body really was Baudette's, how did he get from Lisbon to Paris? And how did he get that ring? Could Pope Clement have elevated him posthumously? An internet search for cardinals raised by Pope Clement V did not include Baudette's name, although the online records were pretty spotty, given how much time had passed.

Determined to get to the bottom of this mystery, Sister Teri pushed on.

∽

MICHAEL'S IPHONE CHIMED. It was time for his lunch with the Holy Father.

Arriving at the pope's outer office in the Apostolic Palace, he greeted Father Nick Bannon, the pope's personal secretary.

"Ah, Michael. Great to see you," the affable American priest said. "And good to have you back from France. Things seem pretty tense there right now, don't they?"

"Yeah, it was a rather stressful trip, Nick. I'm glad to be back, frankly, and putting my mind to work in a less volatile atmosphere."

Bannon took that in for a moment, noticing that Michael had not been directly responsive to his comment. He wondered what had happened to the young priest while he was in Paris.

"Well, I'm glad you were prompt today. The Holy Father's lunch has just been delivered. He's taking it in his study."

Bannon pressed the button under his desk to unlock the doors to the papal suite and escorted Michael into the study.

"Your Holiness, Father Dominic is here."

The pope sat at the head of a long rectangular table in his personal study. He was dressed in a simple white cassock with a white cashmere blanket slung over his shoulders. One of the kitchen nuns was just finishing setting out the lunch dishes. Checking the setting of the table one last time, she quietly left the room.

On the table in front of the pope were a simple bowl of chicken soup, a salad, a small loaf of focaccia, and a glass of wine. Michael's plate was still covered with a gleaming silver cloche. He removed it to discover a steaming grilled cheese sandwich with bacon and tomato, French fries, and a dollop of aioli in a small silver cup. The nun came back in, placed a glass of sparkling cola next to Michael's plate, and again left the room.

"It's just like when I was a boy. You used to fix me grilled cheese sandwiches. Thank you, Father." He glanced at the pope's shawl. "Are you not feeling well?"

"Oh, it's nothing serious, Michael, just a cold. But I'm taking it easy for a day or two. Don't worry about it. Please, do tell me about your trip to France."

As they ate their meal, Michael told him about the funeral of the wife of the pope's old friend, and the demonstrations and riot that followed.

He also explained his invitation from the French Cultural Minister, Lauren Valois, to visit the excavation at Notre-Dame, and the discovery of the crypt and coffin, presumably that of Jerome Baudette, the Bishop of Bordeaux. He described the documents sewn into the sleeve, as well as the cardinal's ring on the finger of the corpse, and added that he had brought the sleeve and the scrolls back to the Restoration Lab for analysis. Reluctantly, he also mentioned the attack at the airport, though he was at a loss to figure out who might have been behind it and what they wanted with documents that hadn't even been deciphered yet. The pope listened carefully, taking it all in with concern.

"That is all very interesting, my son. But you were there with Miss Sinclair, were you not? Did you have the opportunity to discuss your feelings with her?"

Michael flushed scarlet. "Well, I was going to. I asked her to meet me at Notre-Dame for lunch. The night before, at dinner, she told me *Le Monde* had offered her expanded responsibilities in Rome, but her... friend, Marco, seemed rather upset that he hadn't been informed, since their home is in France. He asked me to take a step back and give him a chance with Hana. I agreed. They must have talked that night, because when she came to see me at Notre-Dame—when I was down in the excavation pit—I told her I needed to step back, and she just shouted down to me that she was going to stay with Marco, and then she left. I tried to talk to her later, but it was just too awkward." Dejection clouded his voice, and the pope recognized it.

"Michael, I know it is difficult, this intimate process of discernment. But you must believe there is a purpose to all of it. Everything that happens gives you more with which to determine the direction you must take. Trust me on this."

"Yes, Father. Thank you." That was all they said on the matter.

"So. What have you been doing to identify this person in the crypt?"

"Well, we've assembled a list of people it could be—bishops and cardinals from the appropriate era—and we're trying to backtrack Bishop Baudette's last days. Sister Teri from Vatican Communications is assisting us. I must confess, it would be so much easier if we could just take a DNA sample and identify him that way. But you need something to compare it to in order to make identification possible, and I don't know where we'd get a database of fourteenth-century DNA."

The pope set down his fork, ran a linen napkin across his mouth, then smiled.

"Well, as to that. You know, since that episode with the Petri Crypta, I've been trying to learn about any other things of which I had not been informed since my election. Turns out there have been many. One of them might be of interest and assistance to you. Have you ever heard of VADNA, Michael?"

"No, I haven't. What is it?"

"VADNA stands for the Vatican Ancient DNA project. Apparently, there is a program, a very small one, begun two popes ago, that has been taking DNA samples from relics and building a database from them. We have already discovered several purported relics that do not seem to have come from the person with whom they had been assumed to be associated. Of course, one of the proscriptions is that they are prohibited from typing any relics associated with Christ himself. But I bring this up because technically, it falls under your purview, but only on a need-to-know basis. And up until now, you have not needed to know. The program is highly confidential. I do not want to think what would happen if it were to get out that some highly venerated relics were not from the saint they should be from. At some point, I will have to decide how to handle this, but for now, we are taking things one step at a time. The Vatican's DNA work is now being discreetly tied to modern genealogical databases, to look for familiar linkages. Forgive me, but I had to borrow your technician, Ian, to assist with that aspect of the project. The director of that particular laboratory is someone you might know. She was at Loyola about the same time you were. Nick will put you in touch with her later today."

Michael was flabbergasted. There was a secret Vatican program operated out of his own domain and he had no idea about it?! He supposed he shouldn't be too surprised, since the pope had not been told about the safe in his own office. But still, it made Michael wonder how much other information had been withheld during the last two papal transitions. The Vatican was still such a strange and often unfathomable place.

Dante strikes again, even from the grave, he thought. Fabrizio Dante had been a nemesis to both Michael and the pope in years past but had finally succumbed to his own evil ways. Yet his influence seemed to still follow them in the Vatican.

"Thank you, Father. I am a bit taken aback by this news, but I'm glad there may be a way to help identify the supposed bishop in the crypt. I'll need to speak with the archeologists at Notre-Dame to see if they have a DNA profile on the body, and if they don't, how we might obtain one."

"Yes, let us hope this will move your investigation forward."

The two men spent the rest of their lunch on small talk, discussing the typical rumors and other happenings in the Vatican. The pope often got filtered information and trusted Michael to let him know the word on the street, as it were. When lunch was over, Michael excused himself, giving a last hug to his father as Nick Bannon came in to assist the pope in preparing for his afternoon calendar.

Heading back to the Archives, Michael dropped into his assistant's office.

"Okay, Ian. I've now been read in on VADNA. Of course, you may continue your involvement. Just let me know how much time it's taking, all right? And we'll need to speak with that team about the body at Notre-Dame. Nick is supposed to be setting up a meeting for me with the director of VADNA this afternoon, but since you are already involved, you can come along and give me an update on the way over."

~

As is typical when someone dives into the depths of Google, Sister Teri realized this mission called for some serious internet sleuthing skills. So many questions...

How to find out what happened to a person who died more than seven hundred years ago? Who would have records like that? And what kind of records would those be? Where would they be kept? Would they be indexed so that a search engine could find them?

Her last reference for Baudette was at the Plenary Council of Lisbon. He had to get to Portugal somehow, and then either he died and was buried in Lisbon, or he went back to France. Maybe that was an avenue to pursue.

First, she tried searching for different spellings of Baudette, and his first name, Jerome, with and without the titles *father*, *bishop* or *cardinal* prepended, and then in multiple different permutations. Google's search algorithms were powerful, but they could only work with what you gave them; they didn't read minds.

At least not yet—though when she worked there, she had heard rumors of a top secret project involving menticide, coercive persuasion, and thought reform. She shuddered at the future possibilities.

She did come across some interesting trivia in her search. It was 1,342 miles from Jerome, Idaho to Baudette, Minnesota, in the United States. Baudette has an international airport, just across the Rainy River from Canada, with flights to the Billy Bishop Toronto City Airport. A number of people with the last name of Bishop live in Baudette. Lots of pages on St. Jerome.

Too much noise, and definitely nothing related to the fourteenth century.

Changing tack, she tried looking for websites that might have non-indexed free-form information. She searched for passenger manifests for ships sailing out of Lisbon, or for coaches traveling overland. After finding some records stored in a non-indexed FTP directory, she found nothing useful there.

Then, on a hunch, she tried the same search for cargo manifests. Here, she finally had some luck. In a similar index of scanned but not searchable images, she found a JPEG image of the cargo manifest for the British sailing ship *Shoreham*, which listed "the Bodye of Bishop Jerom Bowdet" as having been among the cargo. But there was no further mention of the fate of the *Shoreham*.

However, the manifest did specify an unscheduled sailing from Portugal to Le Havre, France, at the mouth of the Seine River, and then on to Chepstow, Kingdom of England. Searching for other records from the *Shoreham*, she found an entry in the records of Lloyds of London for a claim against the cargo. In their database, a PDF of the claim revealed that the ship had been lost at sea, with all hands and cargo, reported on April 1, 1314.

Success! Baudette had died in Portugal, and they had sent his body back to France, at least as far as the mouth of the Seine, from which he could have been going to either Bordeaux or Paris. But he never made it to either port.

So, whoever it was buried in the crypt at Notre-Dame, it was not Jerome Baudette!

Exhilarated, she couldn't wait to tell Father Michael.

CHAPTER

FOURTEEN

It wasn't long after Michael had left the pope's office that Father Bannon called saying that Dr. Blake Chaucer, the director of VADNA, would be expecting him that afternoon: as soon as it was possible for him to get there, in fact.

"And where is 'there,' Nick?" Michael asked.

"Ah, sorry. Her lab is in the Genetics Department of Sapienza University, across the Tiber near the Biblioteca Nazionale in the city center. Sergeant Dengler is waiting to take you there."

"That's okay, I'll take the bus, it's not far. And you said 'her,' so I take it Blake is a woman's name too?"

"In this case, it sure is," Bannon replied. "You'll enjoy her company. Like us, she's an American. But, I'm afraid the Holy Father insists you go with Sergeant Dengler... He's waiting for you now at St. Anne's Gate."

Michael groaned. Though he liked time with Karl, being chaperoning was getting tiresome.

After grabbing his backpack, he made his way down to Porta Sant'Anna where Karl was waiting with Ian.

• • •

AMONG THE MOST prestigious public research institutions in all of Europe, Sapienza University had been created by Pope Boniface VIII by papal bull in 1303, establishing it as the first pontifical university in history. Counted among its notable alumni were numerous Nobel laureates, heads of state, distinguished scientists, and prominent religious figures, not to mention a few astronauts and other luminaries. In earlier centuries, most of the ruling Italian aristocracy had studied there.

The Genetics Department was located on the east side of the campus in one of the more modern buildings, distinct from those reflecting the university's more archaic past.

While Karl stayed outside with his Jeep and kept an eye on the entrance, Michael and Ian made their way up to the third floor. At the end of a long hallway, they found a door with a nameplate simply denoting the office of Dr. Blake Chaucer, Department of Genetics, with no indication at all of being identified with VADNA. Opening the door, the receptionist, a young man who looked to be a graduate student, greeted them.

"*Buongiorno*. Can I help you?"

"Yes. Father Michael Dominic and Ian Duffy to see Dr. Chaucer."

"Ah, yes, of course. We have been expecting you, Father. One moment…"

He picked up the phone and rang the office behind him. Michael could hear the phone ring in the adjacent room, then stop when it was picked up. The young man said that her guests had arrived, listened for a moment, then hung up.

Almost instantly, the office door opened and an attractive young woman walked out, wearing a knee-length dress under a white lab coat, her auburn hair pulled back in a bun, with wire-rimmed glasses resting on her nose.

"Father Michael! My, it's so good to see you again."

Michael looked embarrassed. "I'm sorry, you have me at a loss. Have we met before?"

"Well, it's no surprise you don't remember me. It was a long time ago, and I was certainly not on your radar. We had a semester of Latin together as undergrads at Loyola. I was an oblate for the Franciscan Sisters of Chicago at the time."

She took off her glasses, framed her face with her hands, and said, "You might remember me as Sister Mary—"

"*Euphemia!* Yes, I remember now! We used to call you Sister Mary Euphemism. You used to *float* down the hallways! Everyone else walked normally. But somehow you just floated."

"Yes, well, I *had* heard that attributed to me..." She gave a playful scowl. "But the 'floating' came from twelve years of ballet lessons. My parents wanted me to be a dancer, not a nun, nor a molecular biologist. By the way, we used to describe *you* as 'too hot to be a priest.'"

Michael blushed and laughed. "So, how did you end up here?"

"Well, first, I have to confess: I had quite the secret crush on you. One that ultimately made me question my choice of vocation. Then I met my husband—well, future husband—in one of my biology classes, and... let's just say I decided to choose the vocation of marriage instead. I earned a PhD in molecular biology, specializing in the extraction and typing of ancient DNA samples. I was doing a post-doctoral fellowship here at Sapienza when the Vatican contacted us about a relic of dubious provenance. They wanted to know if we could DNA-type it against another relic of known provenance. We did. It didn't match, but that opened a dialogue about other relics, and more testing ensued.

"Ultimately, the Vatican decided to make a substantial investment in the laboratory on a more permanent basis, and the Vatican Ancient DNA lab was born just a few years ago. I was working with your predecessor, Brother Mendoza, at the time. Although with all the turmoil over there, the work has slowed down a bit. Still, your Father Laguardia brings us samples periodically for profiling and comparison to the database we've been building. And Ian has been very helpful with that."

"Wait… Father Laguardia is involved in this too?!"

"Oh, yes, from the very beginning. He is the only one the Vatican has authorized to bring us samples. We are a small operation, strictly on a confidential, need-to-know basis. The Vatican does not want anyone to know we're validating relics. Think of the PR consequences if a congregation found out its sacred relic was a fake. So we do our testing, the Vatican gets the results, and only the pope and the prefect of the Congregation for the Causes of Saints see them. Father Laguardia only knows which relics are coming in, and Ian only knows which profiles are being searched against the external databases. Father Laguardia has even been doing a little traveling to collect samples for us, and he and I have opened more than a few crypts to get conforming samples."

"So you're taking samples from the bodies of saints to compare to known or suspected relics to verify their authenticity?"

"That's it exactly. We *are* building a database of DNA profiles of the saints. There is quite the black market in religious relics, as you probably know. Some of those of questionable authenticity make their way back to the Church. We need to know if it is a genuine relic or a fraud, so we know how to treat it."

Michael was spellbound by Chaucer's explanation. "Fascinating. Have you ever—"

"No," she interrupted him, presuming the question, "we never profile relics associated with the Christ. No Shroud of Turin or Crown of Thorns, no Veil of Veronica or fragments of the True Cross…"

At the mention of the veil, Michael felt a twinge, recalling his earlier encounter with it.

"Do you ever do profiling of people or relics not suspected of being a saint?"

"Well, we certainly could, although there are plenty of laboratories equipped to do modern samples for things like paternity testing, as one example. We are more set up for testing ancient DNA samples. Why do you ask?"

"I just think it's coincidental that we should be meeting now. I'm working with the French National Institute of Preventive Archaeological Research to identify a body in a crypt that was discovered during the rebuilding of Notre-Dame, entombed sometime in the early 1300s. It was assumed to be the Bishop of Bordeaux, but he was wearing a cardinal's ring, so the jury's out on that yet. He also had some parchment scrolls sewn into his sleeve. Our document restoration lab is working on analyzing those now."

"You should know that a DNA profile won't do you any good unless you have something to compare it to, either a sample from the person himself, or perhaps a close family member."

"Ah, I see. That may not help, then, since we have the body, but no idea yet as to who he might be, in order to know who to compare him to."

"Once you suspect his identity, there still might be some way we can help. Let me show you around the lab."

Dr. Chaucer led them down the hall and to a large window separating them from a brightly lit room with a few technicians working in white lab coats surrounded by technical equipment of every type and function.

"The lab is divided into three rooms. The first, this one, is where we receive the samples and extract the DNA. The second"—she pointed through another large glass window into an adjoining room—"is restricted to lab staff only, and is where we amplify the DNA. The last room on the far side of that one contains the profiling equipment. Then we do the profile searching at a secure workstation in the outer office.

"See, Ian?" she added. "This is where all your hard work has been coming from."

Michael's face bore a look of confusion. "You said Ian is

linking your data sets to modern genealogical databases. If we are dealing with saints, what use would that be?"

"Well, since DNA is inherited, even though every human being's is unique, there are elements that are passed on within families. We can often see familiar linkages across generations. So we can associate a profile with the descendants of a saint's family. There is a strong demand from people who want to know if they are descended from a certain saint's family. Right now, that information is only coming into the lab, but at some point, we may be able to put that information into the public sphere. And it helps us validate the techniques and information from both directions. Seeing a linkage in a family lineage is something we can test against known profiles, and vice versa."

"So, if there was a family linkage between our unknown person from the crypt and a modern family, we might be able to use the family genealogy to determine an identity?"

"Yes, something like that," Blake affirmed. "But to make an actual identification, we would need more. All we could determine is that it would be someone in the line of heredity, especially going back so far."

Michael glanced at his watch. "I'm really sorry, but I do need to get back to the office. Thank you so much for meeting with us, Blake, and for your marvelous explanations—*and* for letting me into the circle of trust!

"I just have one more question, though. If the program is run out of the Congregation for the Causes of the Saints, why is my staff being used to assist?"

Blake thought a moment, then met Michael's eyes. "You mentioned the circle of trust. The previous pope, as well as Pope Ignatius, both felt that the staff of the Secret Archives was more trustworthy than the staff of the Congregation for the Causes of Saints. They are a rather large and, from our experience, undependable office, frankly. There's just too great a chance for a leak, which could be disastrous. Your staff had more computer savvy and a better history of keeping secrets truly secret. Father

Laguardia is quite disciplined and very discreet. You yourself didn't even suspect he was involved, and he has been with us since the beginning. Of course, Ian is a very recent addition to the team, now that we are reaching out for data from other genealogical databases. And he's been very helpful.

"Our work is also tied to the European Molecular Biology Lab, but since this project is highly confidential, we couldn't link through their databases. Ian has secured low-profile access to the DNA databases we need, essentially collaborating with relevant data companies to open a back door for us, with, like I said, the hope of someday being able to share data."

"Well, then"—Michael smiled broadly with a twinkle in his eye—"it was great to see you after all these years, Sister Mary Euphemism! I hope our paths cross again soon."

His rather exhausting day nearly at an end, Michael left the office and headed through the Vatican gardens to his apartment in the Santa Marta hostel. As he walked, he noticed Lukas sitting peacefully on a bench beneath the Fontana dell'Aquilone, the Fountain of the Eagle, reading a newspaper.

On hearing Michael approach, Lukas looked up. "Hey, Father Michael. Did you see today's newspaper, with Hana's byline? The Duke of Avignon asked the French Assembly to take a vote of no confidence on the president. That's like calling for a political revolution. He wants new elections immediately to deal with the turmoil in France. I'm sure Hana has her own feelings about it, but it sure sounds to me like an invitation to more turmoil."

"Newspaper?! Cheese and crackers, I almost forgot…"

Michael turned and walked quickly toward St. Anne's Gate. Once through, he retraced the end of his morning run back to the Suburra neighborhood. There he found Luigi, sitting on a tall, three-legged stool under the red-and-white striped awning that hung limply over the Edicola newsstand. The sun was setting, and the last of the workers were making their way home, pausing to chat with Luigi about the comings and goings in the neighborhood—for from his perch, Luigi could see everything that happened in his little corner of the world.

Spotting the priest as Michael drew near, he gave him a wide smile. "Ah, there you are, Father," he said in Italian. "I had almost given up hope. I was just about to look for the number of the pope." He waved his cell phone in the air for added effect.

"Signor Bucatini, I must confess... with the day I've had, I did almost forget. Here, take five euros. One and a half for the paper, and the rest is interest on the loan, and for your faith in me."

"Father, please. It was nothing. I could tell just by looking in your eyes that you were a man of your word. The eyes are the windows to the soul, yes? I could see you have a good soul. Although, it also seemed this morning to be a troubled one..."

Michael recalled his visible worry about not having heard from Hana, given the turmoil in Paris. A shadow crossed his face.

"Yes," Luigi confirmed, "troubled you are."

It seemed as if the old man could see directly into Michael's thoughts. He took the priest's hands in both of his and held them for a moment as if to comfort him.

"Yes, well, I do need to be going," Michael said, withdrawing his hands. "Thank you for your trust, Signor Bucatini. I'm sure we'll see each other again soon."

As he turned away, the old man called after him. "Go in peace, Father. I will pray for you."

CHAPTER
FIFTEEN

"Please hold for His Grace, the Duke of Avignon," the crisp female voice announced after Hana answered the phone.

Sitting at her desk in *Le Monde*'s Paris bureau that morning, she quickly transferred the call to her headset, then opened up a new notepad window on her laptop computer.

As the moments ticked by, she wondered to what she owed the pleasure of a personal call by the presumed presidential candidate, though he hadn't actually announced his intentions yet. Was a scoop in the works? Would she get an exclusive announcement from him? Or maybe he wanted something from *her*…The questions rambled through her mind until she heard his familiar voice on the phone.

"Mademoiselle Sinclair?" the duke inquired.

"Yes, Your Grace, this is she. But please, call me Hana."

"Thank you for taking my call, Hana. It was so good to see you in the Assembly gallery during my speech. I've always admired your work, you know. In my opinion, you are one of the better journalists in all of France. I have followed your career for some time now, in fact."

Initially flattered, Hana knew instinctively that the duke's adulation came with a purpose. He wanted something, that much she suspected. But she was curious too.

"Can you come for an exclusive interview with me this afternoon? I would like to share with you my perspectives and discuss this appalling situation in France just now."

She smiled inwardly, but responded matter-of-factly, "Of course. I can be there this afternoon. When and where shall we meet?"

"In my suite at the George Cinq. My assistant Aimée will meet you in the lobby. Shall we say two o'clock?"

Hana agreed and ended the call.

SHORTLY BEFORE THE APPOINTED HOUR, Hana's taxi pulled up to the white stone façade of the Four Seasons George Cinq, the most exclusive and opulent hotel in Paris. The doorman opened the taxi door and led the reporter into the grand marble lobby. Huge pink and white panicle hydrangeas filled the room, their sweet floral fragrance a welcome contrast to the interminable petrol exhaust lingering outside the entrance just off the bustling Champs-Élysées.

"Mademoiselle Sinclair?" Hana turned around to find an attractive young woman in a smart, dark-blue business suit, a welcoming smile on her face.

"Aimée, I presume?" she asked, returning the smile. They shook hands.

"Oui! Welcome to the George Cinq. His Grace is looking forward to meeting you. Please, this way."

Hana followed her escort to a dedicated elevator, where Aimée inserted a special keycard into a slot, then pressed a button marked "P." The car took them up swiftly to the top floor, which opened into a circular grand foyer befitting royalty, with a round, handcrafted Persian rug tailored to the space, Old Masters oil paintings hanging on both walls, and perfectly lit Carrara marble statuary set back in arched alcoves.

The penthouse itself, easily comparable to her grandfather's 1,525-square-meter suite at the Rome Cavalieri, was divided into living and working spaces. A few people sat in a small cluster by tall windows, chatting quietly as they passed papers among themselves.

A tall, aristocratic figure emerged from one of the bedrooms and walked toward Hana with a broad smile. He wore a black Loro Piana cashmere turtleneck sweater with Ferragamo chino trousers and black Hermès loafers. *Easily a four thousand euro ensemble*, Hana's seasoned eye quickly calculated.

"*Bonjour*, Hana," Jean-Louis Micheaux greeted her, extending his hand. "*Bienvenue!*"

"*Bonjour*, Your Grace. What a lovely space you have here," she said, looking around the suite.

"These days it seems more of a business center," he said amiably, smiling. "We have much work to do, very important work for the betterment of France. Come, we can talk in my office."

He led her down a long hallway to a beautifully furnished office, one clearly designed for a man who appreciates the finer things life can offer the rich: walls of gorgeous, dark African padauk paneling complementing a white-and-gold French Baroque executive desk set in front of a massive radius window, with the Eiffel Tower centered in the distance. Various *objets d'art* were set around the room, each softly lit by spot downlights suspended from the high ceiling.

Inviting Hana to be seated in a cozy sitting area next to a blazing fireplace, he prepared a cup of tea for her without asking, then set the cup and saucer in front of her as he took a seat opposite her. He crossed his legs and placed his folded hands on his lap, looking at her expectantly.

"Your Grace," she said, "I must first ask: are we on the record for this conversation?"

Micheaux sat silent for a moment, still looking at Hana thoughtfully.

"Yes, for the most part, you may use anything we discuss here today—unless I specifically say something is off the record before we speak of it. Is that agreeable?"

"Yes, of course." Hana set out a small recording device and pressed the Record button.

"So… While I have yet to announce my intentions officially, it must be apparent that I am considering submitting myself as a candidate for the presidency."

Hana simply nodded.

"And my reasons for doing so are abundant…" He then took some time reiterating the many points he made during his speech before the National Assembly the day before—things Hana already knew, having been there. But she realized every politician has his stump speech: carefully refined talking points ground into them by campaign managers and staff. She sat and listened politely, though confident—or at least hoping—that something useful would come of the meeting.

"And so you see," he concluded, "not all the people are being well served by their government. I believe the plans I would put into place will constitute far greater freedoms and less public distress. We must take better care of our people and put an end to programs that only serve to benefit people like me—those who already enjoy sufficient financial advantages and don't really need government assistance.

"But enough of the messaging. I asked you to come here so that I could personally tell you face to face that, while I can't go into specifics quite yet, I believe there is a place for you in my campaign, Hana. An important one. We will speak again, soon, at which point I can reveal more, and hopefully convince you that France will be the better with your personal involvement."

Hana sat stock still, blinking in surprise. She hadn't expected *that*.

Micheaux glanced at his watch. "I'm afraid our time is up for now, but I truly hope I can count on your support if and when I make my decision. And if there is anything I might do for you in the meantime, you have but to ask."

Though disappointed that no big announcement was to be had, at least today, Hana was satisfied that she had gotten a one-on-one interview with the most talked-about man in France at the moment. And she *did* have an invitation to call on him—for anything.

Reflecting on their meeting as she left the hotel, Hana was favorably impressed with the duke. Being a person of means herself—thanks to her own noble ancestry and her family's wealth—she had already allied herself with Micheaux's deep-seated notion that those in a position to help have an obligation to those who most need that help, even though such assistance should come from government and not from the more privileged classes personally—except perhaps through their charitable foundations or outright philanthropy.

She was also intrigued by his vague yet tempting offer to be part of his campaign—which likely also meant a post in the new administration. What would that mean? Surely, she would have to leave *Le Monde* if she were to accept such a position... an *important* one, he said. Though she was accustomed to the smarmy world of politicians, she felt that this man was different. She trusted her instincts, and the duke struck her as intelligent and authentic as they come. Yes, she could see herself working with him.

WHEN SHE RETURNED to her office, there were several voice messages on her muted phone, Marco's being the most numerous. She suspected she knew what was coming: he likely had discovered she had gone off without him. As she called him now, she sighed, prepared for the expected skirmish.

"Hey there," she began, optimism in her voice, "I see you've called a few times. I just had an interview with the Duke of Avignon, and you won't believe—"

"Hana," Marco interrupted bluntly, "how many times must I ask you to call me first when you venture out? I have a responsibility to your grandfather, not to mention to *you*, to make sure no harm comes to you while there is still violence on the streets! I get the feeling you aren't taking my job seriously. And it's not just a job—I love you, and I don't want to see you take needless risks."

Taken aback, Hana realized this was the first time Marco had ever said "the words." Though moved by his passion and candor, she felt weary of being tended to, of her independence being hampered, despite his good intentions.

"Marco, you know I appreciate you and all you do, but this is just part of my job. I am completely safe here in the office, and the taxi didn't pass through any protests. And the George Cinq, where I met the duke, has high security around it. So really, your fuss is unjustified. And it was a good interview. I'm growing fond of Jean-Louis and his political agenda."

"It's not just that, Hana. I'm feeling like I don't really belong anymore. First, you failed to mention your apparent plans to move to the Rome bureau. Next, you're trotting off to see the duke without letting me know, not to mention now being under the spell of his misplaced ambitions. I happen to be of the opinion that the government is there to preserve the liberties of the people and protect them from external threats through collective action, such as fire, police, and the military—services too essential for individuals to handle on their own. But when it comes to handouts, why should people get something for nothing? I have had to work hard my whole life to make something of myself. I started on the street, and nobody gave *me* all the things the duke wants to give people now."

Clearly, Hana had touched a nerve. She had never heard Marco so agitated.

"Don't you think you're being a bit harsh?" she asked.

Marco was silent, apparently fuming. She sought to bring the temperature down a bit.

"All right. As best I can, I promise I'll not exclude you in the future, Marco. I don't do it deliberately, you know. It's just an instinctive reaction to being controlled. Self-reliance is too important to me, and I've fought all my adult life to achieve that; to be my own person. It's very much a man's world I work in, and women have to push even harder to make their way through it. And you know me well. I won't tolerate anyone standing in my way. But I'm sorry if you felt trampled. I care for you too much for that to be my intention."

She heard Marco breathing easier now.

"Yes," he said, his voice more soothing, "everything you said is true. I'm sorry I got carried away. And I expect we'll just have to agree to disagree on the duke's politics."

"So, are you free for dinner this evening?"

"Of course, I'm all yours. See you after work?" After Hana agreed, they ended the call.

But now she had a different concern. How would Marco handle the prospect of her working with his ideological nemesis?

MICHAEL SAT at his desk managing the glut of paperwork the Vatican bureaucracy had imposed on his department when the phone rang.

"Hi, Father Michael, it's Sister Teri, and I've got Ian conferenced in as well."

Michael looked through the open door of his office to see Ian down the hall, the phone at his ear, waving back cheerfully.

"Hi, Teri. What have you got for us?"

"Well, I don't exactly know *who* your body is, but I do know who he's *not!* Jerome Baudette, the bishop of Bordeaux, was at a Plenary Council of Bishops meeting in Lisbon, Portugal, when he suddenly took sick and died there. The authorities shipped his body back to France aboard an English sailing vessel called the *Shoreham*, bound for the Port of Le Havre in France and then up the Seine River and on to Notre-Dame.

"But the ship sank during a terrible storm in the Celtic Sea and everyone aboard was lost, including the body of the bishop. Notre-Dame's records do show that Baudette had paid to be interred in the cathedral's crypt, but since he never arrived, they must have assumed this other bishop to be him and proceeded with the entombment as provided. So, whoever is in that coffin, it's definitely not Baudette."

"Hmm," Michael mused. "Not necessarily a bishop, however. He was dressed as such, but what about the cardinal's ring he was wearing? Maybe we should focus now on those who were elevated to cardinal by Bertrand de Got?"

Ian jumped in. "Wait… who's Bertrand de Got? I thought Pope Clement V elevated our guy to cardinal—at least that's what the ring indicated."

"Raymond Bertrand de Got was Pope Clement's real name before he took his regnal name," Michael explained.

"Well, that's curious," Ian ventured. "There's a guy named *Florian* de Got on the list of cardinals I have here. Do you think they're related? Hang on a sec…"

Michael and Teri could hear Ian's fingers flying over his keyboard.

"Yes," Ian confirmed, "Florian de Got was Pope Clement's brother. That's got to be him! No wonder the pope would send this cardinal's body to be buried in Notre-Dame—he was honoring his brother. But… it was no honor to be buried in a casket clearly marked for Bishop Baudette. And why let him be buried in a bishop's attire? And why the secret scrolls?"

"One mystery at a time, Ian," Michael said. "Maybe we have a way to confirm or negate that it is Florian de Got. Dr. Chaucer said we might be able to tell if the body was closely related to someone we can identify in his family. Where is Pope Clement buried?"

After a few more keystrokes, Ian replied, "You aren't going to believe this. Pope Clement V is buried at Notre-Dame!"

At the same time, Michael and Teri said, "You're kidding me?!"

"Well, sort of, anyway. It's Notre-Dame *d'Uzeste*, in the diocese of Bordeaux, not the Notre-Dame Cathedral in Paris. But it says here that when the body of Pope Clement was lying in state, the church was struck by lightning and was destroyed in the ensuing fire. The pope's body was badly burned."

Taking it all in, Michael had an idea. "Okay, thanks for all this. Good work by both of you. Now I've got a couple of phone calls to make."

Michael next called the team at INRAP, the ones responsible for the excavations at Notre-Dame, to make sure they had collected a DNA sample from the bishop's body. They assured him that they had, but their genealogy research had been unproductive. There were no modern relatives of the deceased that they could determine. Michael thanked them and promised to get back to them shortly on a lead he was following.

He called Blake and told her his news. She was excited at the prospect. "Since Pope Clement was never a candidate for sainthood," Michael told her, "it is unlikely there were any notable relics, per se. We would have to get a sample from the remains directly, right? I imagine there may be possible complications from the body being burned in a fire."

"The only way to be sure, Michael, is to run some tests. Where are the remains of Pope Clement now?"

"In Bordeaux, at Collégiale Notre-Dame d'Uzeste, a church in Gironde, France. Up for a field trip?"

"Of course!" Blake enthused. "Sounds like a fabulous idea."

"All right, let me make the arrangements and I'll call back to confirm."

Finding the number for the Collegiate Church of Our Lady of Uzeste, Michael called and spoke to the rector there. Based on his own Vatican credentials, the invocation of Cultural Minister

Lauren Valois's name, and Dr. Chaucer being a prominent scientist at Sapienza, the rector agreed to give them access to the crypt and the body of Pope Clement V.

Calling Blake back, they made plans to leave the following morning. Then Michael sent a text message to Ian saying they were going to meet Dr. Chaucer for a little road trip tomorrow.

God, I love my job! Ian texted back.

Michael smiled at the text as he thought how he, too, loved his job. Instantly, a pang of sorrow struck his chest as he realized that maybe that was what he needed to understand: that he truly loved his work. Maybe Hana's apparent decision to stay with Marco was the best thing for them both. He swallowed back the pain of losing the chance at love with such a wonderful woman. He sighed, forcing himself to realize he didn't need to think, at least at this moment, any more about that. He had a mission to concentrate on.

Michael sat there, assembling all the moving parts of his plan, when it occurred to him he would need to bring Karl along as well. He let out a little moan.

He picked up the phone again and called Nick Bannon to tell him what was going on and ask him to inform the pope of his actions.

"By the way, how's the Holy Father's health, Nick?"

"He's still got the cold, Michael, but he's not any worse. Oh, and as I'm sure he would tell you himself, be sure to have your escort with you."

"Yes, Nick. I know."

WHEN HANA LEFT her *Le Monde* offices for the day, Marco was waiting for her in his usual spot under the gleaming curved arch by the entrance and bike racks, leaning against a cutout in the wall.

She came through the door, kissed him, and put her arm

through his, then they both headed for home as they walked along the Seine, gray skies and the fading light of day making for a pleasant stroll. Streetlights began to blink on as they walked.

"So," Marco said innocently, "you really seem taken with this duke fellow."

Hana stopped and held his gaze, her own eyes nearly blazing.

"Look, Marco. There's a lot going on in the office now, with all the unrest, and I just don't need to deal with your jealousy when I'm out doing my job. I'm a grown woman. I can take care of myself. I don't need a babysitter."

"Hey, hey, it's okay. I just asked a question. I'm not jealous at all, just curious!"

"Well, maybe you just need to take a step back."

Hana was suddenly stunned hearing herself, realizing she had used the same words she had heard from Michael at Notre-Dame.

Marco looked like he had been slapped. Her heart sank as she faced losing both the men in her life. "What do you mean by that?" he asked cautiously.

"I'm sorry. As I said, there's a lot of stress in the office, and sometimes Grand-père treats me like a child. And Michael is getting all weird on me, and I think my godfather is dying, and now you're mad at me about interviewing the duke, and you're jealous, and… it's all just *too much!*"

Marco reached for her, pulling her body close to his. Surrendering to him, she buried her head in his chest and began shedding tears. He wrapped his arms around her, gently rocking her from side to side.

"I'm so sorry," he said tenderly. "I do love you, and I don't want to lose you to anything or anyone. Your independent streak makes me crazy sometimes, yes, but it is one of the things I admire most about you."

Hana looked into the depths of his strong blue eyes. "Marco, please, can we just go home? I need some food, a glass of wine and a long bath. And maybe a massage?"

"Whatever you desire, *ma chérie*. Anything you want is yours."

He paused for a few moments, then said, "Wait, you hadn't mentioned anything about Michael before. What's going on with him?"

"I don't know," she said, shaking her head. "I told him about my opportunity to do more stories in Rome at dinner the other night, and everything seemed fine then. But the next day, it was like he didn't even want to be friends anymore."

"That doesn't sound like him. If anything, I would have thought the opposite. But maybe he was feeling too much pressure and needed to take a step back."

Yes, Hana thought to herself. *I thought there was something there too.*

"You know, those were the exact words he used. Frankly, I'd rather not talk about it. Not tonight. Let's just go home."

CHAPTER
SIXTEEN

At noon the next day, Michael had gathered Karl and Ian, and the three of them drove to Sapienza University to pick up Blake Chaucer for their trip to France. Facing the prospect of either a fifteen-hour drive or a two-and-a-half-hour flight to Bordeaux, Michael chose the latter. On such short notice, the only flight on which he could get four tickets was an afternoon flight at two-thirty. Then it was an hour's drive to Uzeste, home of the Collégiale Notre-Dame d'Uzeste Cathedral in southwestern France, where the body of Pope Clement V had been laid to rest.

Sitting next to Michael during the flight, Blake regaled him with stories of her life since they last met in college: meeting her husband, their world travels together, then starting a family of two children—a girl and a boy, five and seven, the highlights of her life. The young priest listened to her raptly, happy his old acquaintance had found such fulfillment.

Turning to look out over the vast landscape below, he wondered what his own life might have been like had he taken the same path, and naturally, his thoughts turned again to Hana. And again, his stomach churned.

. . .

MICHAEL HAD MADE arrangements for them to stay at the Hotel Cardinal Bordeaux, directly across the plaza from the eleventh-century St. Andrew's Cathedral. Having rented a car at the airport, they proceeded to the hotel, checked in, freshened up, and headed across the plaza to the Cathedral of Bordeaux. They were met there by one of the cathedral priests, who escorted them to Archbishop Allain Fournier's office.

After making introductions, Michael reiterated in greater detail the nature of their mission, and in the time between his phone conversation with the bishop the day before and their meeting today, the bishop's staff had been poring over ancient records in search of information that might be helpful in their quest.

"We have an archivist on staff to serve the three cathedrals here in Bordeaux," the bishop explained, "which house documents going back hundreds of years, some nearly a millennium. This church, the Primatial Cathedral of St. Andrew of Bordeaux, has existed as far back as 814, the year Charlemagne died. The others, the Basilica of St. Severinus and the Basilica of St. Michael, also are quite ancient, but Severinus dates back to the late 300s.

"In any case, we have discovered a letter from the Bishop of Lisbon sent here to St. Andrew's in 1314, informing us of Bishop Baudette's death, that his body had been sent by sea to Paris, intended to be interred at Notre-Dame in accordance with his wishes pursuant to his beneficence toward its construction. I hope that helps solve at least part of the mystery."

"Your Excellency," Michael began, "in our own research we have learned that that ship, the *Shoreham*, was lost at sea in that same year, 1314, and that Baudette's coffin went down with it. So he couldn't have been buried in Notre-Dame. We also discovered that the body we *did* find in the crypt at Notre-Dame could very well be that of Florian de Got, the brother of Pope Clement V, which is why we need a DNA sample from His Holiness's remains, to establish that ancestral linkage."

"Well, Father Dominic, I wish you the best of luck. There is a legend connected with Clement; that while his body was lying in state, the church was struck by lightning and nearly burned to the ground. Some attributed this to God's vengeance for the pope's compromises to King Philip the Fair, and for what he did, or allowed to be done, to the Order of the Templars. I do not know what you will find tomorrow, but I do hope it is what you need. But for now, come, you must all join me for dinner."

THE NEXT MORNING, the team assembled for Mass at St. Andrew's Cathedral. Father Dominic had been offered an opportunity to concelebrate Mass with the archbishop, an offer he gratefully accepted, for his busy life left little time for his expected priestly duties.

While Mass was being celebrated, Michael's thoughts turned back to his struggle with his vocation. As he stood before the altar, raising the golden chalice and the sacred Eucharist, he looked out over the normal, everyday people in attendance. *Were they happy?* he wondered. *Would he be happier down there, rather than up here?* He forced his attention back to the rites, and as he spoke the words of the Eucharistic Prayer, he was struck by the thoughts that had so often plagued him at moments like this. If he had just performed the ancient rite that transmogrified ordinary bread and wine into the actual body and blood of Christ, at the moment the bells rang, shouldn't he feel something? If the full divinity of Christ had just appeared before him, shouldn't the wind blow and the cathedral fill with light, and the angels be heard singing?

And yet he neither felt nor heard anything of such meaning.

Had the Church misinterpreted the scriptures? There was plenty of backing in the gospels and letters of Paul to indicate that the Church was faithful in its understanding. But had the correct words been lost, and was the rite no longer effective? Or was it just that he himself was unworthy?

He was revolted by his feelings. He was no good to anyone stuck in the middle like this. But how could he resolve his dilemma, when the one person who could help him sort this out was barely speaking to him? Unless that was the sign he should be looking for.

Exasperated, Michael tried putting on a passive face, then accompanied by the altar servers and the bishop, proceeded down to the front of the altar to distribute the body of Christ to the faithful.

CHAPTER
SEVENTEEN

I t was a warm, sunny morning, typical of Bordeaux's famed wine-growing region in early autumn, when the team walked across the street after Mass for breakfast at a charming bistro with outdoor seating.

Le Bistro du Musée's dark green awning advertised it as a brasserie, a casual French restaurant whose menu touted its "bistronomic" offerings focused on seasonal produce, freshly baked breads, and local meats and cheeses. The four enjoyed a simple breakfast of charcuterie, layering thin slices of cured hams and aged cheese with salty butter on flaky fresh baguettes to make a slight variation on the traditional French *jambon beurre* sandwiches, with a side selection of fresh fruits and *cafés au lait* all around.

Sated and ready to get on with their day, they checked out of the hotel and—after first stopping at a hardware store to purchase a few things they needed to complete their mission—drove the forty-five minutes down the A62 and through quaint country roads to the church of Collégiale Notre-Dame d'Uzeste, Our Lady of Uzeste.

They were all pleasantly surprised driving through the lovely hamlet of Uzeste, a communal township of just five hundred souls surrounded by lush forests, agrarian fields, farms, and vineyards. Not a very auspicious resting place for so infamous a pope as Clement V, but ignominy had its consequences.

"I've looked at photographs of Clement's sarcophagus online," Michael told the others. "I expect it'll be something of a chore to get the crown of it open to acquire our DNA sample. It must weigh a ton, though we don't have to move it very far. I'm sure Karl and Ian can handle it just fine."

"While you supervise, Michael?" Ian quipped.

"That's right. Blake and I will be rooting for you all the way."

Entering the threshold of the monumental Gothic church, they found and met with the rector, who led them through rows of simple wooden chairs up to the sarcophagus, which was placed in a transept at the head of the central nave.

Surrounded by beautiful stained glass windows behind a semi-circle of towering marble columns lay the impressive black marble sarcophagus of Pope Clement V, clearly the main attraction in the sanctuary. Everyone gathered around it. There was a wide pedestal, the more narrow crypt itself standing a meter above it, and then the top, or crown, which was about ten centimeters thick. Intricately carved on the top of the crown was an effigy of the pope lying on his back in eternal repose, his head resting on an embroidered pillow, all in beige marble. His arms were crossed over his chest. It appeared that the head and pillow had been separated at some point in the past, and the top of the pope's face had been cleaved from the top of his head down to an ear.

The rector excused himself to attend to a parishioner in the hospital in the nearby village of Bazas. He would be gone most of the rest of the day and asked his guests to just leave the doors closed. Before he left, Michael asked him for the use of the hydraulic jack from his car, which he reluctantly provided.

Upon inspecting the sarcophagus, it appeared to Michael that the easiest way to gain access was to lift the crown off the black marble base, head, pillow, and all.

While Dr. Chaucer readied her tools and equipment for making the DNA collection, Michael briefed Ian and Karl about his plan to open the crypt. He brought in the supplies he had purchased at the hardware store: a selection of short two-by-four boards, some wooden shims and a crowbar.

Karl had also retrieved the hydraulic jack from their own rental car, and the one borrowed from the rector. Placing a jack on one side of the pedestal, and placing a two-by-four between the jack and the underside of the crown, Michael raised his jack until the wood just contacted the underside of the top marble slab. Ian duplicated these actions on the opposite side with the other jack. Karl stood at the head, making sure the slab rose evenly and did not tilt sideways or forward.

Slowly, Michael and Ian, guided by Karl, began cranking up the jacks to raise the marble slab. They took their time, careful not to place undue stress on the more than seven-hundred-year-old crypt.

When they had raised it about a centimeter, Karl inserted the first of the shims beneath the slab, and when they had gained two centimeters of clearance, Karl inserted a second set of shims. Blake pulled out an endoscopic borescope connected to her iPhone to see what was inside the sarcophagus. The tiny camera, its LEDs lighting up the interior, fed the roving images back to the phone's display.

"I can see the remains of the body. It's skeletonized, of course, but not badly burned. I suspect the worst of the damage from the fire was made to his soft tissue." She fed more of the cable in so the borescope could peer more deeply inside the crypt.

"Yes, I can see most of the body now, but...*Wait!* There's something else in there...."

PIERRE VALOIS SAT at his desk in the presidential suite of the Élysée Palace, going through his vetted correspondence. The remnants of his lunch sat on the sideboard, growing cold. He just didn't seem to need as much food these days, and he wondered where his appetite had gone. Probably another side effect of the medicines his doctors had prescribed, prolonging the inevitable. He knew he wouldn't last much longer.

He recalled studies showing that when a wife dies, especially after a long marriage such as his own, the husband's life expectancy was typically less than six months. *Well*, he thought, *that was fine.* He had lived a long and full life. If only he were leaving France in a better condition. Still, there may be a few things he could do in the time he had remaining.

Beneath the stack of letters was a flat, slim box wrapped in brown paper. He used his favored letter opener: a miniature French bayonet, a gift from one of the men he had served with in the war, on the occasion of his having been elected president. Opening the package, he discovered a box of gourmet chocolates from Patrick Roger, Paris's most esteemed chocolatier. A note card from the Duchess of Avignon was included:

Cher Pierre,

I hope these chocolates will hit the spot. A goodwill gift and an apology. As a good wife, I must support my husband in his ambitions, even as he seeks to unseat you, but know that I hold you in the highest regard.

Very truly yours,

Sabine Valois Micheaux

Duchess of Avignon

Ah, Sabine, he pondered as his thoughts turned to the past. *I have known you since you were a child. Always the manipulative type, never burning bridges. Nothing was ever enough for you, was it? No wonder you married into money. That Jean-Louis was always the avaricious type, grasping for more at every opportunity...well, you deserve each other. Though I don't know if you deserve the way he carries on with the women here in Paris while you are back home in Avignon. Nonetheless, one does not waste chocolate on sentiment.*

He slid off the top of the box to find a rich selection of truffles, fruit jellies, and ganache-filled chocolates, and selected one with nuts. He placed it on his tongue and began to chew, but sensed the taste was off. It was bitter, as if the almonds had turned. After chewing a bit more of it, he spat it out.

But it was already too late. A few moments later, he began to feel dizzy. His heart started racing, and he wheezed rapidly, struggling for breath. His legs suddenly gave out as he tried to stand, and he fell to the floor, gasping.

IN THE MID-AFTERNOON, Hana Sinclair sat in her office trying to finish up her piece from the duke's interview. She was working hard to make it sound objective, but felt worried that her journalistic objectivity had been compromised by the duke's intimation that he had an important position in his campaign for her; perhaps even in his administration, should he be elected.

Her phone rang. It was the president's secretary, Marcel.

"Mademoiselle Sinclair!" the man said with an anxious voice, "I know you are very close to His Excellency, so I must inform you that he is quite ill. He was on the floor of his office vomiting when I found him. He has been taken to Saint-Louis Hospital and is now in the intensive care unit, being treated for what they believe is cyanide poisoning! Both of his sons are at the hospital now, but he is asking for you. Can you come right away?"

"Of course, Marcel!" Hana said with equal alarm. "I'll be right there!"

As she began gathering her things, the phone rang again.

"*Marcel?*"

"Please hold for His Grace, the Duke of Avignon," the female voice said.

Tempted to just hang up and race out the door, Hana relented and waited. A moment later, the duke came on the phone.

"Miss Sinclair, I hope I haven't called at a bad time."

"Actually, Your Grace, I'm on my way to the Saint-Louis Hospital. My godfather has taken quite ill. I really can't talk now. May I call you tomorrow?"

Without waiting for his answer, she hung up and rushed downstairs to grab a cab.

Glancing at the receiver with minor annoyance, the duke slowly placed it back on its cradle. Then he suddenly grasped something from what Hana had said.

So... given the breaking news, and having seen you at Jacqueline's funeral, I now take it your godfather must be Pierre Valois. Interest-

ing... Mademoiselle Sinclair, you have inadvertently given me a very important piece of information—one I do not intend to waste.

WHEN SHE ARRIVED at the hospital, Hana made her way to the Intensive Care Unit, then paused outside Pierre's suite. Two men in black suits with coiled earpieces stood guard at the door. She had passed two more at the entrance to the ICU who checked her ID before admitting her. As she was about to enter, she heard voices from inside the president's room and paused. Her godfather was speaking angrily. She waited, listening from the hall just outside the door...

"Philip, the prime minister is a weakling and a fool. It would not surprise me, faced with a crisis like my incapacity, if he were to simply resign and let someone else take over, or become their puppet, should he remain in office. You must be ready to take over in my absence. I will use my powers of delegation to place you in charge of as much of the government as possible, and should the prime minister resign, you must take control and prevent immediate elections. Jean-Louis Micheaux is too popular, and you will need time to find his weaknesses and exploit them. But now it is too soon. Much too soon. I was not ready for something like this. You *must* be decisive while I remain here."

"I will, Father. And when I find out who did this to you, there will be grave consequences."

"Do not worry about that for now. I doubt the perpetrator can be found, anyway. Surely, Sabine would not be so bold or foolish as to send me poisoned chocolates with her name on them. Besides, she is family. I would rather suspect her husband over her, but the matter has been turned over to the police, and they will handle it now.

"Philip, you have my blessing. Go, be the leader France needs."

"Yes, Father. You can count on me."

Philip turned to leave. Lauren moved closer to the bed.

"Is there anything you need me to do, Papa?"

"Of course not, my son. There's nothing you can do. Philip will handle things. If you want to be helpful, just go see if Hana is here yet. I want to speak with her."

Disheartened by his father's dismissal, Lauren Valois simply replied, "Yes, Papa."

Walking out of the room, Lauren saw Hana standing just outside the doorway.

"He's asking for you," he said, his eyes glistening with emotion. He turned and walked down the hall, his head hung low.

Hana entered the room, seeing her beloved godfather propped up on the bed, an IV in his arm and EKG lead wires running from electrodes on his chest to a monitor on the wall.

Seeing her, Pierre shouted, "*Stéphane?!*"

The presidential security officer who had been posted at the door promptly entered the room.

"Stéphane, please close the door on your way out. I want no interruptions for ten minutes."

"*Bien sûr, Monsieur le Président,*" the big man confirmed, then turned and left the room, closing the door behind him.

"Now, *ma petite* Hana, don't look so glum. I'm not in as bad a shape as it looks, although the doctors say if I had not thrown up most of the poisoned chocolate, I wouldn't be here now. Plus, cyanide has a couple of very effective antidotes." He gestured at an IV bag hanging from a floor stand next to him labeled "Hydroxocobalamin." "So, don't worry. They missed me this time, though it may not be their last shot.

"But now, I need you to do something for me, something for which your skills as an investigative journalist will be most useful. Listen carefully…"

～

As Hana left the president's hospital suite, she saw Marco and her grandfather, Armand, walking toward her in the long hallway. Armand looked worried; Marco looked angry. Sighing, she prepared herself yet again for another quarrel.

"I can't believe you!" Marco began. "We talked about this, Hana. I must find out you're here from your grandfather? He wanted to know why I wasn't already with you. With you *where?* I ask, since I expected you to be at work! The president's secretary called Armand to tell him about the attack, but you couldn't call me?"

Armand stepped in to reinforce Marco's rant. "Hana, please... I am just concerned about your safety. As you can see now, France is a very dangerous place. You are not privy to all the information I have about what is going on. France stands on the blade of a knife. There is revolution in the air. I would feel better if you would come back to Geneva with me."

"I'm sorry, Grand-père, but my home is here, my job is here, my life is here, and I'm tired of being treated like a child. I don't need a babysitter. And I don't think anyone is trying to start a revolution."

"No?" Armand retorted, glancing up at the TV over the nurse's station. "Look!"

They all turned to face the TV. The duke stood talking to a gaggle of reporters in front of live cameras positioned in front of the hospital. Though the sound was muted, the closed-captioned text scrolled across the bottom of the screen:

"The president lies in this very hospital, critically ill and incapable of exercising the duties of his office. I call on the government to resign at once. And if they will not, I call on the National Assembly to take a vote of no confidence. We need to have elections immediately. France needs leadership now. Leadership with a plan to deal with these difficulties, with compassion and restraint, not brutality and oppression. And I tell you now, I am the leader with that plan. I announce today that I,

Jean-Louis Micheaux, Duke of Avignon, am seeking the presidency of the Republic!"

All three stood there, stunned, along with the few nurses gathered around the TV. But Hana was not as surprised as the others, for while she could not reveal what her godfather had discussed with her, she had suspected that someone would make a move.

Just not necessarily the duke first.

CHAPTER

EIGHTEEN

E ager to see what Blake had spied through the endoscopic camera, Michael hurried around to the head of the sarcophagus to see the display on her phone.

Next to Clement's skull was a thin, beaten sheet of metal, its inscribed lettering glinting in the beam of the LEDs, and beneath it, a sheet of parchment, apparently well preserved by its centuries confined inside the tomb.

"Well, this is intriguing," Michael noted. "What would be so important that such things would be buried with the body of Pope Clement? Perhaps something he valued? And was it interred with him when he died or was it put in later when someone broke the head off the effigy to open the crypt, whenever that was? So many questions. Let's get what we came for, then see if we can get to that document."

Once again, Michael and Ian used the jacks to raise the lid of the sarcophagus a bit higher, until Blake could get a hand inside to manipulate her collection tools.

She looked at Michael and the others uneasily. "I admit to some hesitation sticking my hand in there. Are you absolutely sure those jacks will hold? I really need this arm…"

Karl laughed. "Would you prefer that I do it, Dr. Chaucer?

I've no such fears."

"Thanks, Karl, but I'll manage. And please, call me Blake."

Taking a deep breath, she brought one of the wooden pew chairs over so she had a surface to work from. She began by donning a sterile white lab coat she had brought with her, and then slipped on two pairs of sterile latex gloves, one pair over the other in case of rupture. "Protection from contamination starts at the sampling," she advised.

"All right, Ian, I'm going to have you help me. This is going to be just like surgery. I'll be sanitized while we must assume you are contaminated."

Ian grimaced at hearing that.

"Now that I have my gloves on, I can only touch sterile things, so you will have to handle anything that is not sanitized. I'll give you directions."

"Just tell me what to do. I'm a quick learner."

"Okay, first, I need a clean place to put down the sterile tools, so inside my suitcase are a few packages of sterile items I'm going to need. Those are wrapped in a kind of cellophane. Each one has a clear side and an opaque side. Each instrument within is labeled on the opaque side. It's fine for you to touch the outside, so I'll have you open them and drop the contents either into my hand or on the sterile drape we are going to open first. Find the package that has a blue towel inside."

"Got it," Ian confirmed.

"Now, pull the sides of the package apart until the top opens, then turn the package over and drop the towel into my hands."

Ian did as he was told. "Like this?"

"Yes, perfect."

She took the towel and carefully unfolded it, laying it on the chair.

"Now, the upper surface of the towel is sterile. Try not to lean over it too much and don't touch it. Hand me the extensible probe and the coil of wire. Open the packages and drop the contents on the towel."

Once Ian was done, Blake took the extensible probe—as thick as a pencil, composed of collapsible sections with a small metal loop affixed to the end, and a meter's length of multi-stranded flexible wire—and tied the wire to the loop. Then, passing the wire out through the loop and back again, she created a lasso at the end of the probe, one she could close by pulling on the other end of the wire. She extended the probe to its full length and cautiously inserted it into the gap.

"Michael, would you hold the borescope so I can see the lower jaw?"

Michael came over, took the device, and dropped the cable down into the crypt.

Using the lasso as she watched the iPhone display, Blake grabbed the end of the jawbone in the loop and pulled it away from the skull. Once it was free, she began to collapse the probe until she could grasp the mandible in her other hand and ease it through the gap.

"We're going to have to take a couple of the pope's teeth for analysis. DNA typing of remains this old is a destructive process. I'll have to grind up the teeth and extract the DNA in order to have enough material to profile, and that will have to be done back at the lab.

"Ian, I need the tooth pliers now, and put the plastic bottle on the towel, please."

Ian searched through the suitcase and found the appropriate items, then placed them on the towel using the sterile technique Blake had specified.

"Very good, Ian. If your job in the Archives doesn't work out, maybe we can find you a place in the lab…"

"He's not going anywhere," Michael quipped. "No poaching."

Next, Blake used the pliers to take two molars, a canine, and two of the front incisors from the lower jaw for analysis. She would have preferred the upper incisors, but it would have been too difficult to get the skull out of the crypt to extract the teeth.

Once she had the teeth removed, she placed them in the plastic bottle and replaced the cap. She then reversed the procedure, putting the mandible back in the crypt next to the skull, and removed the probe.

"Now, let's see if I have another trick up my sleeve. Ian, there should be another probe in the bag. This one is labeled 'Magnetic Probe.'"

Ian found it and placed it on the towel. The magnetic probe was considerably stouter than the wire probe, its outer section a centimeter in diameter and twenty centimeters long, with a powerful neodymium magnet at the end of it. Using the probe, she extended it out to touch the metal plate on the middle edge of one side. The plate jumped up as the magnet got close. Slowly and cautiously, she raised the metal plate off the parchment, then slid the plate back underneath it. Retracting the collapsible sections of the probe, she raised both the plate and the parchment to the level where they could be removed through the gap between the tomb and the crown. Pulling them out successfully, she smiled, then placed the plate and the parchment on the towel.

"Whew! That was a nail biter."

"Nice work, Blake!" the others said in unison, applauding her efforts.

The plate was about fifteen by twenty centimeters, hammered to less than a millimeter thick. On observing it more closely, they found it had been finely engraved with elaborate fleurs-de-lis and ornamental feathers around the edges.

The plate had an inscription in Latin on it. Michael translated it aloud.

In the year of our Lord, 1307, I, Clement, Bishop of Rome and Avignon, hereby, with the infallible authority of the Holy Church, do issue this Edict, that Philip IV, of House Capet, is the ordained and rightful king and ruler of all France, and of all lands and territories that shall owe obedience to her, and so shall be his legitimate descendants, for all time to come, and against all pretenders.

Clement V, Pontifex Pontificum

22 November 1307

He then turned to the parchment. It, too, was roughly fifteen by twenty centimeters, and had been written with a fine hand in French, in the vernacular of the fourteenth century. Michael translated it for the others.

My dear Florian,

I have awaited your return to Avignon, but I am afraid that I may not be here when you return. So, I must set down the things I would have told you on your return, some of which you initiated with your trip to Paris.

As you know from my confession to the bishop at Notre-Dame, King Philip had another son, his fourth-born, in 1283. His name is Robert, of House Capet. The circumstances of his birth are in the confession, so I will not repeat them here. His mother is dead, and he himself is now of thirty-one years, and married, with sons of his own, Henri and Hugh. I have sent them to Bordeaux, to be cared for and hidden by Jerome Baudette, the bishop there, who is a good friend and loyal.

I trust you have used the confession to find the third of the treasure not seized by Philip, from the original horde that was secreted at Notre-Dame. The other two-thirds have been removed to Avignon and are hidden safely here. Since I cannot tell you in person, I can only give you clues that will enable you, and nobody else, to find the treasure, which I leave to you. Please see to it that some of the monies I leave you go to Baudette and to Robert and his descendants for their preservation. Use my personal Bible to find the treasures in Avignon with the clues on the back of this letter.

I have also left you the Edict of Avignon for Philip, as mentioned in the confession. I have not given it to him. Make sure it does not fall into his hands. Instead, I have given him the papal bull, *Pastoralis praeeminentiae*. That should be enough for him.

I have not been the pope I had hoped to be, Florian. Philip has been a domineering monarch, and I have appeased him far too much. Be wary of him, and of my successor. May God have mercy on my soul.

Your loving brother, Bertrand

30 March 1314

Curiously, on the back of the parchment was a series of numbers, meaningless on their own but meriting further study. Michael took several photographs of the objects, then asked Blake to return them to the crypt.

"We should be able to compare the hand to other examples of Pope Clement's writing," Michael said. "I am not worried about these being forgeries at this point. And our only authorization has been to remove DNA samples, not anything else. I would think that their value would be in what content they hold, and we have photographic evidence of that now. If their authenticity is questioned, though, we may have to return and retrieve the documents another time.

"But we have a flight to catch soon, and now we have more questions for the bishop in Bordeaux."

Removing the wooden shims and manning the jacks, Michael and Ian carefully lowered the marble crown of the crypt back into place. While Blake packed up her tools, Ian returned the borrowed jack to the rector's office.

The team then loaded themselves and their gear back into the rental car for the trip back to Bordeaux.

Before they had reached their destination, Michael had called ahead to arrange a quick meeting with Bishop Allain Fournier at the Bordeaux Cathedral. When they arrived, as prearranged, the bishop met them outside so they wouldn't have to park and walk in. They had little time left to make it to the airport.

"Your Excellency, we obtained the samples we needed from the body of Pope Clement to do the DNA testing. But we also made the most remarkable discovery."

Michael took out his phone and showed the bishop pictures of the hammered metal plate and the parchment letter.

"Based on the revealing contents of this letter," Michael said, "we'll need to know if there are any records here in your diocese regarding births, deaths, or marriages related to Robert Capet, or his sons, Henri and Hugh." He quickly explained the reason.

"Goodness!" Bishop Fournier exclaimed. "Those truly are remarkable finds. May I ask, what have you done with the items themselves?"

"We left them in the crypt, of course. We didn't have permission from the appropriate authorities to remove historical artifacts from the crypt. I do hope, at some point, to be able to come back and retrieve them for proper study and analysis. But we have what we need for now. Meanwhile, can you have your staff help us?"

"Rest assured, Father Dominic, we will certainly go back through our records and see what we can find. I will have the archivist start on that in the morning. I hope we're able to find something that might help you."

Michael thanked him, and with Karl at the wheel they took off for the airport, paying little attention to the speed limits.

After they had gone, the bishop went back into his office, picked up the phone, and made a call.

But it was not to the archivist.

IT HAD BEEN a long and ambitious day for the duke. He and his staff had been quietly but feverishly working on his campaign, waiting for the right moment to launch.

When he heard that the president was gravely ill, he knew it was time to act. Now, back in the residential portion of his suite at the George Cinq, he relaxed in an easy chair, watching recaps of his press conference at the hospital with a glass of wine in hand. Setting the wine down on a side table, he picked up his phone and pressed the speed dial button for his wife at their home in Avignon.

"Hello, my darling," Sabine Micheaux greeted him. "My, what a day you must have had. I've been watching you on TV all afternoon."

"Yes, my love, it's been quite the day. Only you know how long I've been waiting for just the right moment of crisis to announce my candidacy, and it appears that one just fell into my lap."

Sabine was silent for a moment, an unseen smile crossing her face. "You see, Jean-Louis, this is fate at work. You are meant to be president of France."

"Let's hope so. The country is so split now, I'm not sure you could get more than half of them to agree that the sun rises in the east, much less pick a competent leader."

"Be patient. They will come together. You do inspire them, you know."

"Yes, well, tomorrow will be another display of inspiration for them. I've just been invited to speak at the Simone de Beauvoir Memorial Feminism Rally at two o'clock in the Parc du Champ-de-Mars. The whole event will probably be a zoo. There will be a muster of Yellow Jackets, as well as a *Congrès National Français* counterrally at the same time. Those CNF guys do concern me. They are nothing less than fascists at heart. Oh, and I've also engaged that security company you recommended to augment our personal protection detail. One can't take too many chances these days."

"*Très bien*, my darling. Then I won't have to worry about you so much."

"And how is Margot?"

"Oh, she's fine. She's downstairs watching an American movie. *Chérie*, I agree that she should be bilingual, but really, English? Why not Spanish? Or German? Or even Russian or Chinese... Arabic even? Something useful. The Americans are such bores, and their cinema is trash."

"What is she watching?"

"*La panthère Rose.*" The Pink Panther, she said with a roll of her eyes.

"*Mon Dieu*, not that old thing!" He laughed. "Well, give her a kiss for me. I must be going up now."

"So soon?"

"Tomorrow is a big day, Sabine. I must get some sleep." As he said this, one of the female members of his campaign staff came out of the bathroom, wearing nothing but a towel. He winked at her, putting a finger to his lips.

"I'm sure tomorrow will be even bigger than you expect," Sabine added. "I'll tell all my friends about it."

"*Merci*, my love. What would I do without you? *Bonne nuit* for now," he said, as he stood to meet the young staffer by the bed.

"Good night, my darling."

Hanging up the phone, Sabine then prepared an email to send out to all the people in her immense contacts database:

Tomorrow, two o'clock. The Duke of Avignon will address a feminist rally at the Champ-de-Mars. Don't miss it, and please tell your friends.

A short while later, after several forwardings of Sabine's email, a man in a warehouse just outside Paris received the same message.

He began loading up the white Toyota pickup truck and called his team in. There was work to be done.

CHAPTER

NINETEEN

lack-clad guards arrived at five o'clock the next morning and stationed themselves around the area where the stage was being set near the Eiffel Tower and the Champ-de-Mars.

The local police showed up to begin their own security shifts, and the guards explained that they were the advance team for the duke, who would be speaking later. Having already been briefed on security protocols for the event, the police had expected guards to be there, so no IDs were requested or challenged.

At six o'clock, the white Toyota truck approached the security checkpoint already established by the duke's advance team. The pickup truck had magnetic door signs identifying it as being from the Refuse and Recycling Corporation. The bed of the truck was filled with rectangular cardboard trashcans, still folded, with clear plastic trash bags and a green plastic trash can already full of fast-food bags. The security guards made a show of inspecting the truck, looking under the chassis with a mirror, and checking the driver's paperwork on a clipboard. The police looked on, confident that the security personnel were doing their job.

After the truck was cleared, it was driven into the area where the demonstrations would later take place. Periodically the truck would stop, and the two men inside would get out, each dressed in dirty white work coveralls emblazoned with "Refuse & Recycling" in green letters on their backs. Hoodies covered their heads to warm them from the chill of the morning, and each man wore leather work gloves. Both of them had long beards and mustaches and wore sunglasses.

Each time they stopped at various points in the staging area for the crowds, the two men got out and set up one of the cardboard trashcan boxes, inserting a clear plastic trash bag into it and tying it off. And also each time, they took one of the fast-food bags and dropped it into the trash can before putting it into the trash bag. They fell into the box with a heavy thump.

When the two men were finished, some twenty of the cardboard trash boxes had been dispersed throughout the demonstration area, including two in the area where the stage was being set up. In half of them, the men also dropped in a Pringles potato chip can. These, too, thumped when dropped.

Getting into the truck, they left the grounds back through the security checkpoint.

HANA WAS in her office early that morning, still trying to finish up the article on her interview with the duke, when her phone rang.

"Mademoiselle Sinclair?" a woman's voice asked.

"Yes?"

"Please hold for the Duke of Avignon."

She waited.

Moments later, the duke came on the line. "Hana, I hope I've caught you at a better time now."

"Yes, Your Grace, this is much better, thank you."

"How is your godfather doing?"

Hana paused, thinking about how to respond. "He is in what they call guarded condition," she replied cautiously.

"I do hope he recovers speedily. At any rate, I called to see if you had caught my announcement yesterday."

"How could I have missed it?! You basically dominated the news. In fact, I was just finishing up my piece from our interview the other day, for today's afternoon edition."

"I would hate to take you away from writing about me"—he chuckled—"but I'm speaking at a rally later at the Champ-de-Mars. I was hoping you could attend, and then afterward we could talk about that offer I was hinting at the other day. Now that I have an official campaign, it's time to make bona fide offers, especially for the top spots on our team."

Somewhat flustered at the prospect of a "top spot" on a presidential campaign, Hana replied, "Yes, I think I can get away. May I bring a guest? My grandfather has insisted I be accompanied by a bodyguard when I'm out in public, especially during these unusual times. I don't think I can get away without bringing him."

"That's not a problem, Hana. I will leave word with my protective detail and the security staff to let you and your escort in. You will be directed to a secure backstage area. My own armored limousine will be there to retreat into if things get unmanageable, and I have hired extra security for the event. It will be very safe, I assure you."

"Well, in that case, I'd love to come." They ended the call.

Hana had considered that getting Marco to accompany her to an event where the duke was going to speak might be a tall order. But *he* was the one who kept insisting he be by her side at all times. He would just have to swallow his political leanings in the process, if she was that important to him. She called Marco and asked him to meet her at *Le Monde* at one-thirty.

· · ·

WHEN MARCO ARRIVED ON FOOT, having walked from their apartment, Hana was already waiting at the curb inside a taxi. She called out to him and he jumped in next to her, then kissed her forehead.

"Bonjour, ma belle! Where are we off to?"

Hana looked at him cannily. "We're meeting someone near the Eiffel Tower, and if you are going to be snide about it, you can get back out."

"Sorry, not a chance. There is a big demonstration going on just in front of the Tower, and I even heard that the duke is speak —Wait, we aren't going to the duke's speech, are we?"

"What do you think? I'm a reporter. He's my assignment and I've got to cover him. That means being where he is, hearing what he has to say, talking to other people to see what they think about what he has to say…"

"Well, I can tell you what *this* person has to say about him."

"He's not as bad as you think, Marco."

"Is that a fact? We shall see."

THE DUKE'S prior arrangements made it possible for the taxi to get fairly close to the Eiffel Tower before they had to get out and walk. At the last security checkpoint, where the cab had let them out, a campaign staffer and a security guard appeared to escort Hana and Marco the rest of the way. As they got closer, they could hear chanting coming from the crowd.

The stage had been set up in the Jardin de la Tour Eiffel, the gardens surrounding the Eiffel Tower. The space between the tower and the Bassins du Champ de Mars was a sea of people. The Avenue Gustave Eiffel had been blocked off to provide an escape route for the duke if needed, and his limo had been parked behind the stage, hidden behind the backdrop. Numerous security personnel were stationed around the closed-off area, and two black Ford Explorers were lined up with the limo as chase vehicles.

A casually dressed young woman was speaking on the stage, but the crowd was becoming loud and boisterous. Random hecklers could be heard calling out, and organized chanting was coming from the south end of the gardens. Uniformed police were seen in force, but after the fiasco at the funeral and the riots after the bombing, they had been told to keep a low profile, so they just tried to maintain separation between the various factions in the crowd in hopes of reducing friction: right-wing activists to the east, left-wing to the south, and the feminists in the middle of the gardens. Yellow Jackets were chanting the slogan *"Liberté, prospérité, sécurité,"* while Congrès National Français adherents were chanting *"France pour les Français,"* and *"Congrès Français"* repeatedly. Tensions were rising as the volume got louder.

Marco was clearly on edge. He walked over to Hana.

"Please stay inside the security perimeter. I'm going up to the tower's first-level observation deck to take a look at the size of the crowd, see if I can spot any agitators and check our exit routes. I'll be right back. Don't go anywhere!" He then made a dash for the tower.

Just then, the duke came out of his limousine and walked over to Hana.

"I guess it's showtime now, *oui?* My people tell me the crowd is a little restless. But if I'm going to be their leader, I've got to present a strong face. If things do get unpredictable, though, please get in the limo, Hana. When your man comes back, get him in there too. We are not staying here when the speech is over. We can talk back at the George Cinq. I'll have a car take you both back to your *Le Monde* offices.

"All right, wish me luck!"

On cue, the speaker on the stage transitioned from her stump ramblings to a glowing introduction of the duke. Just before he ran up to the podium, his personal protective detail had taken positions in front of the stage and on both sides.

The duke began speaking, his arms extended as if embracing the crowd.

"People of France! Today we are here to celebrate—"

A sudden series of loud pops sounded from the trashcans, and gasps emerged from the frightened crowd.

Immediately, the cardboard trashcan boxes caught fire as the smoke grenades inside them simultaneously sent billows of thick, yellow smoke into the air. The crowd panicked, turning in all directions, uncertain whether the police had initiated an attack or their political opponents had. Shouts and screams filled the air as confusion reigned.

Suddenly, a second series of explosions erupted from all but two of the trash cans. The canisters inside the Pringles cans launched themselves into the air, bursting when they were about four meters above the crowd. A heavy mist splayed out, as much as twenty meters in all directions from the cans, and then fell down over the crowd with a hiss and a splat.

Everyone stood there stunned, suddenly dampened from some unknown substance. Hideous odors permeated the air; some canisters had emitted the stench of skunk, others of rotten eggs. The demonstrators gagged and choked.

Then the remaining canisters discharged their contents and the demonstrators closest felt their eyes stinging as if from tear gas, their throats burn, and their lungs constrict. Then the nausea came, and with it, uncontrollable vomiting.

The yellow smoke made everything worse since people had no idea which way to go to escape from it. They couldn't see through the smoke and became disoriented. Panic ensued, and people started running. But with the reduced visibility, they all simply ran into each other and fell in heaps onto the ground. The grounds were now slick with vomit, and the smell overwhelmed everyone. Sirens screamed in the distance, coming from all directions.

Marco had just reached the observation deck of the Eiffel

Tower when he saw the smoke clouds start to form. *Merde!* he cursed. *Out of position... Not now! Got to get back to Hana!*

He headed to the elevator, but the cars had been suspended as an emergency precaution. *Stairs.* He made for the stairs, shoving people aside, using techniques from his commando days for rapidly traversing a crowd, pushing people in the ribs, which caused them to jump aside just long enough for him to pass. He was subjected to a slew of curses, but he didn't care. All that mattered was returning to Hana and getting her out of there.

When she saw the clouds of yellow smoke, Hana made for the limousine. The two Ford Explorers were already loaded with security personnel. *How had they gotten prepared so fast?* she wondered.

Moments after she got inside, the doors were thrust open, and the duke was pushed into the back seat beside her, followed by two men from his security team. The limo leapt forward, following the first SUV out through the checkpoint, the other SUV right behind. Each vehicle was equipped with covert emergency lights, which began flashing to clear traffic.

The duke called out, "Is everyone all right?!" His two-man personal security detail was coughing but didn't seem otherwise affected. They had been the two in front of the stage, Hana recalled. She started to tremble. *Where was Marco?*

With panic in her voice, she asked anyone, "Marco? Where's Marco?!"

"Is that your security man?" the duke asked, coughing himself.

"Yes. He went to the tower to get a better view from higher up. But he hasn't come back."

The duke instructed his security detail, "Radio back and see if anyone still there has Marco in sight. See if he made it out with the rest of the detail."

"Yes, Your Grace," the lead agent said.

Marco was not, however, with any of the duke's detail. He

made it down the tower stairs only to see the limo and the SUVs sprinting down the avenue, away from the awful scene. Coughing from the gas and yellow smoke in the air, he took his phone out and called Hana.

In the limo, her phone rang. She jerked it out of her purse and answered quickly.

"Marco! Oh God, Marco, where are you? Tell me you're okay!"

"Yes, I'm fine," he said, coughing. "Tell me you're in the limo."

"Yes, I am. The duke and his security men are here with me. We're headed for the George Cinq."

"Okay, then stay there. I'll get there soon enough, though it may be awhile."

He was still under the tower, but the panicked crowd was now surging in his direction, as were the yellow smoke and the gas. Heading north, he made a run for the river, and when he reached the banks of the Seine, he dove in.

CHAPTER

TWENTY

The next morning, as usual, Ian was the first to arrive at his office in the Vatican. After running out to Caffè Pergamino for a couple of jolts of espresso and a newspaper, he returned to his desk to catch up on the news. Paris's ongoing demonstrations and the violent terrorist attack at the Eiffel Tower dominated the headlines. Knowing his friends had been there concerned him deeply, but he trusted that Marco had taken matters well in hand. He hoped, at least. He had yet to see his boss.

When his desk phone rang, he set aside the paper and answered it.

"Good morning, Ian."

"Hey there, Teri. You're up early."

"Yeah, I was hoping I'd catch you in early as well. Michael has a call coming in now from Bishop Fournier at Bordeaux Cathedral, but he's not answering his phone. The bishop said it was urgent. Would you mind taking it?"

"I expect Michael's out for a run. But I'll take it for him, sure. Put him through."

After a moment, the connection was made.

"Good morning, Your Excellency. This is Father Dominic's assistant, Ian Duffy. May I help you?"

"*Oui, bonjour*, Ian. I have the results of our records search that Father Dominic asked for, but it can be a bit complicated and certainly confusing over the phone, so I'll send this all over by email after giving you the highlights. Ready?"

"As ready as I'll ever be."

Fournier went on to describe the complex lineage of Philip IV's sons and their marriages and children, while Ian did his best taking notes until the bishop wound down his tale.

"Finally, Philip's son Hugh and his wife Marie Micheaux lived here in Bordeaux until her father, Charles Micheaux, the Duke of Avignon, was near death. He had no sons, so he adopted Hugh, who took the name Micheaux, so that Hugh and Marie's son, Louis, would become Louis Micheaux and inherit the Duchy of Avignon. We have Louis' original baptism certificate, in the name of Louis Capet, and after Hugh was adopted, Louis was re-baptized and confirmed as Louis Micheaux, Duke of Avignon. When Charles passed, Hugh, Marie, and Louis went to live in Avignon. That is the last record we have of them."

Ian took a deep breath, letting it out slowly. "You weren't wrong about the confusion, Your Excellency. That's quite the elaborate history, and we thank you for it. I've taken good notes, but your email would still be welcome. In the meantime, I'll inform Father Dominic of your findings as soon as he arrives."

Ending the call, Ian rang the switchboard. Seeing the call coming in from Ian's office, Sister Teri grabbed it before one of the other operators could.

"So, what's the news?" she asked eagerly.

"Can you meet for coffee soon? You'll want to say *yes*."

"Yes it is, then. How about half an hour?"

"Meet you at the canteen in thirty."

Ian grabbed his laptop and headed to the canteen early. When Teri came in later, he was so focused on his research that he didn't see her until she plopped down in the chair next to him. Surprised, he nearly spilled his coffee.

"Easy, Ian. Doesn't it hurt your brain to be concentrating so hard?"

Ian was too excited to take the bait and let the barb pass. "You are *not* going to believe this! So, you know we went to Bordeaux yesterday to get a DNA sample from Pope Clement, right?"

"I didn't know the details, but do fill me in."

Ian explained their trip to Uzeste and unsealing the pope's crypt, finding the Edict of Avignon and the letter from Clement to Florian, and then the bishop's research that tied Robert Capet, King Philip IV's son, to Louis Micheaux, the Duke of Avignon, in the 1330s.

Fully focused now, Teri caught up quickly. "So the House of Capet became the House of Micheaux, while the throne passed to the House of Valois. *Wait...* The current Duke of Avignon, isn't his name Micheaux? Um... Jean Something... Jean-Louis. That's it, Jean-Louis Micheaux. You don't think they're related, do you?"

"Well, that's what I'm looking for now. I'm on the Integrated Ancestry Database I created for VADNA. Oh, shite! Forget you ever heard that name, for both our sakes!"

"You mean Dr. Chaucer's stealth program at Sapienza University?"

Ian's jaw dropped as he whispered, "How did *you* know about that?! It's top secret!"

"Ian, the switchboard is the hub of everything that happens in the Vatican. There isn't much we don't know, truth be told. And what we don't know, we suspect," she said with a satisfied smirk. "And we're usually right. Nuns aren't just pretty faces, you know."

"No comment. Anyway, I developed a program that cross-references the different commercial ancestry databases, looking for matching records, and filling in where one database has information that the others don't. I was just looking here for Louis Micheaux—and I found him, confirming his father was named Hugh Micheaux and his mother was Marie. Since he was landed aristocracy, they kept good records of the family. And get this: there is only one living male descendant of Louis Micheaux. Care to guess who it is?"

"Well, it has to be Jean-Louis Micheaux, right? But that means, since House Micheaux is actually House Capet, Jean-Louis would have a claim to the throne of France!"

"Faith and begorrah, you catch on quick!" Ian exclaimed. "But the other thing we found in the crypt was a hammered plate with writing stamped on it. It read that the descendants of Philip IV were the rightful rulers of France—*for all time!* He absolutely has a claim to be king. Wait till Michael hears about this!"

Just then, Michael came up behind Ian, looking for a cup of coffee to start the day.

"Wait until I hear what? Something good, I hope?"

"Have a seat, Michael," Ian crowed with pride, "and prepare to be amazed…"

DULY AMAZED, Michael had returned to his office later that morning to read Bishop Fournier's email and Ian's notes and ancestral database results when Ian stuck his head in the door.

"Michael, check out CNN on your computer. Things are heating up in France again."

Launching a new browser window, Michael went to CNN's website for their live coverage. The screen filled with an ongoing feed of chaos at the foot of the Eiffel Tower. Michael sat dazed with wonder as he watched the police and firefighters tending to the sick and injured. The camera shook as even the camera operator was heard coughing.

Gas still lingered in the air, irritating people's respiratory systems, even the many officials wearing respirators. An announcer explained that the offending gas had been determined to be DM, or Adamsite, a chemical warfare agent known as a vomiting agent or sneeze gas. The news ticker crawling across the bottom of the screen declared the sensational headline:

Terrorist chemical attacks in Paris... hundreds sickened, no deaths reported... injuries minor but widespread... attack occurred just as the Duke of Avignon was beginning his remarks...

The CNN footage changed to an earlier shot of the duke as he stood on the podium speaking with his hands spread wide to embrace the crowd, when the yellow smoke started to appear. His security detail quickly whisked him off the stage and to his limousine while the network's camera followed his every movement. The shot zoomed in as the duke was ushered into the car, right next to a familiar woman with chestnut brown hair.

My God! That's Hana! Hana was there during the attack! But where was Marco? The CNN footage followed the limo and the security chase vehicles, their emergency lights flashing as they sped away from the scene. Then the screen returned to live images of the tortured audience and demonstrators still assembled in the area. Michael started to call Hana when he heard the announcer state that the attack actually happened a little over two hours earlier. He stopped making the call to listen to the rest of what happened in case there was more he needed to know before he spoke with her.

It appeared the chaos was only now beginning to subside as overwhelmed public safety officials began to get a handle on the scope of the disaster. Firefighters and ambulances from all over Paris had been dispatched to the scene to take the most severely affected to hospitals. Michael was grateful he had seen that Hana had been removed from the scene so quickly.

Acting on behalf of his father, Philip Valois had declared a state of emergency and had called in the military, who had been specifically trained on how to handle a mass decontamination event. It had taken some time but eventually, officials cordoned off the area and funneled the demonstrators through specific channels for treatment and decontamination. Fire trucks sprayed water in arcs over the street as the people were directed through the prepared exits, all getting soaked as the contaminants were washed away.

People had been separated by gender to strip off their contaminated clothing and were given white Tyvek jumpsuits to wear in the meantime. Their belongings were placed in plastic bags and tagged with identifying information so they could be decontaminated later and returned.

The International Red Cross had set up a shelter for people while everything was being sorted out. Everyone had to be interviewed about anything suspicious they might have seen. Michael was mesmerized as he watched, praying through it all, giving thanks that Hana had been whisked away when she had.

He picked up his desk phone and dialed her number. After a few rings, she answered.

"Hana, are you okay?!"

"Michael! Yes, I'm fine. But I wouldn't have been so lucky if the duke hadn't been prepared to leave so quickly. He took good care of me."

"You were with the duke? Where are you now?"

"Yes, he'd asked me to cover his speech. I'm in the duke's suite at the George Cinq. Marco just got here a few minutes ago. He'd been on the lower observation deck of the Eiffel Tower when the smoke bombs went off. He didn't make it back down before we all left. He'd jumped in the river to avoid the gas and the chaos and swam away from the scene. It took him almost two hours to get here, with all the police blockades and emergency vehicles throughout the city. Oh, Michael, it is so awful. The military is everywhere, handling the decontamination so the fire department and medical personnel can focus on treating people."

"I'm so glad you are safe. I actually saw you on TV in the limo as the duke was getting in. I was wondering where Marco was."

"Well, Marco hasn't been with me as much recently. It's getting a bit stifling, this needing a babysitter all the time. Although Paris certainly isn't getting any safer."

"Yeah, I know the feeling. I've had to bring a Swiss Guard with me practically every time I leave the Vatican."

"Michael, I need to run. Marco is getting out of the shower and the duke is getting him some clean clothes. We'll be going home soon. Is there anything else?"

Michael paused. "Well... yes, but it's not important right now. You have a lot going on. Maybe you can call me tomorrow and we can talk then?"

"Sure, I'll call you tomorrow. Thank you for thinking of me, Michael."

And she was gone.

At least she was safe. He had been going to tell her about the duke's genealogy, but it didn't seem like the right time. It was just so good to hear her voice. It was almost like old times. Almost. And he would talk with her again tomorrow.

CHAPTER

TWENTY-ONE

T he next morning, having finished his ten-kilometer run, Father Dominic found himself walking by the Edicola newsstand as he cooled down. Seeing Signor Bucatini sitting on his stool reading, he walked up to the counter under the striped awning.

"*Buongiorno*, Luigi. What's that you're reading?" he asked in Italian.

"Ah, Father Michael. You're not touching my newspapers today, are you?"

Michael laughed. "No, not today."

He showed the priest the cover of the book he had been reading. "*The Meditations of Marcus Aurelius*. I find the stoics helpful in perilous times. Have you seen what is happening in France now? It's terrible!"

"Yes, and my friend is still there. I'm quite concerned about her. Anyway, you're reading the *stoics?!*"

"What? You think a simple newsman cannot comprehend the great works of philosophy? That a street vendor does not understand the difference between a rationalist and an existentialist? *Porca miseria!* You know, I was once a professor of philosophy at the University of Padua. This newsstand is only my retirement plan. I get to sit outside all day, gossip with my neighbors, read all I want to, and get paid to do it. You should be so lucky."

"*Scusi, professore*, I meant no offense. I was just surprised. Even among philosophers, the stoics are not that popular."

"Oh, I don't know. They seem to be having a resurgence of late. But enough of that. How are you doing, my young friend? You look maybe a little better today?"

"Yes, maybe a little. But I do need to get going. I'll see you again soon, *sì?*"

"*Sì, sì*, I hope so. And I wish your friend in France well, under the circumstances. *Ciao, Padre.*"

BACK AT HIS APARTMENT, Michael showered, put on his cassock and collar, then headed into the office. He was anxiously looking forward to speaking with Hana today. He had to clarify, to understand, what had happened at the pit in Notre-Dame that day, and he still needed to tell her what they had found out about the duke's lineage.

He sat down at his computer and opened a browser. He logged on to CNN to see the latest on yesterday's terrorist attack. The live feed was showing army jeeps and troop transports streaming into Paris from military bases throughout France. A camera crew was positioned near the presidential palace, where more soldiers were setting up roadblocks and checkpoints. Two authoritative-looking soldiers came over and told the crew there would be no filming allowed. The coverage showed a soldier reaching for the camera, and then the broadcast went black. CNN quickly switched to another live team elsewhere while trying to regain contact with reporters at the palace.

The live shot cut to another location, the National Assembly, where soldiers were escorting the *députés* and their staffs out of the building. The camera crew zoomed in on soldiers putting chains and padlocks on the doors. The building was being closed.

Reporters at CNN France headquarters cut in: "We are hearing reports that Defense Minister Philip Valois will be giving a press conference very shortly. We will, of course, bring that to you live when it happens."

Michael sat transfixed. He never thought he would see this happen in his lifetime. It seemed like a page out of World War II, or the French Revolution. He was watching history unfold, and not a pleasant one. He wondered where President Valois was. *Had there been a quiet coup? Was he dead? This is completely out of character for him, not to mention France! And where was the European Union in all this?*

His mind turned to Hana. She was there, somewhere in the midst of all that.

I'll bet she doesn't call. She's got to be bogged down by all that's happening there. Where is she?

～

HANA WAS, at that moment, definitely in the midst of it. Soldiers had arrived at *Le Monde's* building and shut down the presses. They also suspended the internet and all telephone landlines. Cell phones remained working, at least for the time being, as well as satellite phones. An army colonel, along with his aides and a security team, marched into the editor-in-chief's office and told him that the paper was being put under military control. Everything would be made clear when the Defense Minister spoke in a short while. Until then, there would be no reporting coming out of the building. All forthcoming news had to be approved by the colonel or his designees before being printed or posted online.

The editor was furious. "This is outrageous! If I have to, I'll use every means at my disposal to get the truth out!"

"I anticipated you might feel that way," the colonel replied steadily. "You, Monsieur, are under arrest—but you will remain here with me for now. We will watch the Defense Minister's speech together. Then you'll understand why these measures are needed."

The colonel flipped on the TV in the editor's office and tuned to channel TF1. It was a live shot on the steps of the Élysée Palace. The large, tricolor flag of France stood behind the podium alongside another featuring the presidential seal. The portico was staffed with military personnel, both officers in dress uniforms and soldiers in camo uniforms carrying rifles and plate carriers with bulging magazine pouches. A small crowd of citizens stood in front of the staging area.

Philip Valois came out the entrance door and walked to the podium, wearing a full military dress uniform with the insignia of a general, his rank before he retired and entered his father's cabinet as Interior Minister.

After a confident pause at the podium, he began his address.

"My fellow citizens of France, and citizens of the world. President Valois, who, as you know, was poisoned in a cowardly act, remains in the hospital in critical condition. And the prime minister, in light of his failure to protect the people of France from the terrorist attack, has submitted his resignation, which has been accepted by the president. As a result, the president has directly authorized me to assume his duties as Acting President.

"Moreover, as both Acting President and Interior Minister, in consideration of the unparalleled acts of violence recently, with regretful loss of life and many injuries—all of which are taxing the civilian emergency response systems to the breaking point— I have taken the inevitable step of imposing martial law for a limited time, effective immediately.

"Until the current crisis is over, the following emergency measures are being imposed: First, there will be a mandatory curfew within the city limits of Paris and every other French city with a population of more than fifty thousand. A list will be disseminated through official channels of those cities affected. Under this curfew, no one will be allowed on the streets without specific authorization from the local authorities. Such authorizations will be provided for those people who work in essential services during evening hours. All other persons must remain in their homes from 22:00 hours to 06:00.

"Secondly, all media outlets are being nationalized for the duration of the crisis. Official announcements and coverage of news events will still be permitted, but the media will not be used to undermine the government's efforts to contain the crisis and stem the violence.

"And finally, all travel into and out of France is prohibited, with requested exceptions to be approved by my office alone. We will not allow any foreign influences to attack us on our own soil. Additional measures may be initiated should these prove inadequate. I enjoin all citizens to cooperate with the authorities and report any suspicious persons or activities at once. Together, we will overcome the forces that seek to divide and conquer us.

"May God bless you, and may God bless all of France." He raised his hand in a balled fist. *"Liberté, Egalité, Fraternité!"*

Then, waving, Valois turned and walked away from the podium to a chorus of jeers and shouts of derision from the crowd at the steps of the presidential palace. The soldiers immediately formed a barrier preventing people from getting close to him as he reentered the building.

Glued to her chair in stunned disbelief, Hana looked at her computer. The website she had been viewing suddenly changed to that of the French government's website. She tried accessing any other website without success. The government had truly taken over, and she was afraid for what lay ahead.

Trying her desk phone, she found there was no dial tone. She took out her cell phone and tried calling her grandfather. A robotic voice reported that all circuits were busy.

She tried calling Marco, but the phone didn't even ring; it just went straight to voicemail. Then she remembered he had gotten the phone wet while swimming away from the attack the day before, and it was sitting in a bag of rice in their kitchen.

She was sure Marco was aware of what was going on, and she expected him to show up at any moment. Who else to try…?

Michael. She dialed the number of his cell phone. To her delight, the phone rang. He picked up immediately.

"Hana, are you okay?! What in God's name is happening there?"

"Oh, Michael, it's just terrible. There are soldiers in the building. They've suspended our presses, even our reporting, and they cut off the internet and all landlines. I'm surprised I got through to you. Can you do me a favor and call Grand-père and let him know I'm okay? I can't get through."

"Yes, of course I will. What else can I do? I'm terribly worried about you. Can you get out? Can you get to Rome or Geneva?"

"No, nobody can travel now. It's restricted. I don't even know if *I* can get out, and I have Swiss citizenship as well as French. It's all so crazy. What is Philip thinking?!"

"Well, he must think the situation requires a pretty strong hand. But this has the feel of a *coup d'état* to me." Just then, he heard a commotion on Hana's end.

"Michael, I have to go. The soldiers are ordering us to go downstairs. What else did you want to say yesterday?"

"Um… two things, though one can wait. But we do have some information about your friend the duke. Turns out Pope Clement wrote an edict that proclaims Philip IV's descendants to be the rightful rulers of France. And based on our genealogical research, Jean-Louis Micheaux is the last living male descendant of Philip IV—which makes him the rightful king of France, at least in name and honorific if not in actual practice!"

"That's hardly even believable! Can you send me proof of that? I think the duke ought to know. I'd want to, if I were in his position, especially now."

"Sure, I'll text it to you, and email it just in case. At least one might get through."

"Thank you so much, Michael. I've been thinking about what happened at Notre-Dame, and I just wanted to say that—"

And she was gone. The connection had been terminated. Michael immediately tried to call her back, but it went straight to voicemail. He texted Hana the photo of the Edict of Avignon, and a copy of the lineage Ian had put together, and then copied them into an email as well.

For now, that was all he could do, but hope and pray.

CHAPTER

TWENTY-TWO

A stern announcement issued from *Le Monde*'s public address system, requiring everyone in the building to immediately proceed downstairs to the lobby. Armed soldiers searched the entire building, ensuring that all personnel obeyed the order by herding them onto elevators and down the stairwells.

On her way down the stairs from her fourth-floor office, Hana managed to call a colleague at their competing newspaper, *Le Figaro*, who reported the same military incursion was happening there; they had to assume all other media were being subjected to the same illegal occupation. Despite her rage at the injustice, all she could do now was go along with the orders—while waiting for her opportunity to take action on her own… and maybe find a way out.

Two folding tables had been set up in the lobby with a soldier sitting at each one. Personnel were sorted into two lines: one for journalists, the other for administrative staff. Each person had to complete a short form identifying him or herself and their position in the company, after which they were handed a color-coded pass.

This is outrageous, Hana fumed. *Where has our democracy gone?!*

The duke is obviously aware of this. Maybe he can help. But how do I get to him? And where's Marco?

After processing, she was ushered outside the front entrance with the others, though for what reasons she hadn't a clue. She observed several soldiers erecting chain-link fencing around the large plaza to contain everyone, but the area was filling more rapidly than the time it took for the soldiers to get the fencing complete.

Seizing her opportunity, Hana moved to an area near the arched frame of the building that had yet to be fenced and, in the confusion, she slipped through the narrow passage.

Seeing her, one of the soldiers started to call after her, but somebody shouting his name from behind made him turn. When he looked back, Hana was gone.

WHAT TO DO NOW? First, home. Marco may be there. Then we'll figure out what to do next.

Walking along the Seine to her apartment, several times she had to duck into an alley or an open shop to avoid being spotted by the increasing number of military police patrolling the streets. She saw them stopping random pedestrians, mostly those of darker skin, and interrogating them. She wasn't even sure what good her so-called pass would do with the MPs. The fact that she was "branded" a journalist could raise an alarm, one she couldn't risk.

Finally reaching her apartment, she entered and called out for Marco. No response, and no note. *Merde! Where was he?*

Pulling a notepad out of a drawer, she started writing a note for Marco, then stopped. What if her apartment was searched in her absence? Unlikely, but who knows what those people were capable of? Thinking about what to write, she had a cryptic idea.

Going to visit a friend to see if your wet clothes are dry. Meet me there.

No names, and only something Marco would understand.

With new determination, Hana left and locked the door, heading for the George Cinq Hotel, a few blocks from her apartment.

As she drew closer, she observed more soldiers setting up barricades at each of the bridges crossing the Seine. *This is getting out of hand!* She could not get across the river at the Pont de la Concorde, Pont Alexandre III, or the Pont des Invalides— all bridges were either closed or had checkpoints. She kept walking along the Quai d'Orsay until she made it to the Pont d'Alma, where the Defense Minister's troops were just arriving, and she quickly made it across the bridge before they began restricting traffic. Before long, the north of Paris would be cut off from the south, and she would not be able to go back home or to work. But really, what was there to work on, anyway?

When she made it to the Four Seasons George Cinq, each of the three arched doorways to the entrance was being guarded by men in black tactical uniforms with military rifles, but no military insignia. They looked like the same security that had been at the demonstration but were now significantly upgraded in both weaponry and armor. She tried going in but was stopped by the guards.

"Excuse me," she said with aplomb and an air of authority, "My name is Hana Sinclair. I was with the duke at the demonstrations yesterday. I'm on his staff and it's very important that I see him immediately. He sent for me, so surely he left instructions for me to be allowed entry."

She waited, feigning irritation—which was no great feat. The guard called in on his radio, while another guard came over with a clipboard.

"*Bonjour*, Mademoiselle Sinclair. Yes, the duke has you on his VIP list. I will escort you to his suite. Now that you are here, I will make sure you are assigned to a vehicle. We will be departing within the hour. If you are not informed upstairs, please check with me on the way out for your assignment. We want to make sure we don't leave anybody behind."

"Where… where are we going?"

"Back to Avignon. It will be safer there than here in Paris."

The guard took her up to the penthouse suite in the same dedicated elevator she had used in her prior visit. In the suite, the chaos rivaled the demonstration, minus the smoke and chemicals. People were rushing back and forth, many carrying file boxes or computers. Some were wheeling stacks of boxes on dollies and carts toward the service elevators. It appeared that the duke was moving out, and doing so with great haste.

Hana stopped a person pushing a cart loaded with banker's boxes.

"Can you tell me where I might find the duke?" she asked urgently.

"He's in the residence. Do you know where that is?"

"Yes, thank you." She walked briskly toward the penthouse residence, separate from the office space.

The duke was sitting at the desk in his personal study, typing feverishly on his laptop. He stood and yelled at one of the workers who had appeared with a furniture dolly.

"No, leave the furniture. If we make it through the week, we can have it moved later. Just get the file cabinets and the computers, and the suitcases in the bedroom."

Turning, Jean-Louis saw Hana standing at the entry.

"Hana! I'm so glad you're here. I was afraid you had gotten swept up in all this. Philip is a damned fool. This will all blow up in his face, mark my words. Did you get my messages, by the way?"

"No, I'm afraid not. The phones and the internet at *Le Monde* have all been cut. I barely made it out as they were rounding up all the reporters. I haven't received anything from you."

"And yet you came here? That must be a sign. Do you have your security man with you?"

"Marco? No. I'm afraid I don't know where he is. His phone

was damaged yesterday when he went in the river to escape the attack. He wasn't in my apartment and he wasn't at *Le Monde*. I left him a note to come here, in a way only he would understand."

"Well, I hope he moves fast. He has under an hour to get here and he can join us, but I fear we cannot wait for him. Avignon will be much safer. My estate there was built to withstand an army. Not this army, mind you, but an army nonetheless. Wait... If you didn't get my messages, why did you come here?"

"To be honest, I didn't know where else to go. They were detaining reporters when I left, even rounding them up in fenced-off areas. And they are closing all the bridges across the Seine, so I can't get back home or to work. It's unforgivable, Your Grace. Something must be done!

"Oh, I nearly forgot! I have some important information for you that my friend Father Dominic, head of the Vatican Archives, discovered. It directly involves you."

"Well, that will have to wait a bit longer, Hana, as will the subject of the messages I sent you."

Hana was about to protest when one of the black-clad guards entered the residence carrying a clipboard and a two-way radio.

"Thirty minutes at most, Your Grace. We're cutting it close, but we'll be ready. The military is expanding blockades and checkpoints throughout the city. We may have to go a little out of the way to avoid them, but as of right now we can still make it to Avignon. We have assets watching the routes to advise us if anything changes."

"Very good, Gerard. Please call down and make sure Hana Sinclair is assigned to my limousine. I need to talk to her on the way. Hana, it might make sense for you to wait for me in the car now. It's going to get even more chaotic as we get closer to leaving, and I don't want you to get lost in the shuffle."

"Of course, Your Grace. I appreciate that."

Making her way to the elevator, she descended the eight

floors, then stepped out into the parking garage, which was a study in coordinated pandemonium.

It was around thirty minutes later when the duke appeared, punctual as always, and the last to enter the armored stretch limo, joining Hana, his aides, and his personal protective detail.

While the driver set the GPS for Avignon, some seven hours south, provided there were no detours, Hana tried to make a couple of phone calls, but the circuits were still busy or blocked. The text message from Michael, with the crucial attachments, had come through, thankfully, and she marveled at the image of the Edict and the pedigree chart depicting the duke's genealogy.

Looking ahead and behind their limo, Hana noted a veritable presidential motorcade of campaign staff SUVs, moving vans, and chase vehicles loaded with more security personnel. She prayed they would be allowed past any checkpoints.

As she looked back at the George Cinq receding in the distance, she spotted a figure running in pursuit of the convoy, which was stopping for no one. *Was that Marco?!* If so, it was too late to do anything about it now, much to her dismay.

The duke was speaking into a satellite phone, giving directions to someone as the motorcade turned onto Autoroute A6. When he was finished, he put the phone down, took a deep breath of relief, and turned to Hana.

"So, tell me, what did your friend in the Vatican have to say that was so important you risked a military coup to tell me about it?"

"Do you really think it's a coup? Philip said the president had given him the authorization to act to preserve the Republic. Not that I believe that."

"While the president may have given Philip some emergency authority, these actions exceed anything even the president himself could order. You cannot disband the Assembly. You cannot censor the press, nor cut off the internet, a clear violation of free speech even under martial law. No, Philip has coveted the presidency for too long, and in his mind, I imagine, his father just wouldn't get out of his way. Now, it's obvious he's found his opportunity. I almost suspect these attacks were his doing, in order to force a crisis, one he could take advantage of."

"I've known Philip a long time, Your Grace. Not well, but for many years. He has always been a patriot, coming from a great family of French loyalists going back centuries, and up to now he has taken that heritage and his current ministerial duties quite seriously. But his behavior now seems uncharacteristic for him. Personally, I don't think he would actually orchestrate such attacks."

"Hana, power and politics make people do things you would never expect of them. But back to your news."

Sitting next to the duke in the back seat, she leaned in closer to him, assuming he may not yet want this knowledge to be shared with anyone else.

"All right," she whispered. "Apparently, during his investigation following the discovery of the body found beneath Notre-Dame, Michael—Father Dominic—undertook extensive research, even going so far as to open the crypt of Pope Clement V in Uzeste to obtain a DNA sample to compare it with that of the body found in the cathedral.

"But they also found documents associated with Pope Clement V and King Philip IV. Clement, it seems, issued a proclamation known as the Edict of Avignon, proclaiming Philip's descendants as France's enduring rulers in perpetuity."

"Yes… But what does any of that have to do with me?"

"It turns out that House Capet married into, or was adopted by, House Micheaux, just after the deaths of the Capetian kings, about the time the Valoises took the throne. And according to the genealogical research, you are now the only living male descendant of King Philip IV.

"And by virtue of the Edict of Avignon and the infallible imprimatur of the Holy Church, Your Grace, *you* are the true and rightful king of France!"

CHAPTER

TWENTY-THREE

F or the second time in as many days, Marco watched as the woman he loved sped away in the duke's limousine. His attempts to hail them to stop were fruitless, understandably. And he was pretty sure he knew where they were going, although he might have a little more difficulty getting there than she would. In the meantime, he took comfort in the fact that she was, for now, safe.

Still, besides his love for her, she was the one he was charged to protect. He would get to Avignon one way or another.

But before he did, there were a few things he needed to do.

As the news out of Paris turned from bad to worse, Michael went from sitting at his desk to pacing his small office while sipping on a rapid succession of espressos. France would find its way out of this mess, but his only concern was for Hana. He couldn't focus on anything else. And the espresso only served to make him more jittery. Bad combination.

Ian walked into his office. "Michael?"

"*What?!*" he snarled. Then, seeing Ian's shocked expression, he settled down. "Oh, Lord, Ian, I'm so sorry. I've got a lot on my mind. What is it?"

"Dr. Chaucer is on the phone for you. She said she's tried reaching you several times today, but your line has been busy."

"Yeah, I've been trying to get back in touch with Hana. We got cut off this morning when martial law was declared in France, and I'm just trying to make sure she's okay. I even tried calling Marco several times. I did speak with Armand in Geneva, though, and now he's as worried as I am."

"And what about, um, Dr. Chaucer?"

"Oh. Right. Put her through, thanks."

Ian returned to his office. A moment later, Michael's phone rang.

"Hi, Blake. What have you found?"

"Well, by generally accepted criteria for DNA profile comparisons, the body at Notre-Dame de Paris is a very close relative of Clement V, and given the time frames, I'd say he was most likely his brother. Given that Clement only had one brother, that would make him Cardinal Florian de Got."

"And you're sure about this?"

"Michael, a scientist is rarely ever completely sure about most things. There's always the possibility that the profiles could be that similar just by chance, although the odds of that happening are one in billions. But if you put enough people in the database, the odds of there being a random match get pretty good. It's called the lottery problem. I know that's probably more than you're asking for, but don't expect a scientist to explain something complex unless you have an hour to spare," she said, chuckling.

"Anyway, we could also just be wrong. Maybe we made a mistake somewhere. We're not infallible, like the pope is when he proclaims an enduring French monarchy."

"Yes, well, papal infallibility isn't all that the world thinks it is," Michael said. "The pope *can* be wrong. Look at the history of the popes and all the wrong things they've said or done. Actually, the Doctrine of Papal Infallibility is specifically limited. It only applies to matters of faith and morals, and the pope must be speaking *ex cathedra*, meaning from the throne of St. Peter as the universal teacher, and with the authority of the Apostles. So, as to that limited function defining dogmas of the Church, the pope is recognized as infallible, when he specifically exercises that authority.

"As it happens, papal infallibility has only been used twice. The first time, Pius IX used it in 1870 to declare the Immaculate Conception as dogma, and then in 1950, Pius XII declared the Assumption of Mary to be dogma as well. Some people point to a few other instances they think qualify, but those are the only two that are widely recognized.

"I could go on, but that's probably more than *you* were asking," Michael laughed.

"So when Clement used the words in the Edict, that wouldn't qualify?"

"Not at all, no, since the French monarchy is not a matter of faith or morals, and Clement was not speaking *ex cathedra*. And since the doctrine hadn't been specifically recognized—even if we said it was something the popes were always able to do— that would not qualify. He could say it was infallible, but it wouldn't be."

"I can tell you," Blake said firmly, "a lot of Catholics, and even those of other faiths, do believe the pope has unlimited infallibility. I'm Catholic, and that's what I learned growing up. So that edict could be used to proclaim somebody the rightful king of France *if* such a person could be identified. By this time, I can well imagine there potentially could be hundreds of qualified people, even if we only restricted it to men."

"Actually, no," Michael clarified. "There's only one."

"How do you know that?"

"Bishop Fournier called yesterday and gave us the results of his search of the records for Robert Capet and his descendants. Turns out that one of Robert's sons married into House

Micheaux, was adopted into the family, and took the name so that his sons could inherit the Duchy of Avignon. Ian ran the information through an integrated genealogy database he created and discovered that the current Duke of Avignon is the only male person alive who is descended from Robert Capet."

"That is pretty incredible. That means if the duke found out about the Edict and his genealogy, he could declare himself king and make the argument that the Church should support it. Think there's any chance he'll find this out on his own?"

Michael suddenly sat bolt upright in his chair. "Oh, my Lord! I told Hana, a journalist friend who's covering the duke's likely presidential campaign. I didn't think about the implications of the Church having to support him, given that language about infallibility. I knew it didn't apply, but I wasn't thinking about how the public might perceive it. And I suppose it was inconceivable to me that anyone would try to declare himself king! France has a strong democracy. At least, I thought it was strong. Now it doesn't look so good.

"But you're right. That could be a powerful argument. Unfortunately, I can't get hold of Hana to clarify things."

"Do keep me posted, Michael, and let me know if there is anything else I can do."

"I will, Blake, and thank you. Hopefully, we can figure out how to put the lid back on this Pandora's box I've opened."

"Well, just remember that when all of life's miseries had escaped from Pandora's box, the one thing left in it was *Hope*, to survive the wickedness that Pandora had released."

"Yes," Michael said with a slight sense of doom in his voice, "although some perceive that more as 'deceptive expectation.' Let's pray it *is* hope…"

TWENTY-FOUR

D uke Jean-Louis Micheaux and his entourage had finally arrived at the Palais des Papes, the ancestral seat of the Duchy of Avignon since the papacy had moved back to Rome in 1377. The seven-hour drive had allowed the duke, his senior advisors, and Hana—whose status in the campaign was still undetermined—to discuss plans for what to do after Philip Valois had essentially seized power and imposed martial law.

It was early the next morning and still dark. Everyone had been assigned guest quarters on arrival, with a favored few in the residence and others, including Hana, in the adjacent hotel in the southern square, which was owned and managed by the Micheaux family.

Built in 1252, the Palais des Papes, or Palace of the Popes, was constructed of two main buildings: a larger one to the south and a smaller one to the north, both featuring lush interior court-yards, numerous crenellated towers, and tall pointed spires. While the southern building had been converted to a hotel and convention center, the northern structure had remained the duke's official residence with adjoining administrative offices. North of the palace was Notre-Dame des Doms d'Avignon—

more commonly known as Avignon Cathedral—and the breath-taking gardens looking out over the massive, white limestone cliffs rising above the Rhône River.

IN HER HOTEL suite later that morning, Hana was summoned to breakfast in the residence. Entering the dining hall, she found many people already seated at a long, family-style wooden table. The duke was sitting at the head, with several aides and other personnel seated on either side. They all looked as exhausted as she felt, especially the duke, whose red eyes were puffy from little, if any, sleep. Since he hadn't shaved, his stubble gave a grayish cast to the contours of his face.

"Good morning, everyone," Hana said, smiling at all the new faces as she took a seat. "Anything noteworthy in the news today?"

"Good morning, Hana," the duke greeted her, courteously standing as she sat down. "I hope you were able to get at least a little sleep. As you might guess from my shabby appearance, I have not even seen my bedroom yet. But that is no matter.

"We have been discussing your extraordinary news from the ride down, and I have come to some decisions with the concurrence of my advisors, to whom you will be introduced shortly—once you've answered a few questions."

Perplexed, Hana turned to him, her inquiring eyes meeting his.

"My advisors tell me I am too trusting, and that you have yet to actually mention whose side you are on, to put it bluntly. You have close connections to the Valois family, that I understand—which would make you the perfect spy. So forgive me, Hana, but I must ask: where do your loyalties lie?"

As she sat there, astonished that the duke would even ask such a question, she felt more than saw two of the black-clad security officers take up positions behind her, a respectable distance back, but clearly there to check her reactions.

She thought back to what her godfather, French President Pierre Valois, had secretly asked her to do for him in the hospital. No, of course she was not there as a spy.

"Your Grace, my loyalties lie with France, and with what is best for France and her future. Right now, I do not believe Philip Valois is acting in the best interest of France, even though he might believe so himself. But given your own political aspirations, in all honesty, I am not yet convinced that you are acting in the best interest of France, either. So, perhaps I can give you a more informed response once you have told me of your own ambitions."

The duke's demeanor shifted from one of serious reproach to cautious acceptance.

"Fairly stated, Mademoiselle, and I would have expected nothing less of you. It is your integrity that I admire most about you, Hana, and why I am hopeful that you will agree to join me in my plans for our country. But you are Swiss, are you not?"

"I am Swiss by birth, yes, but I have lived in France most of my adult life and maintain dual citizenship."

The duke stood and began slowly walking around the table.

"You were in attendance when I announced my candidacy for president, as I recall. I am sorry it had to be at the expense of President Valois, but I sincerely believe that his continuation in power is endangering us as a nation, and that it is time for him to step down.

"But now, it appears that we may never have those elections I called for. As you may know, I am a student of history, and the past has shown us that when people like Philip Valois gain power, they do not easily relinquish it. While his declaration of martial law was couched in language that made it appear temporary, I assure you he will find reasons to extend the contrived 'emergency' indefinitely. It is easy to manufacture invisible enemies: foreign influences, immigrants, crime, terrorism. And as I said yesterday, if there is no actual enemy, one simply needs a crisis to blame on an enemy, no matter who actually caused it."

One of the dining hall servants wove her way past the security guards and laid down Hana's simple breakfast: tartine with quince jelly, *suprêmes d'orange,* and coffee. Hana picked up a slice of orange and nibbled on it as the duke continued speaking.

"Since Philip has taken such desperate actions, I think the only appropriate response would be an equally measured retaliation. Therefore, at one o'clock this afternoon, I will go before the people of France, live on television from the Avignon Cathedral, where the archbishop will proclaim me king, based on the Edict of Avignon as defined by Pope Clement V, and hopefully with the blessing of the Holy Mother Church in Rome."

Hana nearly choked on the orange slice.

"You—you're going to proclaim yourself *King of France?!*"

"In essence, yes, but with the distinction that, based on the Edict, I have the right to be recognized as the ordained ruler of France, by perpetual and infallible decree of the pope. And this is where you come in. I would like you to contact your source in the Vatican and arrange to have Pope Ignatius recognize and validate the Edict and confirm my coronation by the Archbishop.

"I can sense your hesitation, Hana, so allow me to elaborate. I imagine you might interpret this as me being as megalomaniacal as Philip Valois. But I assure you, that is not the case. I already have more wealth than I can use in many lifetimes. I control a vast empire of corporations and foundations. I do not *need* to rule France. Frankly, it sounds like a tremendous responsibility with little reward.

"But I believe my role as the Duke of Avignon, a title that has been in my family since before King Philip IV, bestows upon me obligations to the people of Avignon and, indeed, to the people of France, to act in their best interest and to shoulder the burdens of administering the government of this great country in the fairest and most efficient manner possible should the need arise, which, as we can see, it already has.

"I intend to establish a constitutional monarchy, so that while I am the administrative head—you might say CEO of the country—the people will still have a voice, and their rights and privileges will be fiercely protected. I will be a benevolent king, Hana. What do you say? Can I count on your support and assistance in this great endeavor?"

Hana was stunned speechless. When she had told the duke of Michael's revelations, she never thought he would actually act on them. It was more of a notable familial linkage for a man most people would deem landed aristocracy, if not of noble blood.

But to actually pronounce oneself king and seize control of the government was nothing short of bizarre! And the more she considered it, it did seem to be exactly what Philip had done. While not calling himself king, he had become the ruler of the country—in fact, if not by elected title. And his appearing in his military uniform had all the trappings of a Third World coup. What would her godfather think? And where exactly was he during this constitutional crisis? She wished she could have his thoughts at this very moment.

"Your Grace, your words certainly sound sincere, and I would hope that they are true. I do not know if I can even get in touch with the Vatican, much less arrange for the pope to review the Edict and the lineage and recognize you as king. Those things take time and deliberation, and most certainly would not occur by one o'clock today. Obviously, I'm in no position to make any promises. I'm not sure I should even try, to be perfectly honest."

A momentary flash of anger crossed the duke's face, but then it softened.

"Again, a fair response. But we have little time for such arguments. "By the way, have you met my staff yet?"

The duke went around the table introducing his trusted advisors until he got to the last person, who had been seated at his right: a glamorous woman with a patrician demeanor dressed more elegantly than the others.

He walked up behind the woman and stopped, intimately

placing his hands on her shoulders as he stared at Hana sitting across from her.

"And this is my wife and most trusted advisor, the Duchess of Avignon. Indeed, a Valois herself: Sabine Valois Micheaux."

Once again, Hana struggled to contain her astonishment. Sabine Micheaux was a Valois?! How could she not have known this? Pierre had never mentioned it before.

Sabine extended her hand, clad in a long, black glove that matched her short black skirt.

"*Enchantée*, Mademoiselle Sinclair," she purred. "And yes, my father was the brother of the current president. I'm afraid it is my cousin, Philip, who is causing such havoc in Paris."

AFTER BREAKFAST, Hana was escorted back to her hotel suite by one of the guards, who remained outside her door to make sure she was comfortable—and contained.

The duke had given her a satellite phone with which she was told she could call her colleague at the Vatican, Father Dominic, to effect his wishes. She had immediately thought of calling her grandfather and Marco, and even *Le Monde* to check in with her colleagues, but the duke had anticipated such a move. Instead, asking for Father Dominic's number, he had it programmed into the phone's speed dial buttons to ensure that the phone was blocked for any calls except to Michael and the duke himself.

Sitting in her room, despondent about essentially being held captive, she pressed the speed dial button for Michael. His phone rang several times, but as he never picked up, it eventually went to voicemail. She left a message conveying the duke's instructions and insistence that the pope abide by his wishes. But she was conflicted as to the outcome. She innately rejected the duke's wishes, hoping Michael would take no action. Part of her feared Michael would be upset she had caused this dilemma by confiding in Jean-Louis. And she had. Yet she also longed to hear his voice.

But she knew, or at least she hoped, he would call her back in any event.

B̲UT AS IT HAPPENED, Michael did not call—at least not before the one o'clock deadline.

Shortly before the coronation, the duke came in to check on the Vatican's response. Hana told him she had not heard from them yet.

"I'm certainly not going to wait for them, then," he sputtered with annoyance. "My claim does not require Vatican consent anyway, though the pope may come to regret his inaction.

"And since you were not able to fulfill your mission, you will remain here as my guest and watch the festivities from your room if you wish. I'm disappointed in you, Hana. You led me to believe you had more reliable connections in the Vatican.

"Now, we will decide what to do with you after I address the people of France."

T̲HE CORONATION WAS NOT the typical pomp and ceremony one might expect of a royal accession to the throne, since, after all, this had been rushed in the limited time the duke's aides had to prepare for the investiture.

Emile Renard, the unenthusiastic but pliant Archbishop of Avignon, was advised to locate the historical rites to accompany the *Sacre*—the traditional anointing of the king with consecrated chrism oil, a ceremony legitimizing the crowning. Renard had been unable to make contact with the Vatican for permission to carry out his orders and—apprehensive over Jean-Louis Micheaux's power to make life most difficult for him—reluctantly submitted to the imminent king's demands.

Preparing for the coronation, the duke wore a simple, well-tailored gray business suit, along with an ermine cloak with sable edges which had been handed down from his ancestors over generations. Diagonally across his torso lay the dark blue satin sash bearing his family crest and colors, with a cluster of military decorations over his heart. Even in his simplicity, he cut a striking figure, and the brief ceremony was solemn and regal.

King Louis XX, his chosen regnal name, was now—in his mind, at least—the presumed ruler of France.

AT THE CONCLUSION of the coronation, the king appeared on the portico between the twin spires at the front of the palace's larger building, a squad of black-clad security personnel surrounding the dais. A public address system had been set up along with a live broadcast feed, both of which were streamed directly to the internet and on to world media. King Louis began his speech:

"People of France, two days ago, I came before you to ask for your vote to lead our beloved country. Since then, that opportunity has been quashed by the brash and unfounded seizure of power and declaration of martial law by Philip Valois.

"However, it has come to my attention, through legitimate historical research, that an infallible Edict of Avignon had been proclaimed by Pope Clement V, stating unequivocally that the descendants of King Philip IV, of House Capet, shall always and forever be the rightful rulers of France.

"It has also come to light that I am the last living male descendant of that family line, proof of which will be distributed to the media and found on the royal website. Therefore, I have this day accepted my sacred obligation to lead the country of France as its king, in opposition to the usurper leading a military coup against our people. Mine will be a constitutional monarchy, in which the peoples' rights and privileges will be respected, and in which the people will be served and supported rather than enslaved and oppressed.

"So now I call on you, the citizens of France, to join me in resistance to the military subjugation of France, and to the usurper, Minister Philip Valois. Together, we will restore our country to greatness.

"Vive la France!... Vive la France!... Vive la France!"

CHAPTER
TWENTY-FIVE

Acting President Philip Valois sat at Napoleon's gold-and-white Empire desk in the Salon Doré of the Élysée Palace, fuming.

With a mixture of disgust and admiration, he had watched as the Duke of Avignon proclaimed himself King of France. Philip had been forewarned that something like this might happen, based on information he had been given by the Bishop of Bordeaux, who had heard it from a courier sent by the timorous Archbishop of Avignon.

But as much as he disliked Duke Jean-Louis Micheaux personally—he would refuse to think of him as king—Philip did not expect the man would actually go that far. Yes, he had made it clear that he wanted to be president. But *king?* That was a leap of a different order altogether. For that, he owed the man a measure of grudging respect. That took guts.

On the other hand, he was rankled that he hadn't himself thought of it first. If there were to be a restoration of the monarchy, his blood was as noble as the duke's, and more recent. The last truly Capetian king was Charles IV in 1328. The House of Valois ruled from then until 1589, when the House of Bourbon assumed the throne.

So that was it, then. The duke might have the most legitimate claim to the throne under Salic Law, as the most senior surviving heir of the senior surviving branch of House Capet—but the monarchy had been overthrown in favor of a democratic republic in the late eighteenth century.

Of course, Philip had suspended that democracy by what was in effect a military coup, and he had no intention of relinquishing that control. He would make an excellent beneficent dictator. Clearly, he knew better what was in the best interest of the country than representatives beholden to the whims of the voters and the influence of special interests. He had lived most of his life in the sphere of French power. He had absorbed more theories of governance just by being there than anyone else currently serving or even intending to run for president.

No, the battle between monarchy and democracy, or even autocracy, would not be settled by any court—judicial or ecclesial. It would be settled by public opinion, or by force.

He would try public opinion first. Clearly, a significant portion of the population supported his rule. His advisors had projected that in an actual presidential election between himself and the duke, it would practically be a dead heat. The only unpredictable factor would be the addition of other candidates into the mix, pulling votes from one side or the other. And that would decide the contest: not who was truly better, but which one lost the least votes to someone else, a situation that would depend on who else entered the contest and from which parties. Too uncertain to call.

No, his was clearly the better way. So, if the duke had upped the ante, Philip would have to make the call and raise the stakes.

Let's see what the duke is made of, he vowed, as he headed for the Situation Room.

Situated in the Restoration Lab of the Vatican Secret Archives for much of the day, Michael Dominic oversaw his lab technicians as they gradually negotiated the release of the golden threads from Florian de Got's garment sleeve, carefully separating them from the parchments over many tense hours. It was a tedious process, for they had to use amplified magnifiers over high-precision surgical tweezers to ensure no damage would be made to the scrolls. And the process would continue for another four or five days.

As he sat there, Michael examined the photographs he had taken of the Edict of Avignon and Clement's letter to his brother Florian, reading them over again. *Such a fascinating history*, he considered. *I pray Hana has not shared this information with the duke...*

"I'm heading back to my office, guys," he said to the team. "Let me know at the earliest opportunity if you get even one of the scrolls free."

Returning to his desk, he saw the notification flag on his phone indicating he had new messages—and one of them was from Hana! *Dammit!* He kicked himself for not having taken the phone with him.

Navigating to voicemail, he listened to her message:

Michael, this is Hana... obviously. You should know that, based on the Edict, the duke plans to declare himself king. He wants the Vatican to acknowledge and validate the Edict and recognize his claim to the throne of France! While I favored him as a candidate for president, this whole "king" business has me deeply concerned.

I'm here in Avignon with him, and I'm pretty sure I can't leave. Nobody has said anything specific, but there's a guard outside my room. I expect they want to use me to gain the pope's approval through you. I know these things take time, but please let the Holy Father know what's happening, and try to get an answer back to me as soon as possible.

I do hope we can speak soon. I miss you.

She gave him the satellite phone number she was using, then the message ended.

Michael's stomach tensed up, and he could feel his anger rising. He called Nick Bannon.

"Hey, Nick, it's Michael. I need to speak to both the pope and the Secretary of State immediately. It's an urgent situation."

"Are you able to tell me the nature of it, Michael, so I can better inform His Holiness?"

"Well, you may not believe this, but the Duke of Avignon will crown himself King of France, if he already hasn't! He wants the Vatican to validate the Edict we found in Clement V's tomb and to recognize his claim to the French throne. And while I can't be sure, I suspect he might be holding my friend Hana Sinclair hostage in the meantime."

"All right, yes, I see the urgency now. The Holy Father is in a meeting. He should be done in about thirty minutes. I'll bump everyone else back and ask Cardinal Greco to join you. Be here in half an hour."

"I will, Nick. And thanks."

TWENTY MINUTES LATER, Vatican Secretary of State Cardinal Giovanni Greco entered the Apostolic Palace and made his way up to the papal offices. Waiting for him there was Michael Dominic, chatting with Father Nick Bannon while they waited for the pope to be available.

"Thanks for making time to join us, Your Eminence," Michael said to Greco, shaking his hand.

"When Nick Bannon here says jump, one simply asks 'how high?'" He smiled. "What's this all about, Father Dominic? I was—"

"Sorry to interrupt, *signori*, but His Holiness will see you now," Bannon said, seeing a light flash on his desk. He pressed the door lock release button beneath his desk, and a soft click was heard. Bannon escorted them into the papal chambers.

Pope Ignatius stood and warmly greeted his visitors, embracing Michael as he approached.

"Nick, I'd like you to stay for this, please," the pope said. "You'll likely be involved in handling some of the details to come of it." They all took seats in white chairs centered in a cozy area near the windows overlooking St. Peter's Square.

Michael explained the whole situation to the group, starting with his discoveries at Notre-Dame and in Uzeste, the Edict of Avignon, and the scrolls now being analyzed, and on to the Duke of Avignon's likely coronation as King of France. Each of the men was mesmerized by Michael's story, and when he finished, there was a moment of silence as they took in the ramifications of such a strange turn of events, all based on another of Michael's curious discoveries.

"My, my… you certainly do get yourself in the most complicated of situations, Michael," the pope said with a knowing grin. "As for the duke's request—or is he really a *king* now?—a decision like that would require at least a month or more of research and deliberation. As you know, such things move glacially slowly here.

"In the meantime, we should arrange to have the original Edict recovered and authenticated, as well as the letter to Clement V's brother, Florian. Also, we should have your Dr. Chaucer verify the duke's claim to his family heritage. I do not necessarily believe him to be an impostor, but we have to be absolutely certain before the Holy See can make a final determination. If these documents are, in fact, genuine, he may very well have a claim to an ostensible French throne. But we must not act in haste. France is a democratic republic now, after all, and French courts are certain to weigh in on the matter.

"And where is my old friend Pierre Valois in all this? Last I understood, he was in the hospital. Nick, can you look into that? Maybe arrange a call for us?"

"Of course, Your Holiness, I'll do so at once." Bannon left the room.

"As for Miss Sinclair, Michael," the pope continued, "I'm afraid there is nothing we can do to help her at present. I expect that will trouble you, and I well understand your concerns. But please do not do anything rash, like going to France to try to rescue her. She may not actually be in any danger, and she does have Monsieur Picard looking after her, does she not?"

"I don't believe it's possible for Marco to be with her just now, given the restrictive measures Philip Valois has put in place. That has got to be frustrating for him as well as her grandfather, Armand."

The pope's face turned sullen. Both of his old friends from those long-ago days of war were troubled, and even as pope, there seemed to be little, if anything, he could do.

He turned to the Secretary of State. "Cardinal Greco, I'm putting you in charge of this matter—the duke's monarchical claim—since it largely falls within your sphere of duties. Michael will put the services of the Archives at your disposal. Please keep me informed of your progress, both of you."

As he said this, he pressed a button on a nearby table, and Father Bannon reentered the room. "Nick will show you out. I need a few minutes to prepare for my next meeting."

As Bannon led them into the outer office, he closed the door behind him and, with a look of disbelief on his face, said, "You both need to hear this. I have just learned that Philip Valois has demanded that we *not* recognize the duke's claim, but that we formally renounce it—and that he intends to lay siege to Avignon!"

He held out a piece of paper. "This is an official request for the Vatican's disavowal of the duke's legitimacy. It was communicated to me by the Archbishop of Paris, along with clear threats that we must acknowledge Philip Valois as France's rightful leader and not the Duke of Avignon, or there would be consequences.

"I suggest you conduct yourselves with all due haste, gentlemen. We don't want to come out on the wrong side of history here. I'll inform the Holy Father now."

CHAPTER

TWENTY-SIX

F or the rest of the day, Michael fretted about whether to call Hana on the duke's satellite phone. He wanted to hear her voice, to make sure she was at least doing well mentally under the unusual circumstances of her presumed detention.

But most likely the phone was being monitored or even recorded, and the last thing he wanted was to give the duke's forces any leverage over her—responding to her from the Vatican in any way could make them pressure her all the more. And any hint of his desire to rescue her—despite the pope's caution—was out of the question.

No, for now the best thing to do for Hana was just to wait and see what developed...a desperate state of mind Michael found exasperating at best.

As he lay on his bed that night willing himself to sleep, it was no use. He couldn't unwind.

He got up, threw on sweatpants and a shirt, and headed next door to the Church of Santa Maria della Pietà, one of nine chapels on the Vatican grounds, and the one he always felt most content in, its humble altar encircled by an intimate apse reminiscent of the one he had served in as an altar boy in Queens, New York.

As expected, the chapel was empty at that time of night. He lit two large candles on the altar, took the rosary he had dropped in his pocket before leaving, and knelt at the ancient wooden pew facing the large wooden crucifix mounted behind the altar.

It was at times like this, when he felt most helpless, that he found himself turning to God, beyond the daily obligations of morning and evening Office Prayers. And since he wasn't the kind of man who often felt helpless, that thought alone troubled him. *Why don't we speak more often, You and I? And who's to blame for that, huh?*

Beginning his Hail Marys, he let the intoning repetition of prayer consume him as his fingers moved from bead to bead under the dim, flickering candlelight.

AFTER A LONG RUN through Rome's quainter neighborhoods the next morning, Michael returned to his apartment, showered, and changed into his cassock, then made his way through the papal gardens to the Archives building.

Stopping at Ian's office first, he walked up behind him as he sat at his desk.

"Hey, Ian."

The startled Irishman jumped, flushing as red as his hair. "*Bejazus*, Michael! I didn't hear you come in, I was so engrossed here. What's up?"

"How are you coming with those odd numbers on the back of Clement's letter to Florian?"

"That's what I'm working on now, and it's been a tough one, I have to admit. At first, I wasn't even sure where to start. All I had was a series of numbers that appeared to be in pairs, and the suggestion to use Clement's personal Bible to locate the treasure. There wasn't much else to go on."

"So, I tried finding out where Clement's Bible was. It seems that if it's anywhere, it's likely either at Avignon or Uzeste. I called the rector at Uzeste, and he didn't have it. Then I called the Avignon Cathedral to talk to the rector there, but I couldn't get through, nor could I get through to the rector at Notre-Dame de Paris. So I talked to Dr. Ginzberg. We brainstormed how to approach the problem, like what bibles were available to Clement V that he might have used as his personal one.

"This was prior to the printing press, as you know. All books had to be hand-copied, which was a lot of work and took a lot of time, so there were not that many of them. He would have had a copy of the Vulgate to use, in Latin, but that would probably belong to the Church. What would he have used personally, though?

"Now, Clement was the pope who moved the papacy to Avignon, and he was French. So, I looked up when the Bible was translated into French. Turns out there was a French version, with historical commentary, published before Clement became pope—the *Bible historiale*, produced by a medieval monk named Guyart des Moulins in 1295.

"I'd bet that was the one Clement used as his personal Bible. And as it happens, we have a copy of that one right here in the Archives.

"So, now I have the universe of bibles down to two, the Vulgate, and the more likely *Bible historiale*. But what do the numbers mean? How would you use a Bible to leave a message to someone, and especially using numbers? So we think, what does a Bible have? Books. And the books have chapters, and the chapters have pages and verses, and the verses have words.

"And which of all those are numbered? Well, all of them, really. I was thinking at first that they might reference chapter and verse, but you would first need to know what book of the Bible was being used for that approach to work. Then I found out that numbers for chapters and verses were not added to bibles until 1382, so that was no good.

"But they could be pages and words. I've read spy novels where coded messages were composed of a list of paired numbers representing page and word counts on the page—you know, a common substitution cipher. You could put the code right out there in public because no one could decode it unless they knew which book to use. The secret detail was the identity of the book. And there are many creative ways to identify a book, like call numbers at a library, or an ISBN, or even leaving some kind of mark on a book.

"In this case, however, Clement told Florian *which* book, because Florian would know which book was Pope Clement's personal one—which is why the *Bible historiale* makes much more sense. You follow me?"

"More or less. But go on."

"So, then I tried using the paired numbers as page-count and word-count, starting from the Old Testament. That didn't make any sense. Then I tried using the New Testament, and I got this: '*Half through the crypt of no man. The grave; and the barren womb; the earth that is not filled with water; Half where the waters above the earth were separated from the waters below.*'"

Ian's eyes sparkled with accomplishment, and Michael felt a tingle of memory.

"Some of those sound familiar, like the last passage is from the beginning of Genesis. Have you searched for the phrases online?"

Ian nodded. "'*The grave, and the barren womb, and the earth that is not filled with water*' is a passage from Proverbs. And the part about '*separating waters*' is from Genesis. They bring to mind caves or catacombs to me, but I have no idea what they mean exactly, or how you would find the treasure with these clues."

"I have to get to Avignon, no matter if—" Michael stopped himself, unable to fill Ian in on his frustrated need to help Hana. Avignon stood at the center of all the answers he so desperately needed. "Well, just keep researching how these might apply to Avignon, Ian, and see if you come up with anything. I've got other matters to attend to, so we'll talk again later."

As he entered his office—thinking how best to get into France, and particularly Avignon, without getting caught by either Micheaux's or Valois's forces—his phone rang.

"Hey, Michael, it's Marco. Have you heard from Hana?"

Surprised, Michael blurted, "You're not *with* her? Aren't you supposed to be protecting her?"

"I know, I know," Marco said, chastened. "It's a long story, but no, I'm not with her. Though I think I know where she is. But have you heard from her?"

"Yes, she's in Avignon, with the duke or king, or whatever he is now. And I have a feeling she's being held there against her will. I didn't speak with her, but she left me a voice message and gave me a satellite phone number to call her back, though I haven't yet, not fully trusting the connection."

"Okay, good," Marco said, relieved. "At least I know where she is. Now I just need to figure out how to get her out of there. You don't, by any chance, happen to know how to get into the Palace of the Popes discreetly, do you?"

"Ian and I are working with some documents here that allude to some treasure Pope Clement may have hidden in Avignon—in the palace and maybe the cathedral, too. The clues are fairly arcane, but there are some allusions to caves or catacombs leading into the palace from the river, and that might be our way in. Ian's trying to figure that out. But I'm not sure we can even get into France right now, much less into the palace or cathedral."

"Wait, aren't Lukas and Karl avid cavers? Maybe they know something about caves in Avignon?"

Michael paused, mentally slapping his forehead. "Of course! I even went caving with them one time. Karl's working at St. Anne's Gate now. Hold on while I give him a call..."

He put Marco on hold and called down to the gatehouse on another line.

"*Pronto*, Sergeant Dengler here."

"Hey, Karl, it's Michael. By any chance, do you know anything about caves or caverns in Avignon, France?"

"Sure. Avignon is awesome caving country. There are elaborate and extensive cavern systems all throughout that area. I hear some can actually be accessed from the Rhône River, so it's really more cave *diving*. Others are climbing trips. And a lot of them are full of really sticky mud. You can easily get stuck in them. Not a lot of fun, and usually not very pretty. Why?"

"Might any of them be located under the Palace of the Popes?"

"Hmm. I don't know specifically. I'd have to check the caving boards when I get off duty. Can it wait till then?"

"Actually, no, it can't wait. Is there any chance you could get someone to stand in for you for a bit? It's important."

Karl paused a moment. "Sure, Michael. I can do that. I'll call you back as soon as I find out more."

Michael switched back to Marco's line.

"All right, sounds like the cave thing is a possibility, but it will require more research. Karl will take a look and get back to me. I'll call you back when I learn more."

"Great, thanks. Meanwhile, once you're here, I'll find ways of getting you to Avignon. You don't think I'd let you go it alone on this, do you? Talk to you soon."

GETTING a colleague to hold his post for a bit, Karl went directly to his room in the Swiss Guard barracks and booted up his laptop. Searching the caving websites he followed and asking fellow cavers online about Avignon, he was able to learn a great deal about what Michael wanted.

He called him back. "Okay, Michael, it seems there *are* mentions of an underwater cave that extends from the gardens of the palace down to the Rhône River, but it hasn't been well explored yet. The Rhône is known for being extremely muddy, so the water in the cave would be as well. Which means limited visibility, something I personally wouldn't want to go diving in."

"Would you do it to rescue Hana? It seems she may be held there, in the palace and possibly against her will, by the Duke of Avignon."

"Hana's being held captive? When did this happen? Are you sure?"

"Actually, I'm not sure, no, but all signs point to it. In any event, I'm going to find a way to bring her out safely, and Marco's joining us as well. Are you in?"

"You don't even have to ask. I'll bring Lukas too."

"Okay, get all the gear you'll need and standby. We could be leaving at any time. Marco is working on our transportation now."

When Michael called Marco back, the Frenchman answered promptly.

"So, apparently there *is* an underwater cave that goes to the river beneath the gardens of the palace. Which means we are a Go on that end. There might be some other places to access the caverns. Apparently, the area has a network of caves. Something about having the right kind of limestone."

"*Très bon.* I've got your transportation set, Michael. Be at Rome Ciampino Airport tomorrow morning at five o'clock. Armand is sending his jet to help us out. The pilots are going to fly you in under the radar, literally, and it's a one-way trip. When we get her out, we're going to have to hide in France until things settle down, or find our own way out somehow. The plane won't be allowed to take off again unless you can work some Vatican diplomatic magic—or a miracle, really. A diplomatic miracle. Anyway, France is *my* home court. I may yet have a few tricks up my sleeve when the time comes. I'll see you there when you land."

Things were happening fast now, and Michael felt his pulse racing. He called Karl.

"Okay, we are set for a dawn flight from Ciampino on

Armand's jet. Marco is meeting us when we land in Avignon. You and Lukas will need to call in sick or something for a couple of days. This is completely off the books. The pope told me personally not to get involved."

"You know we've got your back, Michael, and Hana's."

"Thanks, my friend. I knew we could count on you."

CHAPTER

TWENTY-SEVEN

K arl and Lukas had been up all night preparing for the next day's exploits. In order to get all the equipment to do either a cave dive or a cavern climb, they had to call in a few favors.

Contacting the owner of their favorite dive shop in Rome, Karl had asked to rent the specific gear they would need for all possible scenarios. The owner of one of the largest dive shops in Italy, a retired U.S. Navy SEAL, had a lucrative side business of equipping clandestine dives for various military units, intelligence agencies, and private security contractors around the Mediterranean.

Karl already had most of what they needed to do a cavern climb. But since this would potentially be a rescue, and he might need to bring inexperienced climbers up out of a cavern—Hana among them—he added harnesses, helmets, headlamps, and the rest of the gear, enough for three additional people to be on the safe side. He also wanted a tripod and a winch, and a satellite phone as a backup. The total gear took up just about all the space in his Jeep Wrangler as he and Lukas loaded everything up and made it to Ciampino Airport by five o'clock. It was still dark when they arrived at the FBO, or Fixed-Base Operator, terminal, where private aircraft are granted the right to operate at a given airport.

They found Armand's jet parked on the tarmac, with the pilots going through their preflight checklist.

Having taken a taxi down from the Vatican, Michael had arrived before them and then began helping the others load the gear onto the jet.

"You sure we're going to need all this stuff, Karl?" he asked.

"Frankly, I don't know what we're going to need. But I'd rather have it and not need it than need it and not have it, especially where other people's lives are concerned. Me, I'll climb on a shoelace and a keychain if I have to.

"We also stopped by the Vatican Armory on our way out. Based on the intel we're getting, Michael, Avignon could turn into a war zone before we're out of there."

Karl parked and locked the Jeep just outside the FBO hanger, then they all boarded the jet. The pilot came on the intercom as they were taking their seats.

"Gentlemen, I've filed a flight plan to Avignon acting as a humanitarian mission from Médecins Sans Frontières—Doctors Without Borders, for those of you who don't speak French. We have been provisionally approved to land by the French Civil Aviation Authority, but things appear to be pretty crazy over there right now. They sounded reasonably suspicious when I said we wanted to go to Avignon.

"So, here's the plan. We are going to fly the normal pattern, with a route that keeps us over the ocean in international airspace most of the trip, but if we get any signs that they are getting hostile, we'll dive to two hundred feet and shut down the nav lights, transponder, and ADS-B. We don't have any radar, weapons, or anti-missile systems on the plane, so at that point, we just have to fly as stealthily as a Dassault Falcon can fly. I'd appreciate it if everyone could just strap in and stay seated. We should be there in under an hour."

. . .

AFTER GETTING CLEARANCE FOR DEPARTURE, the jet taxied to the end of the runway, ran the engines up to full power, and took off. The pilots fed the Air Traffic Control radio channel through to the passenger cabin intercom so the team could hear all ATC communications during the flight.

The pilot called ahead to Avignon Control. "Falcon Hotel Bravo Four Two Alpha to Avignon-Provence." The air traffic controller responded promptly.

"Falcon Four Two Alpha, fly heading two eight five, climb to flight level two six zero, contact Avignon Approach at one two zero point eight seven five at seven five miles out from Avignon VOR."

"Roger, Avignon. Falcon Four Two Alpha heading two eight five, climb to flight level two six zero and contact Avignon at one two zero point eight seven five at seven five miles out."

"Falcon Four Two Alpha, affirmative. Have a safe flight."

THE PLANE HAD BEEN CRUISING along for about thirty minutes when the team heard the pilot say, "Avignon Approach, this is Falcon Hotel Bravo Four Two Alpha at seven five miles south, requesting approach to land runway three five."

"Falcon Four Two Alpha, descend to flight level one six zero, then turn right heading three five five for runway three five."

The pilot confirmed the instructions back to the air traffic controller. Then, moments later, a surprising new directive was heard.

"Falcon Four Two Alpha, be advised that the Defense Ministry has cancelled your visas, and permission to land is denied. You are instructed to turn right to heading one seven five, then climb to flight level one six zero. Also be advised that two Dassault Rafales have been scrambled to intercept and escort you out of French airspace."

Fighter aircraft?! the pilot wondered. These are serious

cowboys. He had to think fast, knowing there was little time for error.

"Avignon Approach, Falcon Four Two Alpha. We are declaring an emergency. We do not have fuel to return to Italy. We say again, we are declaring an emergency."

"Roger, Falcon Four Two Alpha. Cleared for runway three five. Remain on this frequency, but be prepared for further instructions from the interceptors."

The pilot changed channels to the interior intercom, addressing the team in back.

"Okay, boys. This is where it gets dicey. We have permission to land, but it looks like the French Air Command is not on the same page with civil aviation authorities. We are going to Plan B."

The pilot shut off the plane's identification transponder and navigation lights, then pushed the nose of the plane into a dive, shedding altitude rapidly and then pulling up at sixty meters above sea level. They were now flying below a thick marine layer that would make it harder for the jets above to see them aiming straight for land.

But Avignon Tower was persistent.

"Falcon Four Two Alpha, we have lost you from radar and transponder. Please reply, over."

The channel remained silent. Armand's pilot did not respond. But one of the French fighter pilots did.

"Avignon Approach, Rafale One One Three Hotel Oscar. No joy. We don't see your Falcon... Falcon Four Two Alpha, this is Armée de l'Air One One Three Hotel Oscar. You are in violation of the territorial air space of France. Respond on this frequency at once."

The pilot did not respond. Instead, he brought the jet down screaming over the countryside and landed on Runway Thirty-five of Avignon-Provence Airport.

Avignon Tower notified the French fighter, "One One Three

Hotel Oscar, Falcon Four Two Alpha has declared an emergency and has just landed at this facility. There has been no further radio communication with the aircraft. Maybe radio trouble?"

"Avignon, One One Three Hotel Oscar. Well, if he's on the ground, he's somebody else's problem. One One Three, out."

THE PILOT MADE haste for the FBO. Marco was waiting at the private Signature terminal with a nondescript black van. Even inside the cabin of the taxiing plane, the team could hear two-tone sirens rapidly approaching their position. Avignon airport police and fire personnel were on their way.

The pilot had pushed the jet all the way into the FBO hangar and quickly dropped the stairs before the plane even stopped. On cue, the team made a break for the van, carrying just their packs, without the rest of the gear that was stowed in the small cargo hold of the plane.

Marco turned the van around and headed for the tarmac gate, which was still open from when he had just come in. He gunned it as the young, unarmed security guard, apparently having been given the command, worked feverishly to get it closed before the van reached it. He was unsuccessful—but did manage to get it closed before the airport police arrived, and then had to open it again, by which time Marco and the team had disappeared into the narrow, winding streets of Avignon.

Everyone was exuberant. "*Yes!*" Marco shouted, pumping his fist in the air. "We showed those *bâtards!*

"And don't worry about the pilots. I just spoke with Armand. He's already talking to the Swiss Embassy. They will be fine. We, on the other hand, are probably wanted criminals now.

"I've been doing some reconnaissance of the Palais des Papes. I don't think we have to go in by water at all. It looks like there is a door in the cliff. If we could get it open, we could walk right into the catacombs. I'm taking us now to an old garage owned by a buddy of mine who is vacationing in Greece until this whole political mess sorts itself out. Not much to look at, but at least we can get the van off the street.

"Then I'll brief you on the plan I have to get us in to find Hana."

CHAPTER

TWENTY-EIGHT

" Most likely, Hana is inside the Palais des Papes," Marco asserted, "but obviously, we don't have a clue exactly where she is, which is the main challenge. The entrances to the palace are guarded by those security guys wearing black. I watched from a distance as they rapidly erected fortifications, barricades and sandbags—as if they were preparing to defend the palace against an assault.

"The buildings are divided into the hotel and conference center, the residence and offices, and the church. Then there are the gardens, which lie between the cathedral and the river. The whole affair stands on a hill of limestone with white cliffs facing the river. There is a wide road, the Boulevard de la Ligne, between the river and the cliffs.

"I have been doing some recon since yesterday. There are blue double doors in the cliff at street level, right under the gardens, and there are stairs to the garden east of that. The rest of the north side is all sheer cliffs, with a couple of caves visible, but no way to know how far back they go underground. The rest of the approaches are too well guarded for us to get in, so we are going to have to try the doors or the caves. I looked at the locks on the blue doors.

They are standard deadbolts. I think I can pick one in under a minute."

Karl had been reading something on his phone when he looked up and interrupted Marco.

"We now have intel from the Swiss military and NATO. Philip is mobilizing an entire brigade of light armor and mechanized infantry from Nîmes. They aren't on the move yet, but once they are, it won't take them long to get here; they could actually be here within twenty-four hours. The duke's people must know this too, since they're preparing for an assault. So, we don't have a lot of time to plan or look around once we get inside. There could already be commandos in the area assessing the palace and reporting back to the main force. If Philip is savvy —and with his military background, I expect he is—there will also be drone surveillance, possibly even armed drones and paratroopers. We need to move fast."

"*Oui*, Karl is right," Marco responded. "I'm planning to go in at dusk tonight, which gives us the most time to get in under low visibility. I brought black clothing for everyone. But we can't just sneak in. Too much chance of being seen. So I'm thinking of just going in in plain sight. I've also brought yellow safety vests, helmets, and tool belts for everyone, and a couple of barricades, some traffic cones, and some caution tape. We are going to create a little work zone in the street around the doors, and then we will pick the locks and go in. Nobody will suspect that a bunch of workmen in plain sight are actually trying to break in."

"Good thinking, Marco," Karl said. "Are we going armed?"

"I am, yes, but I'm afraid I was not able to secure any additional weapons on such short notice, so I hope you were able to bring your own."

"Check. Both Lukas and I have our personal sidearms, SIG P220s. We brought some bigger toys but had to leave them on the plane in our haste to get out of the airport. But I'm afraid we don't have one for Father Michael."

Michael huffed. "That's okay. I'm happier *not* being armed.

I'm not sure I could bring myself to shoot someone. Not a very priestly thing to do."

"Understood," Marco said. "Although Jesus himself told his disciples, not long before he was crucified, that they should sell their cloaks and buy swords..."

"I don't know why, but I'm surprised you know that," Michael noted.

"It is kind of a motto among certain groups, especially in the States, but also some military units."

"Well, then, you should know that a couple of verses later in Luke, Jesus said two swords are enough. We have three, so to speak, so we should be good."

MARCO HAD SECURED A SMALL WATERCRAFT, an aluminum Jon boat with a small motor, that would suffice to get them across the Rhône and allow them to tie up at a small nearby dock he had surveyed earlier.

The team carried their gear into the dense trees alongside the river and waited for darkness to come.

A short while after it did, the team carried their gear across the street and set up their sham construction zone, with orange cones surrounding the contained area and caution tape running from cone to cone. The limestone cliffs towered at least thirty-six meters above them, meeting the walls of the gardens above.

Michael held a clipboard, which Karl looked at over his shoulder. They discussed details of the locks in German, just to make it harder for any passersby to hear what they were up to.

Addressing the lock to the doors, with Lukas holding a flashlight for him, Marco inserted a tensioner into the keyway and then used a tumbler rake to nudge the pins into their slots. True to his estimate, it took Marco only about thirty seconds to get the lock to turn. They slowly opened the door. No light or sound emerged from the other side. They opened the doors enough to pass through and went inside, closing but not locking the doors, so they could get out in a hurry if necessary.

Toggling his tactical flashlight, Marco set it at the lowest level of illumination and swept the beam around the tunnel. The walls of the passage were composed of rough-hewn limestone, and the floor was concrete. The passage was a little over a meter wide, a good two and a half meters high, and from the best they could tell, ran over a hundred meters due south, in the direction of the cathedral and palace—but at a hundred meters, that would put them under the center of the gardens.

Keeping his fingers over the end of the flashlight, Marco let just enough light escape to see where to place his feet as he led the others in a staggered formation down the passage. Karl had his left hand on Marco's shoulder, his right holding his weapon. Michael came next, his right hand on Karl's left shoulder. Lukas was last, his left hand on Michael's right shoulder, covering the rear.

The team carefully made its way down the passage under the dim light of Marco's torch. At thirty meters in, a side passage veered off to the left. Since they were still under the gardens, they decided to move forward rather than laterally. No light came from the side passage, which was another fifty meters long, with a single door at the end of it.

They continued until they reached a fork at the end of the passage, where one path led to the left and another to the right. Faced with a decision, they chose left to explore first; they could come back if it was a dead end. There must be something in either direction. The left hall ran about thirty meters and turned right, with a door on the left side of it.

Leaning toward the wooden door, Marco put his ear against it.

"I hear machinery," he whispered to the others clustered around him. "Some kind of motor, with a regular pumping rhythm. But no sounds of people, near as I can tell."

Quietly turning the knob, he found the door was unlocked.

He extinguished his flashlight, slowly opened the door, waited a few moments, then chanced a peek inside.

Nothing except industrial machinery.

Confident the room was empty, Marco entered, turned on his light and shined it around the room. Several pumps were running, with a large filtration system against one wall, and pipes leading up into the ceiling.

"I noticed ponds in the garden when I was scouting the area yesterday. We must be under one of them. This is obviously some kind of service tunnel."

Marco led the way back to the fork and on to the right side passage, which was now dead ahead.

After some fifty meters, the passage ended, where they found a dark red door set inside an arched alcove.

"There's no way we're *not* going through *that* door," Karl said excitedly, anticipating some action. "Hana's here somewhere, and we're not leaving without her."

Again, Marco tried the door. This one was locked. While Karl held a steady beam of light on it, Marco took out his picks and set to getting the lock open.

After fiddling over a minute or so with finding the correct pins and tumblers, the mechanism clicked, and the Frenchman turned the handle.

Extinguishing his light, he pushed the door in a crack. There was a rush of cold air and a dank, musty smell.

They had found the catacombs.

Marco slid the door open a little farther, peering in. It was dead quiet.

He turned his light on and cautiously looked around, finding they were in a large, natural underground chamber with a high, jagged limestone ceiling. Karl and Lukas, both seasoned cavers, were amazed at the variety of speleothems they spotted: dripstones, stalagmites and stalactites, moonmilk, and cave pearls.

"This is a really impressive cave. Rarely do we see cave pearls and moonmilk in French caverns, at least the ones we've explored," Lukas said quietly, pointing out the subjects of his discovery to the others.

A series of niches was carved into the walls of the cavern, with what looked to be ancient bodies entombed in shroud remnants, many with bones poking through the cloth. A few of the earthen pockets were piled with skeletal remains in a jumble, undoubtedly from more than one person.

Set up against the wall at one end of the cavern in a prominent line were twelve marble sarcophagi, the tops and sides of each containing beautifully sculpted funerary art each with a chiseled effigy of the person occupying that crypt, and garlands of oak leaves supported by Victories adorning the fronts and sides. The entire line was set back some one meter from the wall.

"This cavern must have been used to inter dead popes over the decades during the papacy here," Michael conjectured. "They certainly aren't buried in the papal tombs under St. Peter's Basilica. There were seven popes who ruled from Avignon. These twelve sarcophagi must include the others, since we know Pope Clement's body lies in Uzeste. And several of these are identified as past dukes and duchesses. Even the Queen of Navarre is here."

While Michael, Karl, and Lukas admired their respective fields of interest, Marco continued exploring the cavern, some hundred meters long and fifteen meters wide. He noted a door at the far end and a couple more on the sides, built into the limestone.

Since their goal was to enter the palace to search for Hana, Marco decided to skip the side passages and head for the door at the south end of the hall.

Michael hung back a little, though, examining the closest sarcophagus. An engraved plaque revealed it held the early fourteenth-century remains of the Queen of Navarre. He remembered the passage from Proverbs that Ian had decoded... this could be the *"crypt of no man!"* As Michael walked around the crypt, he noted that the stone panel at the head of the sarcophagus was missing, a black expanse of emptiness taking its place. He shone his light inside, now seeing that the bones had been pushed aside to reveal a wooden trap door hanging down through the floor beneath it, and a set of stone steps leading down into what must be a subterranean room. The marble base of the sarcophagus must have been specially removed for some purpose. But what?

Michael called to the others to join him. As they gathered around, he explained about the encoded message, and that a portion of Clement's treasure might be found beneath the queen's crypt.

Marco reminded him that they were there to rescue Hana, not go treasure hunting. Michael had just agreed with him when they heard footsteps coming down the stairs behind the side passage.

Marco whispered quick instructions. "Quickly, down the stairs, turn off your lights and be quiet."

CHAPTER
TWENTY-NINE

They hurried down the stairs beneath the sarcophagus, coming through a short passageway at the bottom and into a large room. In the center was a table, with a large teddy bear sitting on a chair next to it, but that was all that Michael could see before Marco had everyone shut off their lights. He and Karl hid on either side of the room's opening into the passage, while Michael and Lukas ducked behind the table. They waited as the sound of footsteps got closer and closer.

A dim light appeared at the top of the passage and came slowly bouncing down the steps. As the flashlight came through the opening and into the room, Marco grabbed the arm holding it with his left hand and jerked a small person into the room, his Glock trained on the individual as he prepared to fire, finger taking up the slack in the trigger. Karl activated his flashlight as he too pointed his gun at the person—but just as quickly, both men raised their weapons away as the little girl in Marco's grip screamed.

Stunned at finding a child here, Marco instantly spoke softly to the girl in French. "Hey, hey… it's okay. No one is going to hurt you. What are you doing by yourself down here in the dark?"

The young girl looked up tentatively into the glare of Karl's tactical light. Seeing the two men dressed in black, holding guns, tears streamed down her plump cheeks as her chin quivered.

Sensing no danger, Michael and Lukas made their way over as well. Seeing their new visitor, Michael moved in front of Marco and knelt.

"Hi there," he said in French. "My name is Father Michael. I am a Catholic priest, and these men are my friends. Nobody is going to hurt you. You're safe with us. What's your name?"

Michael had unzipped the jacket at his throat, letting her see his white Roman collar. The girl looked up and seemed to relax a little.

"My name is Margot," she replied in a near whisper, also in French.

On hearing the girl say her name in the confined space, Marco suddenly felt dizzy. He stood up and reached for the wall for balance. Karl and Lukas both saw his reaction.

Michael persisted. "What are you doing down here all by yourself, Margot?"

"I came to play with King Teddy," she answered, pointing to the teddy bear sitting on the chair, who Michael now noticed was adorned with gold jewelry, with a gold Viking helmet on his head.

"You know, Margot, let's all go back up the stairs and talk about this, okay?"

She nodded and, without further examining the large, dark room, they all climbed the steps back up into the catacombs.

Michael asked her, "Does anyone know where you are?"

Margot paused, seeming to consider her answer. "I come down here to get away from my au pair, and to visit my grand-père."

"Is your grand-père buried down here?"

"Yes. But I get in trouble if I come down here alone. You won't tell on me, will you?"

Just then, they could hear heavy footsteps coming down the

flight of stairs behind the closest door. They had just moments before the person opened it.

Michael had to think fast. "We aren't supposed to be here either. So, I'll tell you what. If you go with the person coming downstairs and don't tell anyone we're here, then we won't tell on you and get you in trouble. Okay?"

Margot nodded vigorously and smiled sweetly.

"But you should not stay here either," she said. "The guards like to come down here and smoke. They aren't allowed to smoke in the building. They'll be on break soon."

With her little flashlight in hand, she moved toward the door. Michael, Marco, Karl and Lukas hastily moved back behind the sarcophagi and ducked down, turning off their lights just as the door opened.

A large woman was framed in the doorway, light spilling from the stairway as she called out in French, "Margot? Margot, are you down here?" The little girl stepped into view.

"How many times do I have to tell you not to come down here? This is a place for the dead, not for the living."

"*Oui, Nounou.*"

"Now, come upstairs this instant. It is time for your bath. And if *Nounou* catches you down here one more time..." Her voice faded as she herded Margot up the stairs, the door pulling closed behind them.

The team waited in silence and darkness for several minutes, hoping Margot wouldn't say something to alert the guards.

When it seemed that nobody was coming back down, Marco spoke up. "Well, that was too close. The girl might still mention something to someone, and we can't risk it. I think we should abort and reassess."

The others nodded in agreement.

"Were you okay back there, Marco?" Karl asked while Lukas looked on. "You seemed a little shaken when Michael was talking with the girl."

Marco paused, considering his response. "Yes, I just never nearly shot a child before…" He turned away, leaving it at that.

The team made their way back through the crypts and down the tunnel to the entrance. Disassembling their staged barricades and cones, they crossed the street and got into the Jon boat.

As they pulled away from the dock, they observed a pair of military patrol boats coming east up the Rhône. Marco pushed the little boat to its limit as they sped up the river.

Hearing gunfire behind them, all heads looked back. One of the patrol boats had fired several starburst rounds over the palace, announcing their presence with only a warning shot.

They had made it out just in time.

CHAPTER
THIRTY

E arly the next morning, Ian was back at his computer, refining some database document designs, when Giancarlo Borsetti, head of the Vatican Restoration Lab, called for Michael.

"I'm afraid he's away at the moment, Dr. Borsetti, working on a project in France. Is there something I might help with?"

"Ah, yes, Ian. We have finally completed the separation of the gold garment threads from the scrolls, and we are about to start the X-ray tomography analysis. I thought Michael would want to be here for that."

"Well, I can tell you he wouldn't want you to wait on his account. But I'd love to come down and stand in for him if you don't mind."

"Not at all. You'd be most welcome to. We'll see you here shortly, then."

HAVING MADE his way down to the Restoration Lab, Ian was met by Ekaterina, who led him to the instrumentation room where Dr. Borsetti was waiting.

After an exchange of pleasantries, Ian watched as Borsetti set the scrolls inside the microtomography instrument's examination bay, while Dr. Ugo Tibaldi, the other technician in the lab, managed the control station.

Dr. Tibaldi closed the hatch to protect the observers from the X-rays, then started the instrument. There were numerous clicks and hums while the mechanisms moved the X-ray head to collect the data.

As they waited for the instrument to do its work, Tibaldi explained the process to Ian.

"Microtomography is a thoroughly innovative approach to analyzing the contents of parchment scrolls. The process detects the presence of iron gall inks—particularly those from medieval times—then creates a three-dimensional map specifying the ink's exact location on the document, determined by creating images from a series of X-ray slices extracted through the parchment.

"High-level software then combines the data with how the parchment is rolled or folded and calculates the exact location of where ink lies on the surface. Knowing this, we can easily produce an image of the document as it would appear unrolled. It's really quite amazing and is of tremendous value in helping us transcribe the millions of scrolls in the Archives."

Moments later, the large computer monitor in front of them began displaying the first page of the scroll, starting from the top and filling the screen on its way down.

Ekaterina, who spoke French, translated it as each line appeared.

To Guillaume de Baufet, Bishop of Paris, Cathedral of Notre-Dame de Paris

1 March in the Year of our Lord 1314

My dear brother bishop,

I fear I will not be able to travel to Paris, and you would not be able to get here before I am called home to our Lord. So I am sending my brother, Florian de Got, with this, my final confession.

Father, forgive me, for I have sinned. I have not been the good leader of the Holy Church that God had called me to be. I succumbed to the temptations of power and riches. Of the Viking treasure that was discovered under the Cathedral you are now building, as you know, King Philip took the greater part as his royal share. The remainder was split into three parts. One part remains there, buried under the crypts below the foundation. The rest was moved here to Avignon. I have taken the two parts and separated them, hiding both parts in the catacombs and caverns beneath the Palais des Papes. Florian will receive instructions on how to find them when he returns. I have sent you instructions separately about the disposition of the part that remains there. Remember the key verse in the sermon I sent you about greed. Matthew 6:20. That is most important. Your scribe has the means to decode the rest.

Also, I must confess that the Edict of Avignon which I prepared for Philip is false, and I have never given it to him. When Joan of Navarre died in 1305, Philip took another woman and made her pregnant. I officiated at their marriage as soon as it became apparent what had happened. The child was born and was named Robert, of House Capet. He was sent away in haste to the cathedral of Bordeaux for Bishop Baudette to see to his upbringing, for his life was threatened by his cousins, who sought to usurp his place on the throne.

However, on her deathbed, the mother confessed that she was previously married and that her estranged husband was still alive. Therefore, she was not eligible to marry Philip, and their child, Robert, is a bastard and unfit to assume the throne. No royal succession can be based on his issue. You must convey this information to Bishop Baudette at the appropriate time, which I leave to your judgment.

Finally, I have to say that I am ashamed of the whole affair with the Knights Templar. It was all at Philip's behest. I should not have acceded to his demands.

There is little time to make amends. May God have mercy on my soul.

Clement V, Bishop of Rome, PP.

Grasping the broader meaning of this, Ian was stunned. This clearly proved that the duke's claim to the throne was fraudulent. He could not be king! He said nothing to the others, preferring to share it with Michael first.

The second scroll was just an apparently random series of jumbled letters and spaces, with no obvious meaning.

Dr. Borsetti seemed confused by the content of the letters.

"Ian, you were working on the letter to Florian. Does this make any sense to you?"

"Well, I just finished deciphering an encrypted letter from Pope Clement to his brother, but that was a numerical double substitution cipher. Really kinda challenging. This one is different. I guess I know what I'll be doing for a while. I'll let Michael know about the confession and the coded message right away."

CHAPTER

THIRTY-ONE

T he day following his coronation, as soon as he arrived in the Situation Room, Philip gave the order for the Sixth Light Armoured Brigade to take their positions in Avignon.

Shortly after that, thirty-two of the VBCIs—the *Véhicule blindé de combat d'infanterie,* an armored infantry fighting vehicle similar to a light, eight-wheeled tank, equipped with a 25 mm cannon, a .30 caliber machine gun, and grenade launchers—left the military base at Nîmes for Avignon. They were followed by jeeps, troop trucks, fuel trucks, communications vehicles, a mobile field hospital, a mobile field kitchen, and brigade command post vehicles.

However long this conflict might last, Philip was prepared for the duration.

On arrival in Avignon, the VBCIs were stationed all around the Palace of the Popes, with a quarter of the vehicles held in reserve. Soldiers with FAMAS assault rifles spread out and evacuated civilians from a kilometer's radius around the palace, as much for their safety as to avoid hostile locals ambushing the troops.

All roads around the palace had been closed, with barricades and checkpoints preventing ingress or egress. As Philip had ordered, the water, power, and communications had been cut, gas was shut off, and no deliveries of food or fuel were allowed in. Having effectively laid siege to the occupants and operation of the palace, the troops waited for further orders.

The hotel had a diesel backup generator and enough fuel to run for three days—but used sparingly, that could last up to a week. They had satellite phones and satellite internet based in Luxembourg, independent of land-based services which had been cut off by Philip. Solar generators in the courtyards were used to charge the radios security forces were using, so they would not lack for power for some time.

MICHAEL WAS SITTING on the low stone wall surrounding a large white cross monument on the Avenue Île de la Barthelasse, directly across from the Palace of the Popes, watching the complex with his mind on Hana. *What must she be thinking? What do they have her doing? Why the need for her presence at all?* It just didn't make sense.

Marco stood watching the troops moving on the other shore, trying to work out other ways they might get in now that the palace was under military control. Karl and Lukas were catching up on their sleep back at the garage.

Marco raised a pair of binoculars and scanned the infantry moving around their fortifications and armored vehicles.

"They must have brought the whole brigade. I can see six VBCIs just on this side of the palace. There are likely as many on the other three sides."

Michael glanced over his shoulder, acknowledged the troops, and went back to ostensibly contemplating the cross, but all the while still worrying about Hana.

Marco began humming "Sur le pont d'Avignon," a French

children's song, as he continued watching the soldiers through the binoculars.

"Really?" Michael muttered, a bit irritated at Hana's situation. "Humming a tune at a time like this?"

"Oh, sorry, *mon ami*. I couldn't help it. I wasn't really thinking about it. There is a children's song called 'On the Bridge of Avignon.' It just pops into my head whenever I see it."

"Maybe we can—" Michael was interrupted by the satellite phone ringing.

"Hello?" he answered.

"Hi, Michael, it's Ian. How's it going over there?"

"Well, last night we almost got captured by a little girl in the catacombs, and today it seems like half the French army is now encamped around the Palais des Papes. How are things there?"

"Dr. Borsetti finished the extraction of the scrolls from the gold threads, and we completed the X-ray tomography of the manuscript pages. You won't believe what was written on them, Michael! It was amazing, and… Oh, and Ekaterina is really nice. She gave me a tour of all the stuff they do down there and—"

"*Ian!* What did the scrolls say?"

"Oh, yeah. Well, one was the pope's confession. Pope Clement's. He said he was sorry for being a bad pope, but it was really Philip's fault. He said there were two loads of treasure under the Palace of the Popes, and one under Notre-Dame de Paris.

"And maybe most important of all, he wrote that the Edict of Avignon was *false!* That Philip's marriage to Robert's mother was invalid because she was already married, and that Robert was a bastard. In which case, there would be no succession from his bloodline. Oh, and he was sorry about the Templar thing too."

"Ian, you're quite sure Clement admitted that the Edict was false?"

"Absolutely. Philip made him do it, but the pope never officially gave it to him, and then later he found out about the mother still being married. So it's completely invalid, at least as far as Robert is concerned. And since there are no more direct descendants of the Capets, there is no royal succession from Philip. So, the Duke of Avignon cannot be king."

"Incredible," Michael marveled. "I've somehow got to get this information to Hana. I'll call you back later. Thanks, Ian.

"Marco, you are *not* going to believe this…" Since Marco had yet to be briefed on the events at Notre-Dame and the discovery of Florian de Got's body and the scrolls, Michael explained as much as was needed to fill him in.

"We brought the scrolls back to the Vatican to be analyzed, and it took a while to prepare them because of an issue with— well, that doesn't matter. Anyway, what *does* matter is that Ian just told me what's written on the parchments. One was Pope Clement's confession, which confirms that the Edict of Avignon —the single document on which the duke is basing his claim to the throne—is actually invalid, which removes him from the line of succession."

"Then Hana should know, so she can tell the duke to call this whole fiasco off!" Marco exclaimed. "Then we can get her out of there and leave Philip for someone else to deal with."

Michael dialed the satellite phone number Hana had given him. It rang once, there was a click, then it rang again, with a different ring tone to it. As if it was being forwarded. Hana picked up.

"Michael?!" she answered hopefully.

"Yes, Hana, it's me. We've all been so worried about you. Marco is here with me."

"Oh, I'm so glad. I've been kept in my room since arriving. I have no idea what's going on, but from my window, I can see tanks outside. Wait, Marco's there? Where are you?"

"Actually, we're *here*. Right across the Rhône River from the palace. We came to rescue you. We managed to get into the catacombs under the palace grounds last night, but we had to retreat or be discovered."

"Honestly, you guys, I'm fine. The duke, I mean King Louis, isn't going to hurt me. He just isn't letting me go until he hears back from the Vatican about the pope's endorsement. Do you have news on that yet? Will the pope recognize his status?"

"No, I don't think he will, but it won't matter anyway, Hana. There is so much to tell you about what's been happening. Suffice to say for now that we found and deciphered scrolls from Notre-Dame, the reason I was there that day. One of them is the final confession of Pope Clement V. It confirms that the Edict of Avignon is invalid because the pope discovered that King Philip IV's second wife married Philip while she was still married to someone else... which means the duke's ancestor is illegitimate, and no succession can run from his lineage. The duke cannot be king!"

"Oh, my goodness," Hana declared. "I don't know how he's going to take that, Michael. Do you think I should tell him?"

"Don't worry, Mademoiselle Sinclair," the duke's voice came on the line, "there is no need to tell me now. I heard everything."

CHAPTER

THIRTY-TWO

A s Philip's troops surrounded the Palace of the Popes, it had become abundantly clear to Jean-Louis Micheaux —especially in light of what he had just learned—that to proceed further with what had now become a charade would be pointless. It was over.

The first thing the following morning, he called his staff together for a discussion. When his advisors were all assembled, including Sabine and Hana, he took a deep breath and began.

"Last night I received some very distressing information, and I have once again barely slept thinking about what to do. You will all recall what got us to this point: a seven-hundred-year-old decree from Pope Clement V specifying that the descendants of Philip IV were forever the rightful rulers of France.

"As it happens, that is no longer the case. New forensic details of Clement's correspondence have come to light, and it seems the pope had second thoughts about his initial proclamation. He was effectively forced to write it by King Philip IV, but on his deathbed, he actually recanted the Edict of Avignon in his last confession.

"Even if the document could be argued to be valid, it would not assist me. It seems King Philip's second wife, upon whose offspring my lineage and claim are based, was already married when she married Philip. Consequently, their son was born out of wedlock, a bastard, so no royal lineage can proceed from him."

Gasps and moans erupted from those in the room—from everyone except Hana, who already knew, and Sabine, whose steely gaze was fastened on her husband.

"We are surrounded by a superior force," the duke continued, his voice and features those of a man vanquished, "with abundant arms, supplies, and personnel. While we could hold out for a time, we cannot survive as long as they would. If they storm the palace, many of our staff and supporters could be killed. That I cannot abide. So, I have decided to turn myself in on the condition that everyone else involved in my campaign and short-lived sovereignty is granted amnesty."

At last, Sabine spoke. A tall woman already, she seemed positively towering when she stood up in her regal black outfit. And she was furious.

"*No!*" she demanded. "You shall *not* give up now. Not to Philip. Not to anyone. I have done far too much to get you here, Jean-Louis. You cannot so easily squander all my efforts. I will *not* permit it!"

The duke was mystified and taken aback, shocked that his wife would embarrass him so publicly.

"Whatever are you talking about, Sabine? You have been here in Avignon the whole time I have been running the campaign in Paris. Tell me, please, what *have* you done?"

The duchess's eyes blazed as she walked around the table, her voice rising angrily with each divulgence.

"You think those demonstrations, those attacks that you so blithely took advantage of—you think those just happened by serendipity? *I* created the perfect opportunities for you to take advantage of. You needed a crisis, several in fact, to create the social conditions ripe for revolution. Without me, there would have been no chance to be president, no chance to be king. And for all these years, especially these last few weeks, I have pushed you along. I *got* you here. I *made* you."

Speechless, the duke looked at his wife as if she had gone mad. "*You* were responsible for those attacks?! For those senseless deaths?! You murderous shrew! People were slaughtered… Their blood is on *your* hands."

"Better their blood than that of all France. Their sacrifice will make a new order for France, with us at its head. Either *we* lead France out of this darkness—or *I* will…"

Suddenly, the terrifying sound of gigantic helicopter rotor blades was heard just above the palace, shaking the room and rattling its occupants. Everyone looked out the tall, arched windows to see a large Aérospatiale Puma military transport helicopter descend onto the vast courtyard just to the north and east of the buildings. Looking up, they also observed two Airbus Guépard escort helicopters circling the compound, maintaining aerial positions for cover.

Sabine went to the window and looked down. She could see Philip stepping down from the Puma with his military entourage, marching toward the front of the palace.

Turning back to the room, she gave orders to the black-clad security details.

"Take the duke downstairs and shove him out the front door. Lock it behind him." Then, pointing at Hana, she said, "And put *her* back in her room for the time being, until I decide if she is still of any use to me."

The lead security officer and two of his men came up behind the duke and lifted him by the underarms.

"Wait," he protested, "you can't do this to me! You work for *me*, not her! Stop!"

"Actually, Your Grace," the security lead said firmly, "the duchess is our employer. The only times we followed your commands were when we were directed to by her. She holds our contract, and therefore our loyalty. Please, come with us."

Reaching the grand entrance to the palace, the security detail walked the bewildered duke to the front door, opened it, and pushed him outside, closing the door and bolting it as soon as he was through.

Assuming a posture of self-assurance, the duke looked around, straightening his jacket and shooting his cuffs. Philip was standing with a group of men on the other side of the court-yard, along with a contingent of soldiers. They were setting up a sound system, apparently to address those inside the palace. On seeing the duke appear on the steps of the entryway, the soldiers took ready positions, pointing their rifles at him.

The duke stood there for a moment, deciding how to proceed. Then he gathered as much dignity as he could muster and walked formally toward Philip.

He had made it most of the way when a group of soldiers was dispatched to intercept him. They held him at gunpoint while searching him and, finding no weapons, began to place zip ties on his wrists.

Philip interceded. "No need for that. He is alone and unarmed. Bring a couple of chairs and the awning over here. I would like to hear what the duke has to say."

CHAPTER
THIRTY-THREE

T he Duke of Avignon was brought under the portable canopy and held in a standing position until Philip had been seated. Then he was thrust down into a chair by one of the protective detail. Philip crossed his legs, placed his folded hands on his lap, then looked at Jean-Louis for a moment before he spoke.

"So nice of you to join me, Your Grace. To be perfectly honest, I was not looking forward to having to drag you out of your palace in chains. Far too messy, and most decidedly not a good look for the television cameras trained upon us at this very moment."

Philip turned away, looking into the distance back at the crowd of media assembled near the helicopter. His face bore a forced, insincere smile as he waved to them. With a sigh, Jean-Louis assumed his captor had prearranged media coverage of this very event, the capitulation of his short reign. And Philip was preening for the cameras.

Had the roles been reversed, he would probably have done something similar.

"Have you renounced your claim to the throne?" Philip asked.

"Not formally, nor publicly. I was just addressing my advisors when you arrived. There was not yet time to make an official announcement. I suspect you know why?"

"If you are referring to our interception of a certain satellite telephone conversation, then yes. It is now clear that your claim to the throne is based on both an invalid edict and an illegitimate bloodline.

"Thus, my purpose for coming to Avignon to meet with you...to see if we could work out some peaceful resolution to this affair. I may not grant you any concessions, since obviously, I hold the upper hand. But in recognition of your coming out to meet me, I will at least listen to your proposals."

Jean-Louis paused to consider this. Obviously, Philip could not yet have known that Sabine had taken charge; even he himself was still processing that fresh betrayal. No, best to keep that card close to his vest for now.

"I do have something you still want, Philip: the peaceful renunciation of my claim to the throne. I will give this to you in exchange for clemency and pardon for all my staff. They were acting on my account, and do not deserve to be punished."

"And when you say 'your staff,' does that include your wife and Mademoiselle Sinclair? I'm curious what you consider their status to be."

"In the matter of Hana Sinclair, that is easy: she never formally joined my staff and was here not entirely of her own accord. She came to my hotel in Paris seeking safety from the unrest, and I brought her with me to Avignon, but she had done nothing you might consider disloyal to the Republic.

"The Vatican has not been forthcoming with the pope's blessing of my ascension to the throne—to their credit and wisdom, it now appears."

"But... back to your wife?" Philip said.

The duke paused again, looking thoughtful.

"Sabine is a more complicated question, certainly. It appears she was undertaking efforts on my behalf of which I was unaware. I am afraid that, due to our marriage and the confidential privileges pertaining thereto, I am unable to say more at this time."

Philip smiled at his former opponent. "Obviously, I am dying of curiosity now. But you have comported yourself with the honor and dignity of a true gentleman. For that, you have my respect.

"However, as you attempted to overthrow the democratically elected government—even if only for a short while—I am afraid I am going to have to place you under arrest. I would appreciate it if you would make a statement to your supporters, and do so publicly.

"We will set up a podium and a microphone, with a live feed to the media. But before that, you will be taken back inside to notify your staff and top advisors. Those who come out now will be questioned, but not further detained."

"Ah, well, that may present a problem," the duke said, slightly embarrassed. "Perhaps we should do the announcement first, you see, as I doubt they are going to let me back in."

WITH THE MAJESTIC spires of the Palais des Papes as a fitting backdrop, Philip's press office had arranged for a podium with a microphone and broadcast video equipment to be set up in the palace gardens.

Flanked by military officers—giving at least the visual impression of an honor guard for the duke, though they were clearly there for his obedience and containment—Jean-Louis stood proudly on the dais, took a moment to assemble his thoughts, and began.

"People of France,

"I come before you today, a humbled man. I claimed the throne of our beloved country based on recent archeological discoveries which revealed that I was your rightful ruler, and in response to the political upheaval that has gripped the country.

"Yesterday, however, I received news that even more recent archeological discoveries have repudiated that claim, with regard both to the Edict of Avignon and to my personal lineage. Therefore, it is with great regret and disappointment that I must renounce my claim to the throne, and—"

"*Blah, blah, blah...*" Sabine Micheaux interrupted him, her voice amplified on her own loudspeakers as she held a portable microphone standing on the portico of the palace.

Dressed in a Christian Dior black lambskin skort, she also wore a crown of black gold, its oxidized spikes glinting in the sun above her long black hair. Draped across her shoulders was a black cape trimmed in panther fur. Behind her, thirty security personnel in black dress uniforms stood at order arms, their gleaming black rifles at the ready.

"How pathetic!" she continued after a dramatic pause. "What a sad, broken little duke. As they say, never send a man to do a woman's work."

All cameras had quickly turned to Sabine, as the sea of black surrounding her made for a better picture than Jean-Louis's standing apology under an awning—not to mention her scene-stealing intervention.

"People of France...*I* am your queen. I was your queen when my spineless husband was your king, briefly, and I remain your queen in my own right. I am a Valois, of the royal House Valois, a branch of House Capet."

Then, training her eyes on Philip, her long, full-length black gloves pointing accusingly at him, she said, "Philip, I give you twenty-four hours to withdraw your troops. Should you fail, you will find that I possess certain advantages neither you nor my husband could ever have imagined."

Then, turning back to the cameras, "Come, *mes chers*. Come out and show the world how much you love your *reine noire*."

She then left the balcony and went back inside the palace, hurrying down the stairs to the makeshift command center.

"Turn on the TVs for all major French cities, Graham. I want to see my subjects come out for me."

~

PHILIP TURNED TO JEAN-LOUIS. "Do you have any idea what she's talking about?" he asked.

"It's her fashion line. She has a great many followers on social media. She likens herself an influencer. I imagine she thinks her social media followers are going to come out in support of her."

"Is that likely?"

Jean-Louis rolled his eyes. "No, almost certainly not. My people tell me that she is actually something of a joke on the internet. She is almost a parody of herself. There are sites that do mock her. She is portrayed as a rich, spoiled, out of touch fashionista. Her followers do so largely to make fun of her. But she believes they adore her, and that they will do her bidding on command. I strongly doubt it, to be honest. I'm told she hasn't sold any of her horribly over-priced creations in a while. They just fill up displays in galleries where she pays to have them hosted. Frankly, I don't know where she gets the money. I cut off funding her fashion business some time ago. She must have found some other eccentric patron of lost causes to support her or something along those lines. As you might have guessed, we're hardly close as a typical married couple might be. It was more a marriage of convenience among nobles."

"Well, then, I'm done here. I'm going back to Paris. You will be brought there at some point soon to face charges, Jean-Louis. But since you have been so cooperative, I'll make sure we do not throw the book at you."

~

INSIDE THE PALAIS DES PAPES, Graham Halsey—owner and commander of BlackCloud, the private security contractor once affiliated with the Knights of the Apocalypse, and whose code-name then had been "Nimbus"—had been waiting for Queen Sabine, who had just arrived directly from her speech on the portico.

"That was masterful, Sabine," Halsey gushed, though insincerely. He had watched it until CNN posted its "Technical Difficulties" screen, shutting down their live feed when meager images of a smattering of goth teens appeared outside shopping malls.

"Excellent news, Graham, thank you. I'll have my communications director send out the next email soon, staging the mass demonstrations we have planned. Can't you just see it? Supporters in black gathering in every French city, praising my leadership? This could be a great cover for your next mission."

"Yes, I'd thought of that as well. May I ask, though: why black? Don't misunderstand me, it is most striking on you. I'm just wondering what your rationale was in choosing that as your royal color."

"Black, dear Graham, has traditionally been associated with rebellion and melancholy, two psychological states now on the mind of every French citizen. Symbolically, black is unambiguous and not easily misunderstood, conveying certainty and authority. It carries with it elements of power and drama, of mystery, sophistication and formality.

"And lest we forget, the female black widow spider is the most dangerous of them all, known for her cannibalistic sexual appetite…"

Halsey blanched at the thought of such horrid graphic intimacy and quickly changed the subject.

"You said in your speech you were giving Philip twenty-four hours to evacuate. Do you really expect him to?"

"Yes, well, never react as your opponents expect. I want you to launch your attacks as soon as the demonstrations begin. Hit them when they least expect it, and before Philip has his people start hacking our communications."

"It will be done as you wish—just as soon as you make your next progress payment. Waging war is expensive. Those drones are at least a million U.S. dollars each."

"That was money well spent, Graham. Psychologically, Philip now knows we are both armed and determined, and not to be trifled with."

Sabine gestured to one of her aides at the conference table, who bent over, picked up a silver Halliburton attaché case from beneath his chair, and opened it, spinning it around to face Halsey. Inside were stacks of ancient gold coins, sealed in clear shrink wrap.

"I trust this will compensate you for your efforts thus far, and for the foreseeable future."

Graham Halsey, gaping at the riches before him, replied, "Yes, indeed, Your Majesty. You are most generous. We will await further orders."

THIRTY-FOUR

Marco, Michael, Karl, and Lukas were all back at the garage, having failed to get access to Armand's jet at the airport. Philip's forces were using the airport to bring additional troops into Avignon to augment the forces already there.

With their diving gear still inaccessible, Karl had decided to rent additional gear. He called the dive shop in Rome, and was referred to a shop in Marseille that would be able to accommodate them—and a few words to the owner would ensure that no indiscreet questions had been asked. Marseille was an hour away by car, but it was four hours later before they were able to get to the ocean, acquire their gear, and return to Avignon due to congestion on the roads.

The team huddled in the trees across the river from the palace, using the campground as a staging area to get dressed and geared up. Then they crawled into the trees and bushes at the shore to observe and plan their entrance into the castle.

"All right," Karl began as he laid out the plans, "since most of us are seasoned divers, I won't go over basics. I'll be going in first, dragging a rope line behind me. Marco will come next, about ten feet behind and holding on to the rope. If I pull once on the rope, stop and give me some slack. If I pull twice, pull back on the rope slowly. If I pull three times, it's an emergency. Pull me back if you can, but otherwise, break for the surface and head back to the north shore.

"Marco will be my swim buddy. Michael and Lukas are the second team. They will follow the line about three meters behind Marco, with Michael first, then Lukas. It's liable to be pretty murky in the water, and we won't be able to use lights until we are down a little way to avoid being spotted, so we want to get underwater while there is still a little daylight left.

"Based on the look of the cavern leading to where the cata-combs are, there was once a significant flow of water through there. I'm hoping there is either a natural connection or a large pipe to carry us under the gardens and to the catacombs. All we can do is reconnoiter things at this stage. There had better be some kind of way into the castle, or there may not be any way to get Hana out.

"Everybody ready? Everybody check your buddy... Okay, let's go."

Karl dropped into the water, trailing the yellow polyester rope behind him as he used his fins to push himself down into the river.

He shone his light ahead, peering through the murky water as he approached the southern shore of the river, at a spot where the Rhône took a bend to the east.

The underwater bank was an extension of the sheer lime-stone cliffs towering high above the shore. Karl started a little west of the palace, swimming upriver. He found a wide crevasse in the bank with a perceptible current coming from it, wide enough that two of them could swim side by side through it.

He swam inside, and before long found a roof forming over him; he was entering a tunnel. As he continued forward, the crevasse continued to narrow. He estimated they had gone maybe a hundred meters forward when he found a fifteen-centimeter pipe terminating in the roof of the crevasse. He could feel water being expelled out of the pipe. A few meters ahead he found another pipe with a screen over the end; clearly an intake pipe since water was being sucked into it.

Karl figured they must be under the pumping station beneath the gardens. He continued swimming forward, pausing only to turn back and shine the light on Marco to make sure he was okay. Marco gave him a thumbs up, then looked back to check on Michael, who gave him a thumbs up.

Then Michael looked back—but Lukas wasn't there. He pulled the rope three times, signaling the others ahead.

When Karl felt the three pulls, signaling an emergency, he turned and quickly swam back toward the rear. Marco waited for him to pass, then swam after him.

As Karl got to Michael's position, he couldn't see Lukas. A lump stuck in his throat. He couldn't bear the thought of losing Lukas. Concerned for him, his heart rate accelerated, then he saw his partner swimming up from farther down the murky tunnel. He deliberately worked to slow his breathing to counteract it and would talk to Lukas later about letting go of the rope. *He knew better.*

When Lukas caught up to the group, Karl gave him an anxious, questioning shrug with palms upward. Lukas pointed to a gash in the leg of his wetsuit and motioned that it had gotten snagged. He gave his partner a thumbs up as Karl squeezed his shoulder in return.

Karl gave an all-clear thumbs up to the others as he returned to the lead position and kept swimming.

Soon, the crevasse began to widen again. The roof rose until it was no longer visible, and the current slowed considerably. Eventually, after some four hundred meters, Karl shone his light upward and perceived what appeared to be the surface of the water.

Swimming up and breaking the surface, he shone his light around. He did not remove his scuba apparatus in case the air was foul. As the others surfaced next to him, they looked around the chamber. They were in a small, subterranean lake, with a shoreline encircling it. The roof of the cavern was shaped like a bowl some ten meters over their heads, festooned with stalactites.

Up on the shore, Karl spotted in the side of the cavern a door hewn out of the rock and set with concrete at the base to hold the doorframe. It looked to be a hundred years old, based on the style of lock, and was a little over a meter above the water, with stone steps leading from it down into the water. Based on the water line on the walls, the surface of the lake had been much higher in the past, at times right up to the door frame. The shore was littered with old chests and boxes which had obviously been underwater at various times.

As they floated in the lake, their heads barely above the surface, they saw a tall crack of light appear as the door slowly opened. Nobody moved a muscle, not even allowing the water around them to ripple at all.

A flashlight shone through the crack as the door inched open wider. The beam moved along the shore, among the boxes. It was the large woman they had seen previously, the au pair.

In a hushed voice, the woman called out in French, her voice echoing throughout the cavern, "Margot? Margot, are you down here? I swear, *petite fille*, when I find you this time, there will be consequences." Her voice echoed throughout the cavern.

Karl, Lukas and Michael had gradually submerged, leaving barely a ripple on the surface of the lake as they went under. But Marco stayed, his eyes just above the waterline, shielded by the diving mask he was wearing.

He watched and waited, slowly paddling his flippers to maintain buoyancy while holding his breath, waiting for the woman to give up her search. He didn't want escaping air bubbles to give him away.

Marco found himself conflicted. He had hoped to see Margot again, but also didn't want her to get in trouble. But more than anything, he hoped the woman would not shine her light out over the lake.

Turning in a huff, muttering and closing the door behind her, the woman vanished back inside. Marco let out his breath, causing a burst of bubbles from his regulator to pierce the surface. The others also had been holding their breath and exhaled as they rose, causing more bubbles to break the surface, the popping noises reverberating through the cavern.

Confident they were now in the clear, the four men came up onshore, removed and stowed their wetsuits near the door, and from their dry gear bags withdrew and dressed in their black clothing, similar to what the queen's security forces wore.

Then they crowded around the door, listening.

Silence.

Quietly, Karl outlined the plan. They would all go up together until they reached ground level, then they would separate. Michael would go with Marco, and Lukas would be with Karl. They would search the hotel first, then the residence, looking for Hana.

"Move about the palace confidently, as if you own it," Karl instructed. "Hopefully, they'll just assume we're among the other security personnel."

Marco gave Michael a small two-way radio with a coiled earpiece so the two could stay in touch.

"If you get captured and can't talk, Michael, just push the talk button three times. That's the emergency signal. We'll do what we can to help when we hear the squelch. Try to keep us informed as to your general whereabouts, too, and we'll do the same."

Using small tactical flashlights with multiple illumination levels, they entered the stairway, using just enough light to see the step in front of them. The stairway, crudely carved into the limestone eons earlier, wound around in a circle going up.

Reaching a landing with a door on one side and the stairs

continuing on the other, they doused their lights while Marco listened with an ear against the door.

No sound. He gently lifted the latch and slowly pushed the door open. Complete darkness greeted him. He turned on his flashlight, still set to the lowest level, and could make out the sarcophagi and the niches of the catacombs where they had been before.

Crouching, he entered the space.

Suddenly, a light shone from next to him. As it made its way up to Marco's face, he heard a loud and fearful *gasp*, then a woman screamed. Marco quickly jumped toward her, clapping his hand over her mouth. Then—as she began to faint and all her weight fell onto him—Marco broke her fall, then set her down gently against the wall.

Everyone froze, waiting to see if her scream had drawn any attention. But none came.

Quickly, Marco used zip ties to secure her wrists and ankles, and put a cloth in her mouth, holding it in place with another zip tie around her head.

Marco was just standing up when he heard a noise behind him. He turned, weapon in hand, to see a small shape emerge from the back of one of the sarcophagi.

"Bonjour...what are you doing here?" Margot asked uneasily. "Are you soldiers from outside?" She started to back away.

"No, no, Margot, it's okay," Michael said in a friendly voice. "It's us again. Remember me? Father Michael?"

"Oh! Yes, I remember. Why did you come back? You aren't going to hurt Papa or *Maman*, are you?" Her voice had a fearful tone to it.

"No, Margot. We aren't here to hurt anyone. But we can't get caught either, or someone might try to hurt us. One of our friends is being held upstairs, and we are just trying to get her back home with us. Have you seen a tall, pretty woman with long brown hair who might be here somewhere?"

The girl looked thoughtful for a moment. "No, but there are a lot of strangers on the third floor of the hotel. Maybe she is there."

"Do you think you could show us where that is?"

"I could, but *Maman* said I wasn't allowed to go there. Besides, there are too many soldiers up there now."

Michael glanced at the others. Clearly, it wouldn't be wise for them to attempt Hana's rescue just yet.

"Is that your *maman* over there?" the priest asked, gesturing to the still unconscious au pair.

"No, that's my au pair. She was looking for me, but I was hiding. She's mean, I don't like her. I'm glad you tied her up. She locks me in my room sometimes. But I climb out the window and come down here."

Michael noticed the girl was holding something in one of her hands, slightly behind her back.

"What's that you're holding behind your back?"

Margot slowly brought her hand around. It was a teddy bear wearing a necklace of hammered gold discs.

"This is my best friend, Ursa. He keeps me company when I come down here, so I don't get afraid of the queen."

"What queen?"

"The dead queen in the box. You know, where we first met."

"Let's go back there, shall we?"

Margot took Michael by the hand and led him to the queen's crypt. "How did you find this place, Margot?"

"I was down here visiting Grand-père when I was walking along the wall and saw the front of one crypt open, so Ursa and I looked inside and saw the queen, and then we found the steps inside the box.

"It took us a long time to decide to go down the stairs, but Ursa is brave. At the bottom is a room full of gold and stuff. Do you want to see? It's not scary anymore."

Margot scampered into the crypt and began climbing down the hewn limestone steps. Michael followed her, slipping through the familiar open stairwell and down into the subterranean room.

Now that he had time to survey the room, sitting in a corner were several rotting wooden chests: six of them were empty but two had an abundance of riches spilling out: gold coins, jewels, chalices, pearl necklaces…to Michael's eyes, even what was left resembled the classic image of a pirate's treasure.

The priest noticed the large teddy bear was sitting in a chair at a small table in the center of the room wearing a gold bracelet on his arm, gold gauntlets on his legs and a small Viking helmet with horns resting on its head.

"We are sorry, King Teddy, that we had to leave so quickly before, but we have brought some new friends for tea," Margot said sweetly, addressing the bear.

Michael was stunned at the trove of wealth in the two chests. One by one, the rest of the team came down. All four stared at the fabulous bounty of gold and jewels glinting brightly under their torch beams.

"This has got to be part of the treasure Pope Clement V mentioned," Michael exclaimed. "And these empty chests are likely what's funded Sabine's diabolical campaign."

"Look at it all," Lukas marveled.

"Yes, I agree this is amazing," Marco said restlessly, "but again, we need to get about our mission. We can attend to this later. Right now, let's go find Hana."

Michael knelt by the little girl. "Margot, thank you for showing us your secret tea party room. We need to go find our friend now. I know you said that you can't go into the hotel, but can you at least show us how to get there?"

"Okay, but please don't tell *Maman*."

"What is your *maman*'s name, sweetheart?"

"Her name is Sabine. She's the Queen of France."

CHAPTER
THIRTY-FIVE

As Margot led the team up the stairs to the door to the ground floor, she waited at the top landing, listened at the door, then whispered, "There may be some of the new guards there. Some of them are nice, but most of them are bad. You stay here. I'll go look around. *Maman* told them I can go anywhere I want in the castle, and they have to leave me alone. So I can go see where they are, and then I'll come back."

Marco opened the door ever so slightly and, seeing no one beyond it, let Margot through. The others retreated down the stairs and into the dim cavern, waiting for the girl to return.

A SHORT WHILE LATER, the door opened again, with Margot's lithe figure backlit by the interior light. She motioned for them to come up the stairs. Passing through the doorway, they were now in a narrow hall that branched left and right from their position, with stone walls along both sides.

"Be real quiet," the girl said. "If we go that way"—she pointed left—"we would go into the church. But we are going the other way," now pointing right, "along the servants' passage, past the kitchen and dining room and into the hotel. Then we have to go outside, where the deliveries come in, then go into the hotel from the loading dock. Then you can go upstairs in the service elevator to the third floor. That's where *Maman* and Papa are having their guests stay.

"I don't know what room your friend is in. I'm not allowed up there. There are some guards on the loading dock and some more by the gate. But I don't think they will see you going to the elevator."

"*Merci*, Margot," Michael said to her with a smile. "That's very helpful. We'll follow you, okay?"

With Margot leading the way, all four of the team, dressed in black like the palace guards, walked assuredly behind her down the passage. When they got to the door, Marco turned to the girl.

"You have been *très bonne*, Margot! You are a brave and very smart young lady." Margot beamed, relishing the compliments from this handsome soldier. It was clear to Marco she likely didn't get many and was probably starving for affection and attention given the more public priorities of her parents. He assumed both Jean-Louis and Sabine put more emphasis on their careers than on their daughter and contracted out the parenting to an au pair who, at least in Margot's eyes, wasn't very nice.

"Now, Margot, I want you to go someplace safe. Maybe back down to stay with King Teddy and Ursa. Stay there for a while, okay? It might get dangerous up here, and I don't want you to get hurt."

"But I want to stay with you! I'll be good. I'll be real quiet."

"No, *mon ange*. It will be safer for you to go back downstairs. But if we get upstairs and get our friend out, then we will come back and say goodbye."

Clearly unhappy, Margot pouted a moment, but then agreed to do what was asked of her. Turning around, she headed back toward the door to the cavern. Marco watched her go until she was out of sight.

"Hey, big guy, get your head back in the game," Karl said, slapping Marco on the back. "We have work to do."

"Huh? Oh, right. Let's do this."

Marco went to the door, eased it open a crack, and assessed the situation. There was a truck backed up to the loading dock. Two guards were leaning against the front of the truck smoking cigarettes and watching the guards who were at the gate monitoring the street. Everyone was looking away from where the team was. The ancient service elevator was on the other side of the truck, on the opposite side of the dock.

"Okay," Marco whispered, "when I call the elevator, if there are people in it, we push them back inside, close the door, and secure them."

Marco reached inside his dry bag and took out the silencer for his trusty Glock 19, screwed it onto the barrel, then flipped the switch to turn on the holographic sight.

"I'll take point. If we have to put anybody down, let me shoot first with the suppressed gun. We still need to keep a low profile. But if things go sideways, all bets are off."

Opening the door, they swiftly crossed the space between the door and the back of the truck. Marco walked over and pushed the call button for the elevator. They watched above the door as the numbers descended from three, to two, to one. The doors slid open. One of the security supervisors began to step out, looking smart in his black cap and uniform and holding a clipboard.

Catching him off guard, Marco slammed into him, pushing him back into the elevator with a thud with his hand over the man's mouth to keep him from shouting.

The others came in right behind him. Michael pushed the elevator button for the third floor, and the doors began to close. Karl and Lukas dove into the fray of subduing the guard, each holding an arm and leg. Marco switched to a front choke hold, using the man's lapels to leverage his fists into his neck just over his carotid arteries.

The guard squirmed for just under a minute before passing out. Since he was about Marco's size, the Frenchman took his shirt and cap and quickly put them on himself. He also took the guy's radio and clipboard. Karl and Lukas zip tied his hands behind his back, secured his knees and ankles similarly, then left him in a corner of the elevator.

Marco looked at the clipboard. It had room assignments for the "guests" on the floor. Clearly, Hana was not the only person being held here. A number of the duke's staff were being accommodated as well, likely against their will, he assumed.

"Michael, have you got your white collar with you?"

Without asking why, the priest fished in his pack and pulled out his clerical collar, fastening it onto the neck of his black collar and securing the top button.

"Okay, here's the plan. Hana is in room 304. According to the clipboard, there is a guard at each end of the hall, and this elevator opens in the middle. I'm going to take Michael to Hana's room, and we'll tell the guards that he is there to give her last rites before the queen has her executed for being a spy. Then we go in, grab Hana, and if the guards question us, we take them out."

Turning to Karl and Lukas, he added, "You two wait here, and hang on to their radio. Let me know if there is any chatter I should be aware of. Keep the elevator on three and the door open. We'll be right back."

Michael opened the door, then he and Marco walked down the hall.

The guard at the far end, though, started coming toward them. Marco turned, casually glancing behind him, and saw the guard at the other end of the hall was staying put, not paying attention.

The approaching guard met them in front of Hana's door. A padlock hasp had been installed so the door could be locked from the outside.

The guard looked at Marco and Michael suspiciously. "I don't know you. What are you doing here?" he asked in French, then glanced at Michael. "And what's the priest for?"

"You don't need to know me," Marco said authoritatively.

"The priest is here to give the Sinclair woman last rites before the queen has her executed for being a spy. Now open this door so we can get on with our work."

"I'll need to verify this first." He reached for his radio. At the same time, Marco pulled his radio out—the one that was paired with the unit Lukas and Karl had back in the elevator.

Pressing the Talk button, Marco said, "Control, I'm up at 304 with the priest. Can you call the guard up here to open the door?" Then, turning to the guard, "What's your call sign?"

"Sec-12," the man said.

"He's Sec-12," Marco told Karl.

Karl spoke back into the radio he had taken from the supervisor. "Sec-12, this is Control. Approval granted to open 304. Control out."

The guard replied on his radio, "Roger, Sec-12. Copy and out."

He then took out a ring of keys and searched through them until he found one marked 304. He released the padlock, then turned the knob, pushing the door open.

Hana was standing just on the other side. Surprised to see her friends—and before Marco could give her any warning—she said, "Marco! Michael! How did you—"

On hearing the prisoner call them by name, the guard's earlier suspicions were now confirmed. In a flash, he held the radio up to his mouth and pressed the Talk button, intending to call for reinforcements. Marco shoved him into the room, ramming him directly into a wall. As the guard bounced off it, Marco came in low, putting his shoulder into the man's groin and letting the guard's forward momentum lift him onto Marco's shoulders and over before landing on his back. Marco followed the movement, twisting as the man went over and coming down on top of his chest with all his weight, knocking the wind out of him.

The Frenchman quickly grabbed the radio, pressed the Talk button, and said to Karl, "Expect company."

Yanking zip ties out of his bag, Marco secured the guard's wrists and fastened him to a bedpost. Michael had pulled Hana away from the door as the guard came through. The guard's radio chirped.

"CentCom to Sec-12. Come in Sec-12." There was a moment's pause. "Station identifying as 'Control,' confirm."

Taking Hana by the hand and pulling her away from Michael, Marco said, "Let's go. Someone is soon going to realize that unknowns have been talking on their radio."

The voice erupted again, this time with concern. "Sec-10, do you have Sec-12 in sight?"

Another voice came on. "Negative, CentCom. I last saw him talking to the priest and the supervisor down the hall."

"Supervisor Sec-2, do you copy?"

No response.

"They're on to us now," Marco declared. "Let's go!"

As Marco, Hana, and Michael left the room, the guard at the other end of the hall saw them and began running toward them, shouting *"STOP!"* Marco drew his Glock from behind his back just as the guard was passing the still-open elevator.

Suddenly, a hand shot out of the elevator door and hit the guard in the throat. The man went down hard, clutching his neck, gasping for breath and retching. Karl pulled him into the elevator and zip tied his hands just as Marco, Hana, and Michael joined him in the car.

"Time to go," Marco said. "Quick change of plan. We are going to head back to the service passage, take the stairs down to the catacombs, then take the door at the end to the street. If anyone's there, keep going down the stairs and hit the lake— we'll take the wet way out, and I'll buddy breath with Hana."

Hana looked puzzled, then distressed. "We're gonna do *what?!*"

"It'll be okay," Marco assured her.

Suddenly the radio squelched and came alive: *"Code Red! Code Red! Response Team to Hotel 3. Security there is unresponsive."*

Michael repeatedly punched the elevator button for the first floor, as if that could make it move any faster. Almost a full minute later, the old doors slid open, and they ran for the doorway across the loading dock. They could hear shouts from the guards at the gate.

They kept running down the passage toward the door to the stairs. As they drew nearer, they heard the door at the loading dock open. More shouts of *"Stop!"*

Then the thing Marco was fearing most: *gunfire.*

He dove forward, knocking everyone to the floor. As he hit them, he rolled over, drawing his Glock and spinning around to face the enemy. Sitting with his legs splayed out in front of him for support, facing back toward the dock, he could see two guards, one kneeling, one standing, pointing guns in his direction.

They fired, but with their adrenaline-addled minds they were shaking too much to aim effectively, and the bullets passed over all of them. Marco looked through the Glock's holographic sight, put the red dot on the kneeling man's chest, and squeezed the trigger. The man went down.

Marco then took aim at the standing man, who had stopped shooting and was looking at his partner. He grabbed his fallen companion by one arm, dragging him to safety beyond the door. Marco let him go; at the moment, he was no longer a threat.

Karl and Lukas had also drawn their guns and were kneeling behind Marco, ready to fire, with Michael and Hana crouched behind them.

Marco turned and got to his feet. "Let's go!"

They entered the stairway and began running down the steps, Karl and Lukas in the lead, followed by Hana and Michael, with Marco providing rear guard.

They reached the first landing. Karl slowly opened the door and peeked outside. There was no light and no movement among the crypts in the catacombs. He led the way out, turning left and heading for the passage at the end that would lead them outside and to the street.

Marco heard the sound of multiple running feet approaching them quickly.

"Make for the exit," he said hurriedly. "Michael and Hana, you go in front. I'll head over to the crypts and draw their fire. Karl, when Hana and Michael are away, you and Lukas cover me so I can make it over. Then we're going to have to make a run for it up to the street. We're sitting ducks if we try to swim the river."

Karl gave him a quick, acknowledging salute. "You got it, Marco."

The French commando headed across to the crypts and took a cover position where he could see the door. Moments later, a squad of four guards with daunting HK416 military rifles burst through the door.

Marco instantly knew these men were better trained than the guards they had encountered before; they employed smart tactics. They button-hooked through the door, entering the room in two pairs—one pair taking the left side of the door, the other pair taking the right, with both pairs covering their sectors of fire —and began searching for targets.

They saw the rest of the team make it to the far end of the room, just starting to go through the exit door. As the guards were about to fire, Marco aimed for the lead man's head and took his shot. The man went down.

Karl and Lukas got in a few last rounds in the guards' direction before they ducked through the door with Michael and Hana.

The remaining three guards took cover behind the crypts. With the cavern echoing several sources of gunfire—and with Marco's Glock suppressed—they had little idea where the other shooter might be.

Deciding that the escaping targets were the priority, two of the guards started toward the door at the far end, the remaining man checking his now-lifeless comrade. Marco began walking backward, covering his team from anyone else crouching behind the crypts.

He had just reached the next-to-the-last crypt when a small head popped up from the end of one of the closer crypts.

Margot!

Seeing her, Marco sprinted from his position in a panicked rush, blasting cover fire at the guard closest to him as he lifted the little girl off her feet, then charged through the door to the stairs.

Once through the door, he sent Margot up the stairs, telling her to get back home as fast as she could. The girl obediently ran off, frightened by the gunfire.

Marco ran down the stairs and burst through the doorway and onto the shore of the lake. Grabbing his dive tank, he shoved his arms through the buoyancy compensator gear and dove into the water.

GRAHAM HALSEY WAS SHOUTING into a handheld radio as Sabine Micheaux entered the conference room.

"What the hell is going on, Graham?" she demanded.

"We've been infiltrated, apparently through a tunnel from the river that comes up in a lake below the catacombs. It would have been helpful to know before now that there even *were* a lake and catacombs."

Ignoring the insolent remark, Sabine asked, "Have we captured or otherwise dealt with them yet?"

"No. It appears they've escaped. Part of the group went out through the catacombs, and another went back out through the lake."

"Do not fail me, Halsey! I want those people caught."

"I'm afraid Philip has us pretty well tied down. There's still a full brigade out there surrounding us. I assumed this was probably a commando raid assessing entry points and weaknesses. We'll have them shored up momen—"

Halsey abruptly stopped talking to listen to the radio. Then he turned to the boss.

"Spotters on the roof saw the group that went through the catacombs come out onto the street, but they were taken behind the barricades by Philip's forces. They have the journalist now—apparently, this was a rescue mission."

Sabine simmered with anger, her face flushing red as she studied the floor, assessing her options.

"Prepare our troops for battle. We are going to war!"

CHAPTER

THIRTY-SIX

P hilip's soldiers manning the barricades raised and aimed their weapons at the approaching four people running toward them.

"Stop! Identify yourselves," one soldier demanded.

Michael, Hana, Karl, and Lukas slowed down as they got closer and raised their hands.

"Wait! I am Father Michael Dominic, and we're here in your country on behalf of Pope Ignatius at the request of Cultural Minister Lauren Valois. These are my colleagues, Hana Sinclair of *Le Monde*, and Sergeants Karl Dengler and Lukas Bischoff, Swiss Guards from the Vatican on assignment with us here."

While the lead soldier considered this, he noticed Karl and Lukas's holstered pistols.

"Père Dominic, you and the mademoiselle may pass. But the two Swiss Guards must relinquish their weapons before they can enter."

Reluctantly, Karl and Lukas yielded their firearms, then joined Michael and Hana inside the protected area beyond the Palais des Papes.

As they joined the crowd of onlookers and media behind the barricades, live news cameras and reporters rushed up to them, asking what it was like escaping the clutches of the famed Black Queen.

"Well," Hana remarked to a TF1 television reporter, "it is true that with the duke now gone, Sabine Micheaux clearly believes she is running the country, though that's a preposterous claim in my view.

"After all, Pierre Valois is still the legitimately elected President of France."

~

THE TELEVISION in the pope's bedroom was tuned to CNN International, with live coverage of France's current troubles being shown as the Holy Father lay in bed, his head cold persisting longer than expected.

After insisting Papa Petrini get to bed and rest up, Nick Bannon had canceled the pontiff's scheduled events for the day and was sitting in a chair adjacent to the bed, making calendar adjustments on his laptop, while the pope asked him the occasional question.

As Petrini watched for any news that might concern the petitions he had yet to deal with—from both Philip Valois and now Sabine Micheaux, each seeking the Vatican's endorsement for their competing leadership—he picked up the phone to call Ian Duffy for news of Michael's activities.

"Where is Father Dominic, Ian?" Petrini asked. "Has he returned from France yet?"

Knowing the pope had asked Michael not to run off and rescue Hana, Ian's mind raced to come up with some other plausible explanation for his absence, but ultimately felt he could not lie to the pope. "Your Holiness, Michael—I mean, Father Dominic—*was* here, but he returned to France to see if he could help his friend Hana Sinclair. But I'm sure he's doing Vatican business there as well…" His voice drifted off at a loss for words. Even he wouldn't have believed himself.

Petrini sighed. "All right, Ian, thank you for being honest. I suppose I should have expected that, despite my cautions to him. Goodbye for now."

At that moment, looking up at the TV, Petrini happened to see Hana speaking to the TF1 news reporter, with Michael, Karl, and Lukas standing just behind her with a large crowd surrounding them. His heart leapt seeing that Michael was all right.

When Hana stepped away after speaking, though, he watched as two of the soldiers took her, Michael and the two Swiss Guards away, leading them into a tent. *Wonder what that's about?* he thought. *And where is that Picard fellow, Armand's bodyguard for Hana?*

While the pope could not intervene in the internal politics of France, he did ask Nick Bannon to make discreet inquiries into the fate of the team. Perhaps he might be needed to exert the power of his influence in other ways.

Closing his eyes and clasping his hands on his lap, he said a silent prayer for the safety of all of them.

INSIDE HER MAKESHIFT command center in the Palais des Papes, the Black Queen was not pleased, continuing to berate Graham Halsey, founder of BlackCloud, for not having prevented the infiltration by Dominic's team nor capturing the intruders.

"How can five people do so much damage to our troops, Halsey? Account for yourself! We cannot allow Philip and his allies to think they can just sneak in anytime they want without consequences."

"I agree, Your Majesty, but they seem unusually invincible… as if they're somehow getting help from someone on the inside. How they know the palace so well, and especially where we kept the Sinclair woman, is mystifying."

Sabine sat down in a light-blue, elaborately upholstered Louis XIV wingback chair and considered her options.

"Graham, how many drones do we have left in Paris?"

"At the moment, we have ten remote combat drones ready to launch."

"And all ten can be fitted with explosives?"

"Yes, they already are," Halsey confirmed uneasily. He knew where this was going.

"Have you been keeping tabs on Philip's location? Where he is at all times, I mean?"

"As best we can, yes. I understand his last known location was in the Élysée Palace. Our spies report he has not been seen leaving, so it's safe to assume he's still inside."

Sabine was obviously crafting some kind of plan, Halsey thought. His main concern was retaliation; the entire French armed forces against his shorter supply of BlackCloud mercenaries was hardly a match, and he feared for the decimation of his men. Of his entire company, for that matter.

Sabine's musings continued. "Do you think there are more than ten doors between his office and wherever he might be?"

Now how in God's name would I know that?! Halsey swore to himself. But an answer was expected of him.

"Though it's hard to say, I would expect not, no."

"Then here is what you will do...."

BACK IN PARIS, Philip Valois was about to come out into the central courtyard of the Élysée Palace to board a helicopter for a tour of the damage caused by the demonstrators.

While for the most part the so-called queen's supporters had been peaceful, there was still a mob of anarchists and others who took advantage of any unrest to cause mayhem. Windows had been broken in many government buildings and more than a few had been set on fire.

Quietly watching the activity in the courtyard below with its telephoto lens, an armed i9 hexacopter drone had been hovering one hundred and fifty meters up and a hundred meters to the south, beaming live footage back to the control operator in an unmarked van somewhere nearby. When the pilot saw Philip and his entourage exit the building, he radioed back to Avignon. The attack was a Go.

Several of the soldiers spread out and began searching the sky for drones before the helo took off. Philip stood at the doorway, waiting for the all-clear.

Suddenly, everyone heard the faint buzz begin to grow louder as the i9 made a direct line for Philip's position. Troops began firing at the drone, but they all missed the small moving target. Philip's security detail rapidly pulled him back inside the building and propelled him down the hallway, their bodies surrounding him like a human glove.

The drone passed through the still-open front doors, slowed and turned, its camera stalking the hallway like a raptor seeking its prey. Two of the security detail had stayed behind and, taking closer aim at the drone from the end of the hall, they hit it. But the explosive charge detonated, causing extensive damage to the entryway. Both security officers were blown backward, slamming into the wall.

Other soldiers just outside the front entry ran into the blast zone, looking to rescue the security team and anyone else who had been in the blast radius. The loud detonation had caused everyone's ears to ring—which is why they did not hear the second hexacopter come in over the building and zoom through the entryway. This drone turned to the right and swiftly flew down the hallway in the direction Philip had gone.

The rescue team fired on the new drone as it approached them, but the gliding killer sped up, moving rapidly toward them. One of the bullets finally hit a vital part of the drone's rotors and it crashed to the floor, exploding on impact and killing two of the guards while injuring others.

Taking advantage of the chaos, a third kamikaze drone entered the building and flew down the hallway. Soaring down the hall over dead bodies and injured men, past the spots where the first two had detonated, this i9 killer was searching for Philip.

Reaching the end of the hall, the drone veered left. At the end of this hall, two more soldiers spotted the kamikaze and drew their weapons. They continued shooting until it was nearly upon them, their shots going wild as they panicked.

The remote UAV pilot pressed the detonation button and the drone's warhead exploded right in front of them, taking them down as well as the double doors they were protecting.

Now a fourth drone came down the hall, turned left, and approached the double doors now lying on the ground, revealing a staircase heading down.

The pilot carefully watched his monitor as the i9 descended the stairwell. The live camera feed began transmitting interference, with static noise reflected on the display. He pushed it forward in pursuit of Philip, and another set of closed doors appeared at the end of this hall.

Maneuvering the drone up to them, the pilot blew its warhead charge.

Yet another i9 had been waiting at the top of the stairs, having followed its twin in from the outside. It came down the stairs, through the now-open doorway, and spun around, looking for Philip.

Smoke filled the view as the debris of the doorway and beyond continued to burn. Between the smoke and the static from the loss of signal below ground, the hexacopter's pilot could not see his way forward. The drone hovered in place, the smoke swirling from the downdraft of its six carbon blades. Finally, a brief view of the hallway to the right appeared, also revealing a figure approaching with a fire extinguisher and a soldier holding a rifle. The pilot flew the kamikaze toward them, and though the men tried retreating through a door behind them, the warhead exploded, taking them both out.

For such small but lethal devices, the remotely controlled i9s were decimating Philip's troops.

Additional soldiers had been rapidly deployed to the court-yard, with several detoured to the armory to grab shotguns. Making their way outside, those with shotguns easily took out the few remaining drones as they flew toward the entryway before any further damage could be done.

SAFELY HIDDEN in the secure room downstairs, Philip lifted the receiver of a dedicated hotline to General André Bélanger.

"General, we have been under a persistent drone attack here! Drone after armed drone entered the palace, each one getting closer to me down here in the safe room.

"This must stop! I am ordering an attack on the Palais des Papes. Fill it with tear gas, now! Drive them out."

THE FIRST THING the queen heard was the sound of glass breaking. Then the telltale hiss.

"Everybody downstairs!" Sabine shouted. "Nobody goes out. We'll be safe in the catacombs.

"Graham, get on the radio and order everyone to the back of the building. There is only one way to the catacombs, from the service hallway off the loading dock. Have someone get wet towels from the kitchen on the way. We'll have to seal the door once everyone is through."

Most of her team and the BlackCloud guards were able to stagger to the back hall, coughing and choking as tear gas quickly spread throughout the building. Fortunately, as an ancient castle, there were few windows on the first floor, and all were small and difficult to hit with tear gas canisters.

Once people were on the lower floor, the breathing was easier. Some only made it into the central courtyard, which, being open to the sky, allowed some of the gas to dissipate.

Soon darkness fell as quiet settled over Avignon and Paris. Both sides chose to lick their wounds and see how things looked in the morning.

THIRTY-SEVEN

L ong tendrils of dark gray smoke wafted over Élysée Palace in the distance as Lauren Valois stood at the window of Saint-Louis Hospital. He was too tired to care what Philip was up to, having spent the past many hours pacing the corridors, waiting for his father to come out of his coma.

The doctors had told him that Pierre was fading fast, and if there were any goodbyes to be made by family or friends, now was the time. The president had been put on palliative care in the hospice section of the hospital, waiting for the inevitable.

Meanwhile, Lauren knew there was a phone call to make—undoubtedly several in time, but one in particular now: to Armand de Saint-Clair, Pierre Valois's oldest and dearest friend.

Though Lauren had been dreading the expected mutual emotions of the call, Armand had seemed to cope well enough with the news. After all, it was hardly unexpected, since just weeks earlier the baron had spoken to his friend at Jacqueline's funeral, and well knew the magnitude of Pierre's loss and his current failing health, complicated by the later effects of the poisoning.

Lauren assured him that—because Philip had implemented a ground stop on all aircraft in France and restricted commercial air travel into the country—he would make arrangements for the baron to travel from Geneva to Paris via TGV Lyria since trains were still operating.

Philip had only dared interfere so much, and the trains of Europe would run on time. The baron would arrive tomorrow.

ARMAND DE SAINT-CLAIR was preparing to leave Switzerland for France when the phone rang again. It was Marco reporting in. He had been successful in getting Hana out of the Palais des Papes and free of her detention by the duchess, but they had been separated during the escape.

Hana, Michael, Karl and Lukas were now under protective custody of Philip's troops in Avignon, although from the size of the convoy of vehicles he saw leave the command post not long after the four had gone into the tents, Marco suspected everyone was now on their way back to Paris.

Armand promised to check with his sources in France to see what he could find out, to get back to Marco and give him further instructions. But, just in case, Marco should prepare to find a way to Paris himself.

While packing up things for tomorrow's trip, the baron heard the phone ring. His secretary answered it, then brought in the cordless phone from his office.

"It's the pope's assistant for you, Baron," she said, handing him the receiver.

"Hello, this is Armand de Saint-Clair."

"Yes, Baron. Please hold for the Holy Father."

A few moments later, Pope Ignatius came on the line. "My dear friend. How are you?"

"Oh, slowing down, as we all are, Enrico. The years are beginning to hang heavy on these old bones."

"Yes, with me as well. I have a head cold I just can't seem to shake. I would hate to think something like that would be the death of me. I had always envisioned going out in a much more dashing way."

"Speaking of which," Armand asked, "have you heard the news about Pierre?"

"Yes, that's the reason for my call. Lauren called me after he spoke to you. I am glad you are going to see him before he passes. I sincerely wish I could get away too. But I feel I am a prisoner to my office. Perhaps there may be a way, though. We shall see.

"Please, Armand, pass along my love and blessings, and if there is a time when Pierre is more lucid, if you could have Lauren connect me to him, I would like to speak to him one last time. A friendship of over seventy years deserves nothing less."

"Of course. I will make sure it happens. I heard from Marco Picard, my security man who looks after Hana. He said he and Michael, and the two Swiss Guards were successful in liberating Hana from the duchess—I simply cannot bring myself to call her 'queen.' However, they were separated during the escape, and Hana and the others were taken in by Philip's troops. Marco thinks they are on their way to Paris. I have made inquiries. I'm still waiting for further word."

"Yes, I had gathered as much from news reports, such as they are. I did see live footage of Hana and Michael being led past the barricades by Philip's soldiers."

Armand paused for a moment. "Well, I will be departing for France shortly. Perhaps I can convince cooler heads to prevail."

"As to that, I have declined to recognize either Sabine or Philip as the legitimate ruler of France. As far as Vatican foreign relations are concerned, Pierre is still the democratically-elected president of the free France the three of us fought so hard for in the war. You have my full support for a negotiated solution, especially one that sees both of them deposed."

"Then I will count on your prayers, for I think I will need them."

"Godspeed, old friend, and my blessings upon you."

~

BACK AT THE hospital a few hours later, the president's nurse found Lauren in the hall.

"Your father is awake and is asking for you, *Monsieur*."

Lauren hurried back down the hall and into the room, closing the distance to his father's side.

"Lauren? How… how long have I been asleep?" Pierre said groggily.

"Papa, you entered the hospital nearly two weeks ago, and for much of that time, you have been in a coma."

"Where is your brother?"

Lauren looked out the window, uncertain how to break the news.

"Much has happened, Father, since you've been taken ill. I think Philip is still at the palace. But you should know, he has been acting as a dictator."

"Oh, that is absurd! Ridiculous! What has happened, Lauren? Tell me everything."

The president's younger son explained the duke's ascension to the throne based on the archeological finds at Notre-Dame, and Philip's response to establish what amounted to a dictatorship and the duke's relinquishing his crown.

He told him of Sabine herself taking up the scepter, as it were, and holding the Palais des Papes as her seat of power, and the subsequent attacks between Philip's and her forces. And that apparently, from what he had seen on CNN, the duke, then the duchess, and now Philip had variously held Armand de Saint-Clair's granddaughter, Hana Sinclair, in custody, along with her companions, Father Dominic and two Swiss Guards.

"Oh, and Armand will be here tomorrow to see you," Lauren finished off.

"My son, what have you been doing all this time?"

"I have been here, Papa, all day, every day. I sleep in that chair over there. I eat in the cafeteria. I shower in the doctor's lounge. Your position has afforded me a few accommodations, of course. But I have been running the ministry from here and trying to maintain some semblance of your government, despite Philip's actions. The military cannot run everything. I have been holding the rest together for you as best I can."

With tears coming to his eyes, Pierre was moved. "Lauren, my dear son. I have misjudged the two of you. I see that now. I am so very sorry. The leadership I saw in Philip has gone to his head. He has wildly overstepped even what I had thought him capable of, and I now see his sheer lust for power. I had just hoped that the actual mantle of responsibility would temper his avarice. But I was wrong.

"Yet you, to whom I never gave much credit, you have stood by me, and shown true leadership, that of a servant to the people. I will make it up to you, my son. There is still time."

Lauren wiped the tears from his own eyes. "There is nothing to make up, Papa. I only want your love and recognition."

"No, Lauren. We have to set this right while we still have time. What have the doctors said? Will I recover now?"

The tears came back to Lauren's eyes. This would be the hardest thing for him to say.

"No, Papa, they have changed your medications and treatment now to palliative care, as your body is no longer capable of the fight. They give you a few days, a week at most. I'm so sorry, Father." He broke down in tears and leaned over his father, holding his hand.

"There, there, Lauren," the old man said, reaching for his son's hand and pulling him closer. "I am almost ready to go join your mother. I miss her more than anything, and I have lived a long and glorious life, full of meaning and adventure. I have few regrets. That I did not recognize your talents and contributions is one of them. But as I said, if there is time, we must try to set things right."

CHAPTER

THIRTY-EIGHT

The next day, under an unforgiving rain, Armand arrived at Paris's Gare du Nord train station along with his bodyguard and valet, Frederic, who, after collecting the baron's luggage, attended to acquiring a rental car to take them to the hospital and then later on to the Charles Cinq Hotel.

When Armand got to the hospital, he was directed not to Pierre's room, but to the hospital chapel. Inside, he found Pierre sitting in a wheelchair.

Lauren was also there, as were twelve strapping men in dark business suits, half standing on either side of the room and flanking the doors. Armand came forward and knelt next to his old friend.

"Pierre, it is so very good to see you, my friend. But what is going on here?"

"Armand, *mon ami*, come, have a seat. We will be getting started just as soon as one more guest joins us."

They all turned as the chapel doors were thrown open and Philip Valois boldly entered the room, along with General André Bélanger and two other armed officers.

"What in the devil is going on here, Father? I got a message to come to the hospital, that you were dying, and instead of finding you in your room, I am directed here? What is the meaning of this?"

"Watch your tone with me, young man," Pierre said in a clear and strident voice. "But it is good that you have come, for it makes my task much easier.

"Gentlemen, please take Philip and his companions into custody now."

Without hesitation, the dozen men in suits each drew pistols from beneath their jackets and pointed them at Philip and his team.

The lead security agent pulled out a set of handcuffs and said, "Philip Valois, by order of the president of the French Republic, and as chief of the Presidential Security Service, I am placing you under arrest on charges of sedition. General Bélanger, you are also under arrest on the same charges, as are the two of you," he said, gesturing to the other two army officers.

The two officers, their faces twisted in anger, started to draw their weapons, but the presidential security agents quickly surrounded them, holding their arms and promptly handcuffing them. Bélanger ordered them to stand down. The general and the officers were told to take a seat in the chapel. A security agent stood behind each one.

Shocked, Philip resisted. "Father, you can't do this to your own son!"

"You think not, Philip? Why? Because you had the audacity to take over the government as a dictatorship? Well, we are about to fix that right now. Lauren, please bring in the media."

Opening the main door, Lauren requested a television pool camera operator and TF1's lead reporter to join them. Already prepped on what their job would be, they set up over to one side of the chapel.

"If everyone is ready, then, let us proceed."

Pierre turned to speak to the camera, leaning heavily on the podium, but still standing.

"People of France, I come before you now as your democratically elected president. In light of recent events, no one can revive the monarchy on his own authority. Modern government is by the consent of the governed, and the French Revolution was fought for good reasons.

"During my illness, I sought to leave the government in capable hands. To my dismay, I misjudged in whose hands that power should reside. That ends today.

"As your president, I am establishing an independent commission to investigate my son Philip's actions, and the actions of the Duke and Duchess of Avignon, with full power to prosecute any and all of them for high crimes or misdemeanors against the Republic.

"I call upon my niece, Sabine Valois Micheaux, the so-called Black Queen, to surrender at once. She has no better claim to the throne than I do, and as the senior Valois, I supersede and renounce her claim as well.

"Finally, I call for new elections for the position of president, and I will resign as your president at the time of the swearing in of my democratically elected replacement.

"People of France, let us put these troubles behind us, and move forward together. May God bless you all, and goodnight."

Notified that the announcement was over, the hospital staff moved Pierre back to his room, watched over by half of his security service agents, while two guarded Bélanger's team.

The others took Philip down to a waiting vehicle then returned to collect General Bélanger and his officers when suddenly a hexacopter drone crashed through the stained glass window of the chapel and detonated.

Hospital security raced in with fire extinguishers to put out the blaze, but it was too late. Despite the best efforts of doctors and nurses at the hospital, the general, his officers and one of the presidential security agents were killed, with other agents seriously injured in the blast.

. . .

IN HIS ROOM, Pierre listened as Lauren gave him a report of the attack and casualty figures. Then he turned to Armand. "I guess we have Sabine's answer. It appears there is still some work to do."

The baron was about to reply when the presidential security agent at the door opened it and announced, "Excuse me, Messieurs. Baron, there is a Monsieur Picard here. He says he is the your security chief. Will you allow him in?"

Both Pierre Valois and the baron nodded. Marco came in and greeted both men.

"Ah, Marco," Armand said. "Sorry you weren't here for Philip's comeuppance. But we are glad you are here now.

"Pierre," he continued, "I have an idea...."

CHAPTER
THIRTY-NINE

P resident Pierre Valois appointed a more compliant Interior Minister who ordered French troops to pull back from the Palais des Papes, and to stand down from their previous, more authoritarian positions throughout France. Only a skeleton crew of security forces was left in place in Avignon to ensure an orderly transition back to a full democracy, with a Quick Reaction Force in reserve to quell any persistent unrest. But still, there was the Black Queen to reckon with.

Michael, Hana, Karl and Lukas were ordered released and transported to the hospital, where they met with the president, Armand and Lauren. Initial discussion ensued about Hana's experiences with the duke and especially Duchess Sabine, since both Pierre and Armand were most keen to understand the duchess and her current motivations and strengths, and any perceived weaknesses she might have that could work to their advantage.

Pierre designated Armand de Saint-Clair a special Presidential Envoy, with powers to negotiate a peaceful resolution to the situation with Sabine.

But Armand had his own plan, one that Marco had been briefed on before Michael and the others had arrived.

. . .

PIERRE VALOIS CALLED his niece and told her he was sending an envoy to arbitrate a resolution to the standoff, an offer she scoffed at with contempt.

"If he's not coming to tell me you are resigning in my favor, Uncle, then he is wasting his time," Sabine said with mocking reprove. "But feel free to send me fresh hostages, if you wish. I will not yield the crown I deserve."

"Sabine, my envoy comes to you under a flag of truce, with diplomatic immunity, and you will grant him and his entourage safe passage, or you will wish you were still dealing with Philip."

Owing to his heroic past and accolades, as well as his current standing in society, Sabine knew only too well that her fanbase would not take well to her disrespecting this much admired grand old man. Besides, part of her had always been intimidated by her powerful uncle, and she knew he was not one to bluff. Philip might have been a bully, but Pierre was a soldier and an elder statesman, and not someone to be trifled with. So while she considered herself a force of nature in her own right, she was not of his caliber, and she knew it.

"Please, Uncle Pierre, calm yourself. I said I will meet with him, and I will grant him safe passage, along with his people. You have my word—for what it's worth to you."

THE NEXT MORNING, an escorted and well-secured motorcade journeyed south from Paris to Avignon to meet with the pretender to the throne. Armand had brought Hana and Marco with him, while Michael, Karl and Lukas rode in one of the chase SUVs.

During the seven-hour drive south, Armand had been occupied on the phone conducting a particular business transaction that had to be completed before he met with Sabine. Hana and Marco sat with him in the back of the armored Klassen Range Rover limousine, speaking quietly and catching up on what had happened during the time they had been apart.

Hana was moved by the lengths to which Marco had gone in order to try to protect her, even attempting to rescue her when he could not. A persistent guilt plagued her over having acted so independently as to endanger both of them, something she still could not reconcile with her deep-seated need for self-determination. Independence was one thing, but recklessness was quite another. And after all, she knew, Marco himself wrestled with the conflicts of his protectiveness and possessiveness, both born out of his love for her.

Reaching somewhat of an impasse in their conversation—with Marco insistent on Hana's cooperation with his roles in her life—she and the Frenchman spent the rest of the ride in silence, looking out the windows in opposite directions. Armand noticed the chill between them and glanced at his granddaughter questioningly. Hana sighed, then shifted to sit next to the old man. She put her head on his shoulder and closed her eyes, like she had when she was a young girl, finding comfort in the unspoken response.

Already melancholy, her thoughts turned to her beloved godfather on his deathbed, with maybe mere days left, and wondered how much longer she would have him. As she drifted off to sleep under the gentle rocking of the moving car, she heard her grandfather quietly talking to someone on the phone... something about the army, and maybe the pope...

JUST PRIOR TO arriving in Avignon, the motorcade pulled off the A6 and into the small commune of Rochefort-du-Gard to give the security detachment time to gear up in preparation for the meeting—and in anticipation of possible conflict.

Marco, Karl, and Lukas joined the rest of the presidential

security detail that Pierre had sent with Armand. Part of the team was dressed in black tactical gear, with ballistic vests, FAMAS rifles, and black balaclavas covering their heads and faces. The balance of the team was outfitted in black suits and overcoats, with HK MP-5SD suppressed submachine guns slung from shoulder straps under their unbuttoned overcoats.

Now mounted up, they drove the remaining short distance to the entrance courtyard of the Palais des Papes. Meeting no military resistance, everyone got out of the vehicles, the security personnel forming a protective circle around the principals.

Standing on the steps of the portico were several fully armed BlackCloud agents. As Armand ascended the steps, he was stopped by the commander of Sabine's security force.

"I am sorry, *Monsieur*, but though you are expected, I cannot permit you and your team entry while being armed in the presence of the queen. Either your men will disarm themselves, or they can remain outside."

Armand regarded the man cannily but with confidence. "I understand your orders, Commander, but as you will find, your arrangements have changed. Please check with your superiors—and I do not mean your queen. I'll wait…"

Perplexed but unresisting, the commander keyed his cuff mic. "Security Directorate, Sec-2 here. Is there some new arrangement regarding the presidential envoy visiting the queen?"

He paused to listen to the reply. He cocked his head, momentarily confused, then a look of embarrassment crossed his face. Finished with the call, he addressed Armand de Saint-Clair with new respect.

"My deepest apologies, *Monsieur le Baron*. Of course, your men may accompany you in as they are. Would you and your entourage please be so kind as to follow me?"

He led them into the large reception hall inside the palace. There, in a golden throne that had at one time served as the garish seat of state for ruling medieval popes, sat Sabine

Micheaux, the Black Queen, suitably outfitted in her royal stygian color. Two guards flanked her on the elevated dais, and several others were stationed about the room, each holding an M4 carbine rifle.

Young Margot sat off to the side, on the top step near her mother, with her small bear, Ursa, in her lap as she raptly watched all the people paying homage to her mother.

Armand approached the dais. Marco—tall, fit and anonymously seductive in Sabine's eyes—stood on the baron's left, though his face was concealed beneath the balaclava. Karl stood to his right, followed by Hana, Michael, and then Lukas. Both Karl and Lukas were similarly concealed in balaclavas. The rest of the security team stood behind them.

"So, the great Armand de Saint-Clair is the envoy. It figures Uncle Pierre would send you, another puppet past his prime."

"Insults are hardly called for in this situation, Sabine. And since you have clearly dispensed with any civilized decorum, I will get right to the point. You are living a folly. You have no legitimate claim to the throne and your uncle insists that you step down immediately, and gracefully, for the good of France.

"As to why: first, as the senior Valois, your uncle's claim to the throne is superior to yours—*if* he were of a mind and your government was different. He could take the throne from you by asserting that right. And so long as he is alive, legally, you are not Queen of France and shall never be recognized as such.

"Second, the pope has recognized him as the rightful ruler of France, placing the full power and majesty of the Vatican behind him and the French Republic's rule of law. Therefore, if you do not abdicate, you will be excommunicated from the Church. And while that may not matter much to you, it may matter a great deal to your followers. France is still very much a strongly Catholic country."

Recognizing Sabine's not-unexpected intransigence, Armand played one of his last cards.

"There is one more thing—well, two, actually—but this one

must see the light of day." He turned to the man next to him and nodded.

Marco removed the balaclava from his head, revealing his face to Sabine. "There is," Armand continued, "the matter of Margot's paternity."

"*Marco!*" Sabine clamored, standing in fury. "This is outrageous! *We had an agreement!*" Without thinking, the would-be queen turned a glare first at her child and then back at Marco.

Caught in the fire of her mother's angry glance, Margot rushed up to her.

"*Maman*, I'm sorry. I didn't mean to disobey, really. But the man was very nice to me when I saw him in the catacombs. Don't be mad at him."

"He is no one to you, *mon ange*. Pay no attention to him!"

"On the contrary, Margot," Marco addressed the child with great affection. "I am your father. You are my daughter."

Simultaneously shocked and confused, Hana looked incredulously at Marco. "Your *what?!*"

"I'll explain later," Marco said, giving her a look that pleaded for understanding.

Armand stepped in to break the awkwardness. "I realize that adultery is practically a national pastime in France, but its rulers should enjoy at least a veneer of respectability. And there is the little girl to consider. Imagine the shame of this being made public. It doesn't have to be, Sabine. This can all end quietly."

"Marco, we had a confidential agreement. How dare you break your word!"

"I'm afraid you've made choices that compel me to overrule you on that, Sabine. You are clearly not in your right mind, and I've watched that get worse over the past few weeks. I will not have my daughter subjected to your madness and these delusions of grandeur you've taken on. What in God's name has happened to you?"

The Black Queen was furious now, the full force of her crazed personality revealing itself in the twisted features of her face.

"Guards!" she shouted. "Arrest all of them at once! Get them out of my sight."

The guards snapped to attention, boot heels clicking smartly, rifles pressed out to port arms. They waited at attention—but they made no moves toward Armand and his people.

Sabine looked around. "What are you just standing there for? *Did you not hear me?! I said arrest them. Now!"*

Graham Halsey, the head of BlackCloud, had been standing at the side of the room, waiting for his moment. Armand nodded to him, and he stepped forward.

"I am sorry, Your Grace, but my people will not be arresting anyone today—except for you. You see, my company has just been acquired, and the new owner will be withdrawing his troops momentarily."

"What do you mean, 'new owner?' BlackCloud is under exclusive contract to me!"

"All prior contracts have been vitiated as part of the acquisition. You will have to speak to the new owner about renegotiating yours, I'm afraid."

"And who is this new owner of BlackCloud you speak of?"

Armand turned to glare at the Black Queen.

"That would be me, Sabine. I acquired BlackCloud this morning, on very generous terms with Mr. Halsey. These men now work for me, and I'm not in a negotiating mood just now. Mr. Halsey, would you care to do the honors?"

"It would be my pleasure, Baron." Turning to two of his trusted men, Graham Halsey gave the orders. "Please take the duchess into custody."

"No! You cannot do this to me!" Sabine shrieked. Jumping off the dais, she ran up to Marco, rage creasing her face.

"You're involved in all this, I'm sure of it. You'll pay for this, Marco Picard. If it's the last thing I do."

"I wish it didn't have to be this way, Sabine, I truly do," Armand continued, "but you brought it on yourself. You will be turned over to a presidential tribunal for investigation and prosecution and face the consequences of your actions."

Armand took his phone out of his pocket and read a text message. He turned to Karl and Lukas. "Take her outside. Her transportation has just arrived."

Margot ran down from the dais toward her mother. "No, *Maman! Maman*, come back!"

Two guards reached for Margot, trying to prevent her from getting to her mother.

"Let her say goodbye," Armand told them. "It may be some time before she sees her mother again. We will have to make arrangements for her care until we know of Jean-Louis's and Sabine's fates."

"Until those arrangements can be made," Marco stepped in, "I will take care of her. She is my daughter, after all."

Hana looked at him, a sly smile curving her lips. "Yeah, we definitely need to talk."

CHAPTER
FORTY

Hana was remarkably cool when Marco pulled her aside in a quiet corner of the palace. She folded her arms across her chest as they both stood in the shadows.

Marco grimaced, pursing his lips in a contemplative frown. *Where to start? How to say this?*

"When I was in the military," he began, "my last assignment was in dignitary protection. It was considered a safe position for commandos to finish out their tour after a particularly dangerous assignment. A rest stop, so to speak, between ops.

"I was assigned to the duke's household, and specifically to the duchess, since the duke was away much of the time. Even eight years ago, the duke was prominent in politics, and there were threats to him and his family. He spent a great deal of time in Paris, and the duchess was left alone in Avignon.

"She was certainly aware that the duke had relationships with women in Paris. And of course, she had informers. Friends in high places. So, she figured if he could have an affair, she could have the same freedom.

"Sabine is a ninja seductress; she's mastered the art. And

eight years ago she was even more aggressive. She was never one to take 'no' for an answer, and I was in her employ.

"I had no one in my life at the time, Hana, and after a long, lonely and fearsome operation in Afghanistan, I… well—French commando, lonely woman, lots of time together: you do the math. There were liaisons. And a few months later, we found out she was pregnant. The duke hadn't been gone *all* the time, of course, so the baby could have been his.

"Secret DNA tests were done later. The duke was not informed of the results, of course, and as it turned out, Margot was mine."

Hana listened respectfully with understanding. Marco went on.

"Sabine contacted my command. Nobody wanted a scandal. I signed a termination of parental rights and a non-disclosure agreement. I agreed to never come back to Avignon. To never have any contact with Margot. I left the military early. I floated around for a couple of years, doing the odd security job, and a few off-the-books missions for French Intelligence when they needed deniability and an expendable asset.

"Then I got hooked up with your grandfather. He offered me a job. He did a comprehensive background investigation on me…found out things that even I had no idea how he uncovered, including Margot. He has known the whole time. With all that he knows about me, he is assured of my complete loyalty, just to avoid any of that being released. And because of that, he trusts me, even to the point of assigning me to protect you.

"But I don't think he ever expected me to fall in love with you. So you see, I couldn't tell you, even if I wanted to."

"But Marco, where we were in this relationship is something you should have told me."

"Where we were?" Marco asked, incredulous. "Where was that? Somewhere in the limbo between the guy you have but don't want, and the guy you want but can't have? You know what it's like trying to save the woman you love from wasting her life chasing a false hope? A fantasy? I had to ask Michael to step back just to give me a fair shot"

"You didn't!"

"I did. I love you. Don't you get that? But now I have responsibilities to Margot, too. We could be a family. Isn't that what you want?"

When he was finished, Hana stood there stoically, a single tear tracing a line down her cheek.

"I'm actually happy you have a new love in your life, Marco. But I need some time to think. Too much is happening."

"I have to go now," he said dejectedly, but mustering determination. "I would like to discuss this further with you. Can we meet for coffee when we return to Paris?"

"Of course," Hana said, already sensing what Marco wanted to talk about. "I'll see you then."

IAN SAT FORLORNLY in the Vatican cafeteria, staring at his laptop, lost in thought. On her break, Teri was walking through with a cup of cappuccino when she noticed him sitting there so dejectedly.

"Hey Ian. You look like a 404 error. What's up?"

"Oh, hi Teri. Yeah, I've been looking at this encrypted letter from Pope Clement to the bishop at Notre-Dame—the one we found in Clement's crypt in Uzeste—but I just can't seem to crack it."

"Can I have a look?"

"Sure, see what you can make of it."

Teri looked at the page. It was just a string of letters and spaces a couple hundred characters in length.

"Okay, so what have you tried so far?" she asked.

"Well, since the other letter was a numerical double substitution cipher—kind of an unusual one, since it was based on both times and degrees corresponding to letters—I was thinking this one might be just a letter substitution cipher. The Caesar cipher was already well known at the time of Clement, and the Vatican scribes were adept at using it, as well as numerical ciphers. But it seems that Clement's scribe must have been a little ahead of his time, and very creative. I devised a program that ran the cipher text through every iteration of the Caesar cipher, but nothing decoded the message. I thought about using a polyalphabetic cipher, but there are just too many options, and besides, they weren't in use until another hundred years or so later. Plus, they would need a key, which I don't have."

"What else do you know?" Teri asked. "Were there any clues in the other letter?"

"Maybe. The letter was directed to the bishop. It was Clement's last confession. He said the rest of the treasure was hidden in the church. He reminded the bishop of the sermon he sent and told him that his scribe had the means to decode it. But we don't have the sermon or the tool."

"Is that it? Nothing mentioned about a key?"

"Wait…the confession did use the word *key*. It said there was a key verse in the sermon, in the Gospel of Matthew. You don't suppose that could be it? A passage from Matthew about storing treasure?"

"Matthew 6:20 does say *'store up your treasure in heaven…'*"

Ian turned back to his computer and started typing. "I really need the verse in Latin. He would have written it that way, or in French.

"In a polyalphabetic cipher, you use the Caesar cipher tool to encode the message, but for each letter, the key tells you where to index the wheels, then you encode or decode the letter, according to the indexing revealed by the key. It would have been impossible to break at the time unless you had the key. And the key and the message could be sent separately to prevent people from getting both. That's apparently what the pope's scribe did: sent the key in a sermon from the pope, and then sent the coded message with Florian. Let's see what we get using the passage from Matthew as the key…"

Ian fiddled over his keyboard a bit, his hands accelerating the more he instinctively knew he was on the right track.

"It worked!" he cheered, looking over at Teri with a victory smile. It reads, *'I know what you did with the treasure. Numbers 4:11. Pray that nobody else does, especially Philip. Hide it better. Genesis 11:4.'*"

Ian used his computer to get the verses.

"The Book of Numbers reference is about *'a golden altar covered in blue cloth and goatskin…'*"

Teri added, "And the Genesis passage says, *'Let us build ourselves a city and a tower that reaches to the heavens.'*"

They stared at each other in wonderment. Ian spoke first.

"You think there's a golden altar in the tall tower at Notre-Dame?"

"Well, not anymore. The spire was destroyed in the recent fire. I don't remember anything about a golden altar being found during the recovery period.

"But I do think we should tell Father Michael about this at once."

FORTY-ONE

With the Duke and Duchess of Avignon and Philip Valois all in custody—and President Pierre Valois still alive and in command of his senses and, with the assistance of Lauren, the government as well—the team took a collective sigh of relief.

Only sporadic protests had broken out in Paris of late, and the local police were more than capable of monitoring and containing them without state assistance.

Armand, his valet Frederic, Michael, Hana, Marco, Karl, and Lukas had all stayed in the Palais des Papes Hotel for their final night before returning to Paris. They had all gathered in the dining room for a celebratory dinner, cooked by the hotel's executive chef, Lucien Boudreaux. Though not yet famous, Boudreaux was hoping to earn his restaurant its first Michelin star, and knowing he had important state guests in his dining room for the evening, he put on a meal fit for a king. Fine wines and aged cheeses were brought up from the cellar. Steak tartare, duck confit, venison and Mediterranean salmon were featured main courses, along with local asparagus, fougasse, fresh salads, and apricot sorbet, a local favorite, for dessert.

After dinner, everyone retired to their rooms, fatigued but relieved that the worst seemed to be over.

THE NEXT MORNING, as the team packed up and prepared to return to Paris, Michael got a call from Ian.

"Father Michael, about that coded letter in Florian de Got's sleeve… It seems it held clues about the portion of the treasure that had been hidden in Notre-Dame Cathedral. The coded message included passages from the books of Genesis and Numbers, which had been decoded by using references from the Gospel of Matthew.

"The passages from both Matthew and Genesis each mention Heaven: Matthew says to store your treasure there, while Genesis tells of a tower built to reach Heaven. Then the passage from Numbers speaks about a golden altar, one covered in blue cloth and bound in goatskin. But I have to say, I don't have a clue what all this means.

"Oh, and as for the Avignon treasure, one part is in the catacombs, or can be reached from there, through the '*crypt of no man*,' or '*no man's crypt*,' whatever that means. The other part was referenced in Genesis again: the verse that says *God separated the waters above from the waters below*. Don't know what that means either."

"Now that's interesting, Ian," the priest enthused. "The treasure we found with Margot's help is beneath the sarcophagus of one of the queens of Navarre, which can certainly be described as a '*crypt of no man*.' So that makes sense. And there is a subterranean lake beneath the catacombs, which fits with what you just said.

"We will have to coordinate with Lauren Valois about how his ministry wants to handle the treasure. It is certainly part of the cultural heritage of France, or at least that's what I expect he'll claim it to be. But, since it once belonged to the Church, or Pope Clement V—who seems to have acquired it during the course of Church business—I expect there could be an argument that it actually belongs to the Church. But others can deal with that.

"Meantime, I'll ask Armand to station some of his security people here to protect the catacombs until the Cultural Ministry can get their people down there to manage things.

"But for now, I think we should be heading back to Paris. We need to talk to the archbishop."

~

ON THEIR FIRST morning back in Paris, Michael and Hana attended early Sunday Mass at the Church of Saint-Germain L'Auxerrois in the 1st Arrondissement, where Notre-Dame's services had been moved until reconstruction could be finished in the coming years.

Having earlier made an appointment to visit Cardinal Gauthier, the archbishop of Paris, they then took a taxi that delivered them to his residence promptly at eleven o'clock.

Historically, archbishops of Our Lady of Paris lived adjacent to the cathedral, but a century ago a special residence had been bequeathed to the Church in the shadow of Les Invalides, the seventeenth-century military complex, museum, and final resting place of Napoleon Bonaparte.

The archdiocese of Paris, in the country long recognized as the "eldest daughter of the Church," oversees more than a hundred parishes throughout the greater metropolitan area. And Gauthier's office reflected the wealth of his diocese, with its opulent furnishings and abundant rooms in a grand palace.

This kind of lavish display of grandeur always disturbed Michael as a renunciation of Christ's instruction to vanquish man's inordinate desire to accumulate wealth in ways that distort human nature, and to guard against these desires diligently. But with few exceptions, the roughly two hundred princes of the Church had each become so accustomed to enjoying sumptuous surroundings and prestigious societal positions that it was de rigueur for most cardinalates around the world.

"Thank you for seeing us, Your Eminence," Michael said. "How are restorations going after all the unrest in the city?"

"We sent most of the workers home for the last couple of weeks, hoping that the troubles would pass us by. We did hire security personnel, but actually, Philip's roadblocks kept people off of the Île de la Cité, so we were spared the worst of it.

"What brings you to see me, Father Dominic? Mademoiselle Sinclair?"

"We thought you'd like to know that Pope Clement's letters, and the treasure trove we found in Avignon, would seem to indicate that the original treasure was of Viking origin. They also reveal that King Philip IV had become aware of the treasure and had taken a portion of it. The remainder was split into three parts: two parts were taken to Avignon, and the last remained here. By any chance, would you have any idea what became of it?"

The cardinal paused before responding, then couched his answer in the tangle of a non sequitur. "Well, we have re-interred Florian in the crypt beneath the foundations. In the process, we discovered there were additional spaces found under the crypt, and chemical analysis indicated traces of gold, wood, wool and horn. Though the spaces had been cleared out, we suspect it was the original hiding place for this treasure of which you speak. Sadly, there were no such riches remaining."

Michael was circumspect, glancing at Hana as he spoke. "Perhaps not. But my staff was able to decipher the other letter, the one Florian had in his sleeve when he arrived here. The instructions he was given were to have the scribe then in residence decode it, using a variant of the Caesar cipher in the form of a wheel which the scribe was familiar with, and a decoding key hidden in a sermon the pope sent to the bishop."

"Now that is very interesting," Gauthier said, looking

beyond Michael as he spoke, not meeting his eyes. "Sorry to tell you, we have no records of sermons dating back that far, so I'm afraid we wouldn't be able to help in that regard. But I can check with the diocesan secretary about whether any decoding wheel is extant. It might be in a museum if it still exists."

"That's not particularly essential at this point, though I would be interested in learning if such a wheel from that era did exist. But using our computer technology, we were able to duplicate the function of the cipher wheel. It was the key that was more important. The second letter, the one that was buried with Pope Clement, had clues that we were able to use to deduce the key."

Gauthier's head tilted. "So, are you telling me that you *do* know the location of the treasure?"

"Yes, in a manner of speaking. We were wondering if we might have a look at the great spire?"

The cardinal sat back with a smug smile. "As I'm sure you are aware, Father Dominic, the spire was destroyed in the fire, but even if it had not been damaged, it is not the same spire that was in existence in the 1300s. The original spire was built between 1220 and 1230 and was taken down in 1786 due to damage and decay. The new one was built in, oh, about 1860, and lasted up until the recent fire. So, the old spire you are looking for has been gone almost two hundred and forty years. I'm sure that anything that had been hidden in the original spire would certainly have been discovered when it was dismantled, or long before."

"Of course, yes. So, since the spire did not survive, would you happen to know if there had ever been an altar built into it?"

"Goodness, no. It was originally built as another bell tower, though for some reason the bell had been removed. I'm not aware if there was ever a chapel in the spire itself, but I seriously doubt it."

"Eminence, would you mind if Hana and I wandered around the grounds here for a bit? We'd like to see some of the chapels."

"Well, there are twenty-four chapels and side altars in the cathedral. Is there something in particular that you are looking for? Perhaps I might help."

Michael, noticing the cardinal's earlier reactions, chose to exercise caution. "Oh, it's just a description we found in the letters, something quite vague, but referring to a tower to heaven, and storing up one's treasures there. It made me suspect that the rest of the treasure might have been in the spire since it reached closest to heaven. But perhaps when they dismantled it, they moved the treasure somewhere else in the church, not realizing what it was."

"As you can understand, Father, most of the cathedral is off limits to all but the restoration staff and construction workers. It's still rather hazardous in places as they rebuild the structural components." Gauthier offered a smile tinged with impatience, then crossed his arms as if the audience was over.

Michael said nothing, and the two of them waited patiently for the next move. Finally, the cardinal sighed and said, "Of course, I would be happy to walk you around those that are safe to view."

The archbishop's limousine drove them all from Les Invalides to Notre-Dame, and before entering, each of them donned a hard hat dispensed by one of the site foremen.

Cardinal Gauthier took them around the church, engaging Michael and Hana in small talk while discussing the history of the cathedral and the restoration plans for the chapels, many of which had been in various states of disrepair prior to the fire. As he looked closely at each of the chapels, nothing that Michael saw fit the description in the letter.

Finally, Michael and Hana took their leave of the archbishop, thanked him for his time, and left the building.

"I guess we might never know what happened to this part of the treasure," Michael said. "Hey, how about we get that lunch we promised each other a few weeks ago?"

Hana smiled. "Sounds like a great idea."

Cardinal Gauthier watched them leave from the steps of the cathedral, then got back into his limousine for the return trip back to the residence.

RETURNING TO HIS OFFICE, he closed and locked the door so he wouldn't be interrupted by his staff, then opened a hidden door on the bookshelf wall next to his desk. Beyond the door was his personal chapel.

And inside the chapel was an ancient golden altar, wrapped in blue cloth and bound in goatskin leather.

It was small but weighed significantly more than any other altar, a fact due to its nearly solid gold construction. Much of the gold in the original treasure trove had been melted down to create the resplendent work of art.

On either side of the altar was a pair of golden lampstands, and on the altar itself were golden candlesticks. A picture of the Virgin Mary holding the infant Jesus hung above the altar in its lavish gold frame.

Archbishop Gauthier knelt on the padded velvet kneeler, its carved mahogany creaking under his weight. And he prayed.

He prayed that the secret treasure of Notre-Dame would forever remain a secret, one known only to its current archbishop.

CHAPTER

FORTY-TWO

T rue to his word, President Pierre Valois set in place the mechanisms to conduct an election for a new president as rapidly as possible. While there were several lesser-known candidates from different parties running against him, Lauren Valois was widely recognized for his devotion to his father, for his steady stewardship of France's cultural heritage, and for the leadership and courage he had exhibited during the recent crisis. He won in a landslide.

Having lived to see his son elected president, but before he could be sworn in, Pierre Valois died peacefully in his sleep at Saint-Louis Hospital, with Lauren and his oldest friend, Armand de Saint-Clair, by his side.

The state funeral cortège was a somber affair, with the streets of Paris lined by thousands of appreciative citizens who applauded and cried when the black horse-drawn hearse passed them by.

Pope Ignatius had secretly flown into Paris on Armand's jet, with a small contingent of plainclothes Swiss Guards as his discreet security detail. There was no public mention of the Holy Father's presence at the funeral, and the few who recognized him, dressed sedately in a simple black suit, were stunned that he was able to pull off such a public appearance so quietly in honor of his friend—but even the press honored the gesture and let him grieve without their interference. He was not the pope today; he was the man once codenamed "Achille" of the Maquis, in the secret French Resistance group known as Team Hugo, composed of Armand, Pierre, and himself.

As the procession ended at Montparnasse Cemetery, the deafening sound of three Dassault Mirage fighter jets from the French Air Force streaked overhead, with one jet breaking away higher into the heavens in honor of Pierre Valois's taking leave of Team Hugo, and of France.

In a televised special report on TF1 later that evening, Lauren Valois addressed the nation and the world as France's new president.

"You have heard many eulogies about my father today, his time in the resistance in World War II, and his decades as a public servant and as your president. He put his love of country and his love of its people above all else.

"I loved him, and I will miss him terribly. We will all miss him. And I hope that I can live up to the standards he set.

"People of France, we have been through much recently. These were perilous times and people were afraid. We had been beset by radicals on both sides, extremists who had been stoking that fear. And when people are afraid, they will give up their money, they will give up their freedom, they will give up their power to anyone who will reduce those fears.

"Such fanatical voices have been amplified by the internet and social media. But today I tell you that I am here to amplify the voices of everyone else, those in the middle. I hear you. I hear you all, and I know you. I know the people of France. Not just the wealthy who come to the opera and the ballet, but also the people who play football in our parks, who hike in our forests, who swim in our seas and rivers. Even the ones who live under a bridge. I know you all. And I tell you that the worst has passed.

"Today we begin to rebuild our future. A future built on moderation. Everyone's voice will be heard and considered and tempered by reason.

"To those who would close our borders to those seeking better lives in France, I remind you of our history. We all came from somewhere else. There was a time when we were not French, but Celts and Gauls, Goths and Visigoths. We were Anglos and Saxons and Etruscans. But borders cannot be porous, so the exercise of due diligence will ensure that those who wish a better life here will actually contribute to the good of France.

"To those who would cut off the poor from government services, I tell you we were all poor once, and we have a duty to help those who are less fortunate. France will help you, but you will help France in return.

"There is also value in work. There is pride in work. We must have free trade and open markets. But not the abuse of unregulated capitalism.

"And to all of you, I say, we will find our way forward, together, down the middle path."

JEAN-LOUIS MICHEAUX, Duke of Avignon, was detained longer than expected in order to determine how much he knew of Sabine's activities on his behalf, the protests and the bombings, but was released and returned to his home.

Once he had discovered Sabine's betrayal over Marco's paternity, the duke quickly lost interest in Margot and posed no challenge to Marco's taking responsibility for her.

After a brief trial, Sabine Micheaux was sentenced to ten years in prison for treason, sedition, and several other crimes.

The only time she would see her daughter—if she cared to at all —would be through a thick pane of glass in the prison.

∾

THOUGH HE INSTINCTIVELY CARED FOR little Margot a great deal and was committed to supporting her in any way he could, Marco Picard realized that he was not cut out for full-time fatherhood, and his obligations to Armand de Saint-Clair required him to be able to travel at a moment's notice and to be armed most of that time—not the circumstances in which he wanted to raise a child. But he would be able to see her as often as both of them wanted.

He enrolled Margot in a Catholic boarding school for girls in Paris, near his own new apartment in Ménilmontant, a hip area in Paris's 20th Arrondissement, with narrow, cobblestone streets and grungy artists' studios populating the hilltop hamlet. It was here he could spend time with his daughter when possible and learn how to be a parent.

As PLANNED, Marco had asked Hana to meet him for coffee. That afternoon they met up at Le Procope Brasserie near her office, and as each ordered café-au-lait, Hana couldn't bring herself to meet Marco's eyes, for she knew what had to be said.

Finally, he broke the tension. "The three of us cannot continue like this, Hana. One of us has to go."

And there it was, finally out on the table in the sun-dappled cobblestone alleyway where they sat. Hana reluctantly turned to meet his gaze, her face a mixture of pain and shame, yet determination.

"I'm so sorry, Marco. This is terribly unfair to you, to all of us, actually. I just can't reconcile my feelings. I'm in an impossible situation. I do care for you—a great deal. But...well, I think you can gather the rest."

"Michael is a good man," Marco said. "One of the best I've known. But he's a *priest!* And there's your impossible situation. I suppose I'm equally to blame, though. You were a job, and the first rule of my work is to never get involved with the client, much less fall in love with her.

"So, until you can make up your mind, or even if you can't, I need to step back."

Those words again, Hana reflected.

Without waiting for a response, Marco continued. "I'll stay here in Paris with Margot while you go on to Rome. With your grandfather's approval, I can find a suitable replacement as your bodyguard. Or, if you think we can both handle it, I can stay on and continue my job. Armand knows everything, so he'll understand either way."

"It's good you're staying for Margot's sake; she needs you now. I expect she hasn't had much proper love in her young life, and we both know you can give that to her.

"As for my needing a bodyguard, with Paris more or less at rest now, I really don't need protection here. And you already know how I feel about that anyway. But I have decided to take this new job in Rome, so I'm making plans to leave Paris shortly.

"But for those times where Grand-père thinks it essential, I would be honored to have you as my escort, if that's something you feel you can handle, Marco. I leave that entirely up to you. But we can at least be friends, can't we?"

"The words no man wants to hear at moments like this," the Frenchman said, his eyes feeling tight and reddening as he attempted a smile. "*Mais oui.* Friends it is. Always."

HAVING ACCEPTED the job in *Le Monde*'s Rome bureau, Hana packed up her office and her apartment in Paris and moved to the Eternal City, taking a modest top floor apartment overlooking the Tiber River.

Settling into the Trastevere, a picturesque working-class neighborhood just south of the Vatican—its narrow alleyways and medieval houses making it particularly lively at night— Hana could stroll along the banks of the river or relax on one of the many café terraces. She already had one friend there. And she would make many more.

EPILOGUE

On Michael's earlier return to Rome from his exploits in France, he had found both Ian Duffy and Sister Teri having cappuccinos together and discussing code breaking in the Vatican canteen.

"I'm glad I found you two. I just want to say how much I appreciate having both of you working behind the scenes with me over the past few weeks. I could not have done any of this without you."

Reaching into his backpack, Michael took out two red and blue snow globes, each with a model of Notre-Dame Cathedral resting inside.

Shaking the snow globe, making the little white flakes swirl around the cathedral, Ian chuckled, "Gosh, boss, you shouldn't have. We are definitely coming with you next time, if for no other reason than to make sure we get better souvenirs!"

"So," Teri asked, "whatever happened to the Pope Clement's treasure? You did find it at the Palais des Papes, right?"

"Well, what little was left of it, yes," Michael said. "I expect most of what was found in Avignon went to support Sabine's failing fashion empire, as well as her bid to rule France. The rest likely belongs either to the family or to the Church. Lauren is handling that now. As for what might have been at Notre-Dame, who knows? It could still be there, somewhere. I suppose we'll never know."

~

As THEY SAT among the ruins on Palatine Hill, Michael and Hana looked out over the most ancient parts of Rome, with the modern city in the distance. It was an unseasonably warm, early autumn day, and they had stopped at a street vendor's cart offering that classic Italian delight, artisanal gelato, then chosen a shady spot beneath the broad umbrella canopy of one of the many stone pine trees dotting the ancient landscape.

They were both silent, with things unsaid circling their minds.

Hana smiled. Michael looked up from his gelato and caught her eye and her coy smile. He blushed and smiled back. After a few moments, he spoke softly.

"Okay, so I guess I'll just get this out there," he began. "I'm sorry about what happened at the cathedral a couple of weeks ago, and I'm hoping that you can forgive me. I thought maybe you were thinking about taking this Rome assignment so you'd be able to spend more time with me. I missed seeing you. But then Marco stopped me after dinner and asked me to step back and give him a fair shot at having a relationship with you. He's saved my life more than once, so I thought I owed him that. And I only want you to be happy."

The priest stopped for a moment, unable to go further. He covered his embarrassment with a bite of gelato.

"I was thinking about taking this Rome assignment to spend more time with you," Hana responded candidly. "I do want to be closer to you. But Marco had called me right then and chewed me out for leaving without him. He's been really over-protective. I guess with all that's been going on, he had his reasons, but he can also be a bit jealous. He didn't tell me he had asked you to step back, and he hadn't told me about Sabine nor about Margot. I found out after we confronted Sabine. I thought you didn't like me anymore, and I couldn't understand why. He lied to me. And in a way you did too.

"I know. Marco asked me to step back and *not* to tell you why. I guess he knew how you would react. Again, I'm very sorry. It's not what I wanted."

"I forgive you, Michael. But if there is one thing that these last few weeks have taught me, is that I'm not sure what I want now. The job is changing. Paris is changing, hopefully for the better. Marco has a child; I didn't see that one coming. We sort of broke up the other day. He's staying in France, with Margot, and I'm now here in Rome. We decided to stay friends, and he may still provide protection services when I need them, but we won't be together. So at this point, I don't know where that leaves us. You and me."

"I'm going to be honest with you, Hana. Always, from now on, no matter what. I have strong feelings for you. Feelings I sometimes have trouble reconciling with being a priest. You have no idea how much that kiss in the Archives shook my world. But as you say, these last few weeks I've been giving thought to my own future, and at this point, I don't have a firm idea of what that looks like. I feel in limbo. I am certainly not ready to make any commitments. I need to think through a lot. I was going to tell you at lunch that day at Notre-Dame before everything got messed up."

"I thought so. And I have strong feelings for you, too. But I couldn't live with myself if I took you away from the priesthood. I would feel so guilty. I know how important being a priest is to you, and I have mad respect for your vows. And you're right, things are too unsettled now. But I'm so glad we got that cleared up. I hated to think I had driven you away. You are too important for me to lose as a friend."

"And you to me. So…where *does* that leave us?"

"For now, let's just go back to being great friends, friends who actually talk to each other and clear up misunderstandings before they bring France to the brink of civil war! And then, who knows?"

They looked at each other lovingly, as only the closest of friends could. Then Hana leaned over, put her arms around him, and gave him a warm kiss on the cheek.

"I know we have been put in one another's lives for a reason. Let's take some time to figure out exactly what that looks like."

Then she sat back up, ruffled his hair, and grinned.

"I've always wanted to do that," she said.

Michael grinned, too, then finger-combed his hair back into place.

"I don't know. Any more of that and I may have to ask you to *step back...*"

Hana lightly punched his shoulder, and they both broke into laughter.

FICTION, FACT, OR FUSION?

Many readers have asked me to distinguish fact from fiction in my books, and where the two meet. Generally, I like to take factual events and historical figures and build on them in creative ways—but much of what is written here is historically accurate. I'll review some of the chapters in this book where questions may arise, with hopes it may help those wondering where reality meets creative writing.

SPOILERS AHEAD: If you prefer to sustain the illusion of fiction as presented in the book, it is suggested you stop here and not read what's real and what's not.

GENERAL

As in all my books, vehicles, trains, airports, transportation schedules, restaurants (and their menus), locations, time zones and travel times are all consistent with reality. As reasonably as possible, events take place in real time, using actual locations and mentioning local buildings and businesses where suitable. All cities and streets, landmarks, buildings and their respective interiors and exteriors, wherever located, are described as accurately as our research confirms. Avid readers often comment that in their travels they have come across specific places described here, making their reading experience that much more realistic and enjoyable.

European time is normally spoken in military time units. For example, in the U.S. we would say three o'clock or three p.m. But in Europe (and elsewhere) it would be referred to as fifteen hours (or 15:00): three hours past noon. In light of the vast majority of readers being in the U.S., I have for the most part used the more commonly understood expression of time here, except in descriptions of military-type maneuvers, and ask the indulgence of my European friends and other readers around the world.

The attentive reader will have noticed this is the first book where I've begun using "Michael" instead of "Dominic" when referring to the main character. I did so by popular reader demand—since I do listen to reader feedback.

PROLOGUE

The entire first scene is completely factual. King Philip IV was quite the shrewd monarch and exerted firm control over the papacy during his long reign.

Though Pope Clement V did die from lupus, and he *did* have a brother named Florian de Got, the scene depicted here is fictitious.

In a mix of both fact and fiction, Jerome Baudette is an imaginary figure, but the English ship, *Shoreham*, was indeed real—though it didn't sink in the Celtic Sea but in Widemouth Bay, North Cornwall.

The deaths and details of Pope Clement, King Philip and his sons are all accurate, including the crown passing to the House of Valois—which is purely coincidental in relation to my long-time character Pierre Valois, the president of France—but fits perfectly into the story. Serendipity, prescience or divine intervention? Make of that what you will.

As it happens, excavators refurbishing Notre-Dame de Paris Cathedral in 2022 did, in fact, discover a previously unknown fourteenth-century lead sarcophagus, as described here. And they also found another pit beneath that—but the "discovery" of another coffin, along with the parchment scrolls, was solely derived from our imagination.

CHAPTER 4

King Louis XIV, the renowned Sun King, did, in fact, star in scores of ballets while serving as France's monarch, and expanded on his country's long-lasting cultural legacy consequent to his support for the arts.

As Lauren Valois describes, that lower pit was indeed discovered in 2022 while building a thirty-meter-high scaffolding to reconstruct the great spire that was destroyed in the 2019 fire. Excavators also did find a fourteenth-century lead sarcophagus, and a lower pit beneath the floor of the cathedral, all as described. The crypt for Jerome Baudette was added fictionally as part of the story.

CHAPTER 5

The description of the reconstruction of Notre-Dame has been reworked from numerous original sources but remains accurate as it appears. Completion of the project is expected to be in 2025.

Though why this odd custom existed is a mystery, boxwood leaves were actually used in caskets to preserve the heads of deceased religious figures and the social elite in the Middle Ages.

All popes do, in fact, bestow engraved rings on the cardinals they elevate, symbolizing their renewed vows of fidelity to the Church, a tradition that goes back to at least Pope Innocent III.

CHAPTER 10

While the Vatican does have an extensive array of many unique laboratories for the restoration of paper, wood, stone, metals, ceramics, paintings, mosaics, tapestries and textiles, the "Authentication and Restoration Laboratory" used here is an imaginative amalgam of all those, and then some. Whether the Secret Archives actually has or uses tomographic X-rays is unknown, but the Franciscan Missionary Sisters of Mary do, in fact, manage the Tapestries and Textiles Restoration Laboratory.

CHAPTER 13
VADNA, or the Vatican Ancient DNA project, is fictional.

CHAPTER 14
The description of Rome's Sapienza University and its history of illustrious alumni is accurate, and they do have a Genetics and Molecular Biology lab, though its internal descriptions are imagined.

Although the extended discussion of DNA and its processes are all authentic, the VADNA operation and work on the DNA of saints is not (at least to the best of my knowledge).

CHAPTER 17
The sarcophagus of Pope Clement V, as shown in the photograph, is, of course, authentic, as are the descriptions surrounding it in the church of Collégiale Notre-Dame d'Uzeste, or Our Lady of Uzeste, France.

CHAPTER 18
Pastoralis praeeminentiae was the papal bull that authorized the arrest of all Knights Templar and the seizure of their property.

CHAPTER 20
While Philip IV had no fourth son named Robert, nor grandsons named Henri and Hugh, the reigns and genealogy of his other sons occurred as described.

CHAPTER 24
The Palais des Papes, or Palace of the Popes, is the actual

castle where the Avignon papacy held residence for sixty-seven years and is largely as described, except for certain fictional elements. The blue doors in the cliffs below the garden are actually there.

CHAPTER 30

Microtomography as described here is a brilliant and fairly recent technology used for reading rolled-up scrolls and other such "inaccessible" material, something the Vatican most certainly employs in its archival processes.

Guillaume de Baufet actually was a notable bishop in Paris in 1314.

CHAPTER 31

The French Sixth Light Armoured Brigade is headquartered at Nîmes and is equipped with the VBCI armored personnel carriers as described.

AUTHOR'S NOTES

Dealing with issues of theology, religious beliefs and the fictional treatment of historical biblical events can be a daunting affair.

I would ask all readers to view this story for what it is: a work of pure fiction, adapted from the seeds of many oral traditions and the historical record, at least as we know it today.

Apart from telling an engaging story, I have no agenda here, and respect those of all beliefs from Agnosticism to Zoroastrianism and everything in between.

Thank you for reading *The Avignon Affair*. I hope you enjoyed it and, if you haven't already, I suggest you pick up the story in the earlier books of The Magdalene Chronicles series—*The Magdalene Deception, The Magdalene Reliquary,* and *The Magdalene Veil*—and look forward to forthcoming books featuring the same characters and many new ones in the continuing *Vatican Secret Archive Thriller* series.

When you have a moment, may I ask that you leave a review on Amazon, Goodreads, Facebook and perhaps elsewhere you find convenient? Reviews are crucial to a book's success, and I hope for The Magdalene Chronicles and the Vatican Secret Archives Thriller series to have long and entertaining lives.

You can easily leave your review by going to my Amazon book page. If for some reason that link doesn't work, just head over to *The Avignon Affair* and scroll to the reviews section at the bottom of the page. And thank you!

If you would like to reach out for any reason, you can email me at gary@garymcavoy.com. If you'd like to learn more about my other books and my background, and receive occasional exclusive offers, visit my website at www.garymcavoy.com, where you can also sign up for my private mailing list.

With kind regards,

ACKNOWLEDGMENTS

My special thanks to pilots Mike Phillips and Peggy Phillips for their assistance in refining the air traffic control communications in portions of this book, and to Greg McDonald for helping make that happen.

To our valued beta readers team, whose insights into the story and helpful feedback always makes for a better book, with special props to Ben Cheng, Don Reiter, Lisa Knapp Treon and Donna Marie West.

As always, to my fantastic editor Sandra Haven-Herner for her thoroughly spot-on recommendations and improvements to the manuscript.

CREDITS

Image of the Sarcophagus of Pope Clement V is used under the Creative Commons Attribution-Share Alike License 3.0, attributed to Szeder László.

Made in United States
North Haven, CT
22 March 2024

50355524R00182